For The Lost Soul

Michael Andrews

ISBN: 1492859281
ISBN-13: 978-1492859284

DEDICATION

For all the lost souls in the world, there is hope.
It does get better.
Keep faith and belief in yourself.

ACKNOWLEDGMENTS

To Sue B, Andy F and Liam C, thank you for your proof reading and support throughout my journey writing this story.

To Rebecca for the full and final edit.

To Jessica at Coverbistro for the wonderful new cover

To Neil B for creating the music for the trailer.

To Phil D for the conversion of the prophecy into poetry form.

To my parents and family for supporting me through all the highs and lows.

To my friends for being the type of guys that I want to spend my time with.

MICHAEL ANDREWS

Chapter One

Blackness gave way to a sort of hazy white light. My head was a bit groggy and I shook it, which was a mistake, and I groaned as pain shot across from one temple to the other. I raised my left hand to touch my head, and saw that my usual attire of a dark, long sleeved hoodie had been replaced by a grey robe. What the fuck was going on?

I sat up on my bed, only to find out that I wasn't in my bed. I looked around what I thought was my room, to see it was a smaller room, with no windows and bad lighting. There was a hospital smell about it. I looked down and saw that I was lying on top of a single bed, dressed only in a grey singlet robe. I looked at my wrists and I saw the scars.

I looked around the room again, thinking it was a pretty shitty hospital. I mean, there were no monitors, no windows, not even a table with some flowers. I guess that my parents must have skimped on the cost and just put me anywhere that would take me. I wondered how long I had been there. I wasn't hungry, which was strange because I couldn't remember having any dinner.

I heard the door open. Finally a doctor or nurse, I can ask them. I looked over and was shocked to see my Uncle Dylan. Why was I shocked? Because he'd been dead for three years!!

"Oh my Joe, my sweet little Joe," he said to me, coming over to take me into an embrace. "What have you done?"

"Uncle Dylan? Wha… what's going on?" I stammered.

"Why did you do it Joe?" He asked. "It's the one irrefutable law that He Himself passed down."

Huh? Uncle Dylan was never really that religious. I looked at him, and for the first time saw things on his back. Things? Wings?

"You're dead Joe," he whispered sadly to me. "You succeeded in killing yourself."

He hugged me into him again and, as I let my tears course down my face, I sobbed into his chest as my life replayed itself before my eyes.

It was at the age of twelve that I guessed something was different about me. I was smart for my age, scoring highly at school but, despite that, I still maintained a good set of friends. I wasn't overly geeky by any stretch of imagination but never made it on to any of the school sports teams either. However, I found myself taking a great interest in the sports teams, and I came to the realisation that I was attracted to the boys who played in them.

At the time, it wasn't widely accepted that kids of my age could know their sexuality at that point so I kept it quiet, and played along with the pretence of being straight. Other boys in my school year were at the awkward point of realising that there was more to the girls at the school other than being there for us to torment. It was easy enough to play along, pretending to be interested in this girl or that one, without actually having to do anything about it. Boys would boast about kissing this girl or the other, which many times was refuted by the girl in question.

On my best mate Jimmy Johnson's thirteenth birthday, we had a big party for him. We did the usual things of meeting up at his house, giving him the presents we'd all persuaded our parents to buy for us, before heading out to the local shopping centre which housed a Laser Quest arena, cinema complex and various junk food outlets. We spent all day messing around, having a blast before saying our goodbyes and splitting up to head back to our various homes. Jimmy had begged his parents, my parents and me to arrange a sleepover that night, something we hadn't done for over a year, but the thought of spending some time alone with my best bud, watching the latest horror DVDs that we weren't supposed to be allowed to watch was too good of an opportunity to miss and it had all been arranged.

It was that night that he asked me if I was gay. It stunned me into silence. Whilst in my head I could see the end of our friendship, the reality was that Jimmy just gave me a big hug and told me it was okay. He told me that he wasn't but he didn't have any issues with me being that way. After all, "it left more girls for him," he giggled. He did ask if I fancied him; and while he was nice to look at, with short, spiky blonde hair, deep blue eyes and a smattering of freckles across his tanned, slim face, I could honestly say that I never thought of him in that way. I loved his friendship and he was like a brother to me. From that point on, we became even closer than before, and were soon nicknamed 'The Deadly Duo' as we seemed to sync our minds and pranks and were soon terrorising our friends with our escapades.

8

A year of research on the internet followed, mainly at Jimmy's house as I didn't want my parents to find out just yet, and I felt that I had all the facts about it. I was certain that I wasn't just going through a phase and was ready to come out to my parents and my sister. My sister Gill and I had always had a close relationship, she confiding her secrets to me as she broke rule after rule set down by our parents, and me, in return telling her about the antics that Jimmy and I got up to. So, at the age of fourteen, I came out to my sister, who shocked me to the core by completely rejecting me. She couldn't understand how her perfect little brother was suddenly this pervert. Despite my begging, she promptly dragged me in front of my parents, whose reactions were much the same as those of my sister. I became an object of shame for them. My internet use was constantly monitored, my activities outside of school were curtailed and they watched me like hawks ready to pounce on anything that could bring shame on to them.

Due to closeness of our friendship, Jimmy became the number one target of their suspicions as to why I had turned out that way, and whenever he came round, we were never allowed to be in a room on our own. I tried explaining to my parents that Jimmy wasn't gay, that he was totally into the girls but to no avail. Jimmy soon twigged on to what was occurring and, as much as he didn't want to do it, we agreed that he would start spending less time around my house.

I spent the next couple of months keeping a low profile, playing everything by the strict new rules that my parents enforced upon me, whilst Gill, my sister who was older than me by a couple of years, was given almost free rein. Nothing that she did was ever wrong. She dated a string of boys, even having sex with some of them at our house when my parents weren't there, but she was now their golden child. I kept my head down and improved my grades at school even further until I was maintaining a straight A average.

It was one of the times when my parents were away for a weekend that the really big trouble started. As usual, Gill had completely disobeyed the rule about not having anyone to stay over, and she was happily getting it on with Tyler Walford, the captain of the school football team, when I came into the lounge to watch the television. Tyler, who was the same age as Gill, had been a long time fantasy of mine, but the fact that he had lowered himself to the standards of my sister lessened his appeal to me. As much as I tried to ignore the smooching noises coming from the sofa as I watched a documentary on the solar system, I couldn't help but keep glancing at them. Gill soon spotted my attention was being focused on the shirtless Tyler. She sneered at me and promptly warned Tyler that he needed to watch out or I would try to jump him.

I couldn't believe that she had just outed me to the school's most popular boy and, when he jumped up off the sofa to confront me, I could only nod in agreement that I was ogling him. Two swift punches to my face and one in my stomach and I was left crying on the carpet as the laughter of the pair echoed up the stairs and into her room where they would, no doubt, spend the night together.

The next day, I was amazed my parents were totally unconcerned over my apparent lack of self-coordination. My sister explained away the now prominent black eye I was sporting was down to me not watching where I was going and walking into a door frame.

Monday morning came round far too quickly for my liking and, with no small amount of fear, I walked to school, meeting Jimmy at the gates and heading towards our lockers. A sense of apprehension came over me as I noticed the looks being directed at the pair of us and, sure enough, as we got to our lockers, there it was. Someone had taken a permanent marker pen and had scrawled the word 'FAG' across my locker door. I looked around and sniggers were easily heard, as well as some snide comments. I looked at Jimmy, who had a sad look on his face, and I knew that he was about to reach for me to offer me a comforting hug. I pulled away, not wanting him to get labelled as well, and I saw a hurt look flash across his face. He stepped up to me, pulled me into a hug anyway, and said quite loudly that he didn't care if I was or wasn't gay, I was his friend and always would be.

Unfortunately, not all our friends were quite so accepting. In fact, once the bullies started on us, we were deserted. Boys from older age groups thought that tripping us up, pushing us into lockers, or punching us in the ribs or our backs in the crowded corridors was now an acceptable part of their daily routine. Even some of the younger students started to give us verbals.

I started to withdraw into myself, but the knowledge that Jimmy was by my side was my salvation. He was a rock. Yes it hurt him that, despite not being gay himself, he was now as much of an outcast as I was, but he remained by my side none the less.

During all of this, the teachers looked the other way. I thought that they were supposed to help but, living in a conservative suburb of the city, I guess I shouldn't have expected any less. It was just another obstacle in our daily suffering.

Just two weeks after my fifteenth birthday, Jimmy landed the bombshell on me that would alter my life for the worse. Somehow, it had reached his parents that he was being tormented on a daily basis and, while they had sympathy for me and my situation, it was their job as parents to consider the welfare of their only son. They had decided that his father would take a transfer to another division within the multi-national company that he worked for, and they would be moving out of the country. They would leave for a new life in the Far East within the week. To say I was devastated was an understatement. I had lost my rock. We said our tearful farewells and, with the exchange of email addresses for us to remain in contact, a contact that I knew in my heart wouldn't last, Jimmy departed for the Land of the Rising Sun.

So I was completely alone in my misery. I tried to become the invisible student. My grades dropped to a C average as I tried to stay off the radar of everyone, students and faculty alike. Most of the students had long since gotten bored with the daily torment I was put through and I became a fixture in their own daily grinds. Most schools have the same idiosyncrasies, and ours was no different. We had the teacher nearing retirement, who took more comfort in the small bottle of vodka hidden in his desk drawer than the achievements of the next generation of students he was faced with. There was the female teacher, not too long out of her latest failed relationship, who took delight in seducing one of her willing, underage male students. There was, of course, the grumpy caretaker, muttering obscenities at the student body as he roamed the corridors armed with his trusty brush. The different cliques of students made themselves known. The sporty jocks with their hanger-oners who lorded it over the school. The geeks who moved from class to class, folders crammed full of their work notes under their arms. Punks and Emos added their own kaleidoscope of colour to the normally uniform dress of the swarm and, finally, the normal kids made up the balance. You know the ones, the lucky ones who go through the day with no-one to hold them on a pedestal, no-one looking down at them, no-one expecting anything from them except to turn up, put in a decent day's schooling and go home again to their family, friends and game consoles.

I used to be one of them. Now? Now, I was the outcast. The kid who ate his lunch in a shaded corner of the school, far away from anyone who may decide that they have a few spare moments to torment him. The kid who the jocks decided they needed to humiliate at every opportunity in order to massage their already over-inflated egos. The kid who no-one dared say hello to, to ask if he was alright after, once again, being knocked down in the corridor, or to help gather his now spilled books before they were kicked in all directions and trampled on. Why was I this boy? It was because, for some reason, it had been deemed acceptable by society that if you were different, you were not normal and so no-one cared enough to stand up to any injustice. What was the great crime I had committed? I was simply accepting that I liked other boys.

After a year of bullying, and of being forced to face it daily on my own, my final straw came on my sixteenth birthday. I had just finished my last lesson and, with my head kept down and all eye contact avoided with the masses, I was on my way out of school when around a half a dozen of the football team grabbed me and forced me into the sports changing rooms. I was punched in the stomach and forced onto my knees. They took it in turns forcing me to give them blow jobs, telling me how much of a faggy slut I was and how much I must be enjoying having the dicks of the hottest studs of the school in my mouth. Of course he was there. Tyler Walford. Despite everything he had done to me, he was still number one on my list of fantasies. I looked into his eyes and thought for a moment that they flared as red as his flame coloured hair. I begged him to leave me be, but he went one step further and, with his dick still out, he let loose with a stream of urine all over me, soaking my clothes and my short brown hair.

Laughter greeted my ears from the older boys and, after a couple more punches to my face, they left and I slumped to the ground. I looked up and over to the coach's office to see that he had witnessed the whole thing and had done nothing to stop it. He glanced at me with a look of disgust and told me in no uncertain terms to 'get my gay fag ass out of his changing room.'

I dragged myself up and stumbled out of the changing rooms. I ran straight out of school and home to tell my parents what had happened. Ok, they didn't like that I was gay, but their son had just been raped. They had to find some compassion surely? How wrong could I be? It seemed that phone calls had already been made by the coach and my parents were under no illusion that their "piece of filth" offspring had in fact willingly gone in and begged the boys to let me give them blow jobs.

I cried, pleaded and begged them to believe me, but was told that as I had already eaten, then I should go to my room and have no dinner.

I gave up and, with tears streaming down my face, I stumbled up the stairs to my room, with the sound of my sister's voice taunting me in the background. Instead of going to my room, I made my way to the bathroom. I stripped off my school clothes and started the shower on hot. I waited until steam was billowing out of the cubicle and stepped in, flinching as the scolding water sprayed over my naked body.

I found the shower gel and soaped my body, making sure I was as clean as I had ever been. I even shampooed my hair to get rid of the urine that was still present. Funny how you think you have to be ultra clean for what is going to happen next.

I looked into the mirror as I picked up the pack of razor blades that I had bought only last week from the corner store. I saw my brown eyes staring back at my image, a defeated and haunted look showing through. My brown hair was plastered to my face, which I brushed out of my eyes as I struggled to open the pack, ending up using my teeth to do so. I held one up, looking at the reflection of light shining off the silver metal. I returned with it into the shower and held it underneath the spray of the hot water.

This was it! Was I really going to do it? I thought about my life, my family, my school. I had no friends. No-one dared be associated with the school gay for fear of finding themselves being targeted as well. My parents and sister hated me. My best friend had left me. I had no-one. I had nothing. I was nothing.

"Dear God, I know you that you haven't answered any of my pleas before this, and I guess you are tied up with other things like the Middle East or other worse shit going on in the world, but I can't take anymore. I know what I am about to do is the cardinal sin. The worst sin ever. Please can you find it in your heart to forgive me and don't condemn me to Hell. I beg you. Father, forgive me for I shall sin."

I took the razor blade and sliced it across my left wrist, gritting my teeth as the pain shot through my body as the sharp metal pierced my flesh.

"I have had thoughts of lying with other boys, but your son Jesus Christ said that we should love each other. Please forgive me."

My left wrist dripped blood down onto my hand, making it difficult to grip the now slippery blade. I held it against my right wrist. This was it, once I've cut this one there is no backing out. If anyone cared for me, if anyone was going to save me, now was the time.

"Father Almighty, I love you and I forgive those who have hurt me. Please forgive them their sins too, even if you cannot forgive mine."

I sliced through my right wrist and more red liquid sprayed forth. I looked at the streams of red flowing down my hands. I began to feel light headed and my legs wobbled. My knees gave way and I fell backwards, slumping down under the spray. For a moment, I thought it's true what they say, that sometimes, death doesn't hurt anywhere near as much as the pain of life.

I felt my eyes getting heavy as the water started to pool at the bottom of the cubicle. I tried to move my foot that must be blocking the plug hole, but I was rapidly losing strength. The water was turning from a light pink to a darker red as my lifeblood poured out from my cuts.

"Forgive me."

I felt the blackness well up around me. He hadn't heard me. I didn't want to go to Hell but, as I was already living it, how much worse was it going to be? I blacked out to the noise of the bathroom door being broken down and my Dad shouting profanities at my naked unconscious body.

I looked down at the ground, not wanting to look my Uncle in the eye.

"Did He hear me? Did He forgive me?" I asked, fearing the worst, but hoping for the best.

"Not exactly," Uncle Dylan replied. "He did hear your prayer, and He reviewed your life with Saint Peter and He has decided He should not be quite as strict as He normally is, given the circumstances."

A glimmer of hope sparked in my eyes, only to be extinguished immediately as the door opened again and a tall, dark robed figure walked in. He had horns on his head for fucks sake!! (Sorry Father!)

"Is this the boy? The player?" the demonic figure asked.
"It is he, Yeqon," Uncle Dylan answered.

The demon called Yeqon looked at me, and suddenly I was blinded by a flashing light and, in the place of the horrible form was a youth of stunning beauty. He looked to be about 17 or 18 years old, platinum blonde hair, pale eyes and pale skin. He wore a tight fitting black top and black jeans. I couldn't understand how a demon could transform into a figure of such beauty.

"Yeqon, play fair!" Uncle Dylan complained.
"Oh yes, he will do," Yeqon said as he leaned forward and caressed my cheek. Uncle Dylan smacked his hand away from my face, and I saw Yeqon's eyes flare red for a moment.
"Remember your place, Angel," Yeqon almost spat at my Uncle.
"And remember yours, Fallen One," Uncle Dylan shot back. "You are here only at His forbearance, as by the terms of the agreement."

Yeqon broke eye contact and looked over at me. He smiled a killer smile, which I could not help but return.

"We will meet again, Joseph Harris," he warned me. "Of that you can be sure."

To my surprise his body faded from sight, though why anything is surprising me at the moment is a surprise in itself!!

"Uncle Dylan, please will you explain what's going on?" I begged.

He looked at me sadly, sitting next to me on the bed.

"You have been chosen Joe," Uncle Dylan started. "Chosen as the most important soul in a hundred generations."

I gulped.

"Our Almighty Father has been hurting for decades over the fate of the lost youth, those who cannot bear the pain and suffering that is forced upon them simply for being homosexual. However, by His Own Law, and the agreement He made with Lucifer, all souls who commit suicide are cast down to Purgatory."
"So why am I still here?" I asked.

"Well, He heard your prayer, and saw your life and decided that enough was enough. However, He cannot change this law on His own. As it is an agreement, He had to offer Lucifer something in return."

"WHAT??" I exclaimed. "God is all powerful, He should be able to do whatever He wants!"

"Well in the old days, yes He could," Dylan said. "However, with all the evil in the world today, Lucifer is growing stronger and stronger, and his influence is everywhere. He is the reason that rapists and child molesters exist, that homophobes beat up gay kids. He remembers being the beloved of our Father, and despises that he is no longer favoured."

"So he takes it out on everyone else?" I asked.

"He finds ways to inflict pain on those who have found love," Dylan replied.

I thought for a moment.

"Who was that other guy? That Yekkon?" I asked.

"Yeqon, you mean?" Dylan responded. "He is one of Lucifer's Chosen, a fallen angel just like him. He supported Lucifer against our Father and was cast down. He is Lucifer's agent in this... situation."

"What situation? I'm confused Uncle Dyl, what has all this to do with me?" I questioned.

Uncle Dylan gave a sigh and hugged me to him, folding a wing around my body.

"It's a wager, nephew. There is a soul being conceived as we speak, who will grow up into hardship, into fear, into pain. But also, there is the chance of friendship, of freedom and of love. Yeqon will be doing everything he can to force the soul into the darkness, into following what you have done, into the cardinal sin."

"What is God going to do?" I asked.

"He is sending you," Uncle Dylan replied. "You are to guide the soul to safety and happiness."

"ME?" I was shocked. "Why me?"

"This is your chance to redeem yourself and find a place in Heaven. By saving the soul of another, you gain redemption, and Lucifer has agreed to give back the souls that he taken for committing suicide in the past, and to waive his rights to them in the future."

"What happens if I don't succeed?" I asked.

"Well, we lose you to Purgatory, along with the rest of the souls who commit suicide for the rest of eternity," my Uncle replied.

Yeqon suddenly reappeared, back as his demonic form, holding a cruel looking dual pronged spike.

"And should you lose the soul, my young opponent, not only will I be given you for eternity, but that of your charge as well." The spike glowed, a burning white hot, and his evil laughter filled the room as he once again faded from sight.

Chapter Two

I spent the next few months being trained to prepare for my mission. I was schooled by the muses on how to inspire people. There were Angels who taught me about compassion and empathy. There was the Angel Haniel, who is the Angel of Harmonious Love, the Angel Malcheldiel who inspires courage, something I will definitely need. and the Angel Verchiel, the Angel of Affection.

I even got to meet the Archangel Metatron, the voice of God. He showed me how to communicate with humans. There is a special trick to it. Ever since the serpent tricked Eve in the Garden of Eden, there are only certain levels in the hierarchy of celestial beings that can be heard by mankind. There are some tricks to get around it, which is why the Angels of Darkness succeed in their diabolical plans, and now I was being taught them because. despite my assignment, I hadn't been granted Angel status. As I am in limbo between acceptance to Heaven, and damnation to Hell, I am classified as a 'protective spirit'. I think they actually needed to come up with a new name for me.

The coolest Angel though was the one called the Angel Forcas. He is the teacher of mathematics and logic. Boring I know, but I forgave him when he also showed me the ability of invisibility. Yup!! No Harry Potter cloak needed!! I can phase in and out of the visible spectrum at will!!

I was studying with one of the Angels called Jackson. He had been human and was elevated to the celestial choir upon his death because of the life he had led on Earth, working selflessly for charity organisations. He was teaching under privileged children in war torn areas of the world when a stray bullet from an ambush attack on the village he was in hit him and killed him instantly. He was teaching me about which humans can see or identify us.

"Now not every human is capable of seeing the ethereal beings, both good and evil. In fact, only a small percentage truly believe in the existence of God and the Heavenly Host. Of those, an even smaller percentage can hear our whisperings and a fraction of those can see us. Something has happened to the Human mind in the last few thousand years that make it incapable of believing that, all around them, Angels and Demons battle for their souls." Jackson told me.

"But some can right? You know, like psychics and stuff?" I asked.

"Yes, we are able to influence all humans to an extent, and there are those that can hear or see us. We call them 'communers', they call themselves psychics and most humans call them crazy"" Jackson said with a chuckle.

"Children however are another group altogether," he told me.

I looked questioningly at him.

"The raw imagination of a young child has no limits, no boundaries. So while many people remember having an imaginary friend from their youth, what they do not realise is that their friends are, in fact, real."

"You mean Angels? They're our imaginary friends?" I asked.

"Yes, they are on Earth to protect the children," Jackson told me. "However, we are not the only beings interested in the fate of humans."

"Demons?" I queried.

"Yes, why do you think there are so many stories and memories of the monster under the bed, or in the closet?" the older being told me.

"So why don't we remember that they are real?" I asked.

"When a child is born, they are truly innocent. No-one is born evil, or good for that matter. It is all about how we are raised that decides that fate. When we reach the age of five, innocence is lost and we lose the ability to see the beings around us, unless they make themselves known to us," Jackson explained.

I filed that information away for later use. If I could be seen by my charge and become his friend in his very early years, maybe I would be able to help him and influence his choices better.

The area in which we were studying suddenly glowed with a golden light and a fanfare erupted in my ears. I looked around to see a staircase appear from nowhere and a figure marched down it, confident and upright. It was a tall male, blonde hair and dark looks, clad in a suit of golden armour. Wings adorned his back and I knew instantly that I was in the presence of a major hierarchal figure.

"Protector Joseph?" the armoured figure asked.

"Yes sir," I said, jumping to my feet and bowing as best I could.

"It is time for your training to take a more militaristic approach," the Angel told me.

"Has the vote finally been decided Saint Michael?" Jackson asked the now named figure.

I gulped, and looked at the armoured figure in awe. This was Saint Michael, one of the higher Archangels in the throne room of Our Father himself. This was one of God's Generals, who leads the Celestial Army in their battles against the forces of Lucifer.

"Yes Teacher Jackson, we finally persuaded the Muses to cast their lot with us," Saint Michael said, with a smile.

"Um, excuse me Sir," I said reverently, "but why has there been a vote if you can teach me or not? I mean, aren't I meant to go and be God's representative on Earth against Yeqon?"

"You are indeed, but there was a section of the Council who were arguing that, as you had not been granted entry into Heaven and the reasons behind it, you should not be taught that which the Demons do not know," Saint Michael told me gently.

"You mean 'cos I killed myself?" I said sadly.

"Simply put, yes," the armoured Angel responded. "There are those on the Council who believe that Humanity, and indeed all living things, have been granted a gift by our Father, the Gift of Life, and to choose to take your own life is seen as a rejection of God's Gift and an insult to Him."

"But it wasn't like that," I started to whine, but the Saint held his hand up to interrupt me.

"I know and I do agree that in certain circumstances, the taking of one's life is a plea to our Father to be gathered up from despair and brought into the light of His Love."

He wrapped an arm around me and, where I thought it would be cold with the armour next to my bare arms, I could feel warmth flowing from him.

"So you have been arguing over whether or not you can teach me stuff?" I asked, feeling more confident and at ease with him. After all, he was obviously on my side.

"Yes, for many weeks now we have monitored your training and progress. I brought into the discussions that it is Yeqon himself that you will be competing against and that he, despite the depths to which he has fallen, is still an adversary to be feared."

"Whereas some of the others think you shouldn't teach me stuff 'cos if I fail, I'm going to Hell, which is where they think I belong anyway?" I stated, realising the extent of the discussions that had been taking place unbeknownst to me.

"That is correct," Saint Michael answered. "We have debated this for some time."

I sniggered as the easiest of all comments sprung to my dirty little mind. Jackson and Saint Michael looked enquiringly at me. I couldn't resist and so I said it.

"So you Angels have been sitting there having a mass debate about me?" I said, smirking and trying to hold in laughter.

"Yes, I told you that we have," Saint Michael said, confused at my repeating of his previous statement.

Jackson, being formerly human on the other hand, let a smile spread across his face, as for the first time since my death, I had shown signs of humour.

"Joe, tell me you seriously did not just say that to a Saint!" Jackson sighed.

"Sorry, but I couldn't resist it," I chuckled, a couple of tears beginning to fall down my cheeks.

"I am confused," Saint Michael stated. "Why are you finding humour about the Council having a detailed discussion about this subject?"

"No, no, no, Saint Michael," I giggled. "You were all having a mass debate about me!"

I fell to the floor, unable to hold in my laughter. I saw Jackson approach Saint Michael and whispered into his ear. His eyes grew large and he looked at me with an amused look.

"I see the misunderstanding now Protector Joseph," Saint Michael said. "You assumed that we celestial beings, born of Angels, have the certain human appendages that you find so enjoyable to exercise. Alas we do not, so we do not pleasure ourselves that way."

I looked at him in surprise. I had been learning something new every day, but this certainly was something unexpected. There went my plans for kicking Yeqon in the nuts, given the chance!

"You mean if I do get into Heaven, I'm gonna lose my dick?" I squeaked in horror.

"No Joe, you're not," Jackson laughed, reassuring me. "Humans brought into Heaven keep everything in working order. I mean, it wouldn't be Heaven if we lost one of our favourite past times now would it?"

I gave a big sigh of relief.

"Well I will leave you two to it," Jackson said, gathering his books that he had been using to teach me.

"Teacher, why do you not stay a while?" Saint Michael said. "There are certain exercises that could use a helper."

Jackson looked at Saint Michael, narrowing his eyes at the now innocent face of the Saint.

"Hmmm, I've heard about some of your new exercises, General Michael," Jackson said lowly. "I'll sit over here and watch, and don't you think I'm going to get up and get my butt kicked again!"

"It was just that one time, Teacher Jackson, and when will you forgive me for it?" Saint Michael chuckled. "You do know that forgiveness is a virtue, and you do wish to be virtuous do you not?"

"Ha!" Jackson shouted. He looked at me. "His Saintliness here used me as the sparring partner of the last Guardian Angel in training. I had bruises for weeks."

"I will be more gentle this time, my friend," Saint Michael promised him.

And with that my physical training started. As a being that I had believed had no physical form, I found myself breathing hard for the next couple of weeks as Saint Michael drilled my body and my mind. I found myself in better shape than I had ever been, and my mind more alert. I was taught how to sense danger and identify it, how to cast my mind around in an open net and how to close it in on different beings. Jackson was a constant companion, helping to explain when the Archangel used terminology that I didn't understand. He was a willing target for my new found abilities of mental attack and, as much as he had jokingly complained at the beginning about being the focus of the attacks, he did so without question. I gained a new respect for him and thought that it was a great loss for Earth that he had been killed before his time.

Eventually, Saint Michael told me that I was as ready as I could be and, with the training he had given me and in light of the lack of any new teacher coming forward, Jackson remained with me and turned my training to more studious affairs. Book after book was plucked from thin air and, while I had enjoyed reading when I was alive, I now ploughed through books like Heaven's library had an hourly rate.

"Hey Joe, there's someone I'd like you to meet." I turned my head as I heard my Uncle Dylan enter the room behind me, where I was reading a book called 'Death in Venice' by a German author called Thomas Mann. I had been given it to read as it was all about a man who falls in love with a teenage boy, and stays in Venice despite an outbreak of cholera, to which he finally succumbs. What was really sad about the story was that the guy, Gustav, didn't even talk to the boy, just fell in love from afar and even gave up his life to stay near him. I guess the moral of the story is about how far people are willing to go for love, and at times why we act the weird way that we do for the ones we love.

A feminine figure of beauty walked in beside Uncle Dylan. If I had any doubts that I may not be gay, this proved my homosexuality because, as stunningly beautiful as she was, I still felt nothing. Mind you, maybe I shouldn't be having these thoughts about God's Angels anyway!!

"Protector Joseph, I am Lailah," she said to me, holding out a hand as way of greeting. I took it, not knowing what to do otherwise. She was the first Angel to offer me a hand in greeting. In fact, the only other Angel besides Jackson to actually touch me was the Angel Forcas, who had proven to be very adept at high fives while I was practising my visibility shifts.

"Um, nice to meet you ma'am," I replied, self-consciously straightening myself to look presentable.

"There is no need for formality my young spirit," she said, obviously trying to set me at ease. "Come, let us walk. I have things to discuss with you about your charge."

I glanced at Uncle Dylan, who nodded for me to go with her, so I left my book and walked alongside her. The room suddenly phased out and we were walking by the bank of a silver river, along a path of golden grass. I looked up at her and a smile crossed her face.

"I'm sorry, but I can't understand why they keep you in the dingy grey conditions that they do, this is much better do you not agree?" Lailah asked.

"Absolutely ma'am," I replied respectfully. Hey, if she can change the scenery with just a thought, then what could she do to me if I upset her??? Self-preservation here guys!

"Joseph, please call me Lailah," she told me.

"Okay, but only if you call me Joe," I responded with a smile. She had a disarming attitude that certainly was making me feel relaxed, or was it the feel of her right wing as it stretched and covered by back?

"Do you know who I am?" she asked me.

"Um, the Angel Lailah?" I replied.

She smiled and let out a small laugh. "No young spirit, I meant my responsibilities," she queried.

"No, not really Lailah," I answered. "I've seen so many different Angels over the last few months that I've sort of lost track as to who does what." I bowed my head slightly at my confession.

"But I am sure you remember my brother Forcas," she chuckled. "He speaks very highly of you and your commitment to learning."

I felt myself blush at the compliment. We continued to walk for a few moments before coming across a bench by the edge of the slowly winding river. Lailah motioned for me to sit and she took a place next to me, keeping her wing around me, almost protectively, almost to stop me running away. I wasn't sure which.

"I am the Angel of Conception, which means I look after the souls of those conceived from embryo until birth. I was directed by Our Heavenly Father to keep a special watch on a certain soul, for it is his destiny to change the Universe." Lailah looked at me and held out a hand. A silver bound book appeared from nowhere. "In here, is the history of your charge, his parents and family and the history that surrounds them. You are advised to study and read it until you know it by heart, as it is your heart that can save the soul."

She held the book out to me, and I reached forward with shaking hands. It seemed like I was reaching out to take someone's past, present and future which, in a way, I suppose I was.

"Um, no offence meant Lailah, but if you are responsible for looking after and caring for them until they are born, why are you passing this to me now?" I asked, as politely as I could. "I mean, there is still another month before the baby is due to be born. A lot could happen in that month."

A sad look took the place of her gentle smile as she said quietly, "Alas the soul is now in danger. He is required to leave his protective womb early due to the first of many dangers that will befall him."

I felt an unknown force slam into my side, but I was held in place by Lailah's wing and was prevented from falling off the bench. I looked up in surprise to see two figures materialise in front of us.

"Angel Perpetiel, Saint Peter," Lailah acknowledged reverently in greeting, as she stood and bowed, her wing encouraging me to do the same.

"Have you passed on the Chapter of Life to the Protector?" Saint Peter asked her.

"I have Saintly one," she replied.

"Then come with me young Protector," St Peter commanded. "For now is the time for your assignment to begin."

I looked at the tall figure in shock.

"But, but, but I still have a month to go," I stammered. "I'm not yet fully ready."

"Be that as it may, but the forces of the Accursed One are abound and have caused an accident which has put the soul's earthly protectors at risk." Saint Peter informed me. "Our Heavenly Father suggests you are despatched to watch over the soul during the first struggle of his earthborn existence."

"But Lailah has only just given me this book," I told him. "Aren't I supposed to read it before I go?"

"There is no time young Protector," the Saintly figure told me. He bent down so he could speak into my ear. "Fear not for, although by terms of the wager with the Accursed One you are supposed to be on your own during this battle, help will find its way to you."

That reassured me slightly, as I had been told I was completely on my own against Yeqon, but this at least offered me a glimmer of hope. After all, I was a sixteen year old boy spirit about to do battle with one of the most ancient and formerly higher angels.

The angelic form of Perpetiel came and stood beside me and covered me with a wing. I looked up and saw the faces of Saint Peter, Lailah and Uncle Dylan, and for a brief moment, a blinding light behind them. I felt it was a good omen that the angel who was to transport me back to the earthly realm is recognised as the Angel of success.

As I felt myself begin to phase out of the celestial plane that had been my home for the last eight months, I suddenly shouted to Lailah that I didn't know how I was to recognise my charge, or what the name was.

Lailah smiled at me.

"As a protector, you will know your charge as soon as you set eyes upon the soul," I heard her voice whisper as my phasing continued.

"As for the name, his name is Adam."

Chapter Three

Sirens were blaring all around me as I materialised back on the earthly plane that had been home for the sixteen years of my previous life. Boy, if I knew then what I know now, how much of my life would I have lived differently? I would definitely have gone to church a lot more, but I guess hindsight is a wonderful thing.

I was brought out of my musings by the shouts of a man who, when I looked at him, was wearing the green and yellow uniform of a paramedic. The scene in front of me was one of carnage. There were at least half a dozen cars smashed, crumpled or overturned. A lorry was embedded into the wall of a building by the side of the road. Obviously, it had smashed through the cars on its journey to the edge of the road.

Police cars and ambulances were interspersed between them and paramedics and firemen fought the crushed metal vehicles to try to free the occupants. I walked in between the cars and felt a pull towards an overturned blue BMW. I used my inner vision to see through the crushed metal and saw a male, slumped unconscious behind the driving wheel, blood freely pouring from a large cut on the side of his head where the airbag had pushed him sideways into the side window. A dark haired woman was moaning in pain, holding her bloated stomach. At first, I thought it was just a woman who had obviously let herself eat too much and exercised too little, but then I felt a pain in my own stomach and realised that this couple were Adam's parents.

I turned to see where the paramedics were, but there simply were not enough of them at the scene to cope with everyone. I tried my empathic powers to try to persuade the nearest medic to leave his current patient to go and attend the couple who had my whole attention. However, the pull of his current patient overrode my insistence. Desperately, I looked around, and heard a low chuckle behind me. I turned and saw the red and black skinned form of Yeqon materialise before me.

"Having trouble my young opponent?" He said, still chuckling.

"They won't let me in their heads to persuade them"to help," I complained to him, though why I was telling Yeqon this, I didn't understand. "How can I save them if I can't get help?"

"Not my problem, Protector," he said with a sneer at the name assigned to me.

I growled in frustration, turning away and looking at the crowd of people gathering, watching the scene as though it was the latest episode of some drama on television. Remembering the words of Angel Hamael, who taught me the art of persistence and practicality, I opened my mind and allowed myself to scan the people watching. I felt slight disgust as some of the minds were enthralled by the pain and suffering that was occurring in front of their eyes, before I touched a mind that opened possibilities to me.

I brought my mind's eye back to my normal ones and looked at the body of the mind that I had touched. My confidence faded slightly as I saw a boy of around fifteen or sixteen. He was standing, watching with pain in his eyes and a look of desperation on his face. I could see he wanted to help.

"Well, he's all I've got to work with so I'd better make the most of it," I said, more to myself than anyone else.

I let my mind touch his again and sifted quickly through his feelings and memories. I discovered a young man who had suffered the loss of a brother in a car accident a couple of years previously. His inability to help his younger brother had hurt him deeply, and he had set his future to learn how to become a first aider and then to study to become a doctor. I found the part of his sub-conscious that dealt with his confidence and gave it a little nudge.

Suddenly the boy was on the move, past the outstretched arm of the policeman who was attempting to prevent the watching audience from encroaching on the scene. He dodged his way to the BMW and peered in through the windscreen. He saw Adam's father passed out and bleeding. He managed to open the car door slowly and supported the injured man's head as it threatened to slump out. He reached in and undid the seatbelt that had save the man from instant death and lowered him to the tarmacked surface. The young man wiped the blood from his face with a cloth he found inside the doorwell of the car and quickly inspected the wound. He undid the man's tie and using the cloth as a makeshift bandage, tied it to staunch the flow of blood and rested the man's head back down, using his own coat as a makeshift pillow.

"Interesting choice of helper," Yeqon announced, appearing by my side once more. "How did you decide on this one? His looks?"

I looked properly at the youth for the first time as he scooted around the car and made his way to Adam's mother. I noticed his blonde hair and tanned complexion. His now bare arms had a firmness to them. I felt myself begin to get aroused at the thought of him. A desire to take him away from the scene and ravish his body crossed my thoughts. I saw him stumble as he opened the passenger door and looked inside. A look of doubt flashed across his face. I felt my hold on his mind begin to crumble.

A shiver ran through my being, and a sudden feeling that I was being manipulated hit me. I growled in anger and looked at the beast standing not far from me, watching and enjoying the pain of a woman in her twenties finally losing her battle against her injuries.

"Yeqon, I reject you and your thoughts," I spat at him.

Yeqon's grin turned into a scowl and he hissed as he turned to me.

"You're learning, my young opponent," he said to me. "The last object of my attention was not nearly as strong as you."

He motioned to the cabin of the truck, where I could see the paramedics carrying out the mangled body of a half-naked young boy and that of the truck driver, whose faded jeans and underwear were down by his ankles. I whispered a small prayer for the soul of the boy before returning my attention to my young helper. I reached into his mind again and tweaked his confidence once more. The young man's shoulders straightened and he reached into the car.

"Hi there missus, I'm Jake and I'm gonna help you okay," he said to the dark haired woman, who was beginning to groan in pain.
"Urgh, Jake, you need to get the belt off me," I heard her say. "I'm pregnant and it's pressing into my womb."
"No problem, I can do that," Jake reassured her. "What's your name?"
"Penny," she said. "Are you a paramedic?"

Jake reached across her, unclipping the belt from its holder and eased it up and over her, releasing its hold on her.

"Not quite Penny," he said, "but I'm getting there."

She let out a loud groan of pain and gripped Jake's hand tight. I saw Jake's expression turn to pain as the woman's hand crushed his under her own agony. Again, I felt pain stab through the middle of my being and for the first time, I felt fear. Not my own. I was used to my own feelings of fear, but this was something different. Something primal. Something innocent.

"Adam!" I whispered under my breath.

Somehow, the unborn child knew of the danger he was in and was reaching out for help. I turned in frustration to where the nearest paramedic was finishing bandaging the wound of a young girl who had several cuts on her arm that had been forced through a side window.

I tried to gently enter his mind but, once again came across the feelings that he had to help his current patient. Knowing it was something that I would not be too proud of later, I tore past the barriers of his mind and forced my thoughts into his. 'Help Jake!'

The man stiffened, looked around and saw the young form of Jake holding Penny, supporting her as she started to convulse. He got up and sprinted over to the upturned car and started an examination of the woman.

"Who are you?" he asked Jake as his hands were checking Penny's pulse.

"I'm Jake Warburton and I have a first class award from the St John's Ambulance," the blonde haired boy answered.

"Good, I need your help here," the paramedic told him. "This woman has gone into labour. We need to deliver the baby now."

"What?" Jake exclaimed. "I can't deliver a baby!"

"You can and you will," the paramedic reassured him. "If we don't, we will lose both of them."

I touched their minds and gave the pair of them a boost of confidence and laid my hands on each of their shoulders, sending healing energies through their bodies to make sure that they were in the best condition to help save the lives of the Adam and his mother. I watched nervously as they battled with the injuries that Penny had sustained, and the imminent entrance into the world of my charge. I heard Jake going through the motions of every midwife from every movie that he must have seen, telling Penny when to push and when to breathe.

Suddenly I saw a flash of light streak across the heavens and felt my heart expand with joy. A cry came from the car and I knew instantly that Adam had made his entrance into the world.

"It's a boy!" I heard Jake shout. "Penny, you have a son."

I saw the woman turn her head weakly and gaze lovingly at the bundle in Jake's arms.

"Adam," Penny whispered. "My son."

Her eyes rolled back in her head and I saw her body go limp. The paramedic shouted in distress to his colleagues and one of them joined him and they worked on trying to resuscitate Adam's mother. Eventually an ambulance pulled up and Penny was transferred to a stretcher and into the back of the vehicle. Jake was ushered into the vehicle holding the crying form of Adam. I willed myself inside the moving truck and was shocked to see another celestial being in there with me.

"Ezekiel?" I asked.

The Angel of Death and Transformation looked at me, and then sadly at the woman whom the medics were desperately trying to save. The slow beeping of the monitor suddenly turned into a monotone and continual noise.

"Flatline!" one of them shouted.
"Charging!" the other said, holding paddles in his hands.

I had seen this on television often enough to know what was about to happen. I glanced at Ezekiel, who shook his head. I focused on Jake and the baby boy he was holding. The baby had grown silent, almost as though he knew his mother was in mortal danger. I looked at his face and into his deep blue eyes. I opened my thoughts to his and allowed feelings of love and safety flow from me into him, trying to reassure him that he would be okay.
I heard a gasp and a cry from a female form and turned back to where the paramedics were still trying to save his mother's life and was shocked to see a shining form next to Ezekiel.

"Are you real?" the spirit of Penny asked.
"We are," Ezekiel replied. "You have been called by Our Father."
"But who will look after Adam? And what of my husband, John?" she asked.

I phased myself to become visible to her.

"Hello Penny, I am Joe," I said of way of introduction. "I am Adam's protector."
"I knew I felt someone helping us," she said with a small smile on her face. "Is that Jake?" she asked, motioning towards the brave young man whom I had commandeered.
"Yes, he was a great help to you," I told her.
"And his help will not be forgotten," Ezekiel said. "Saint Peter has already scribed his actions into his Chapter."

Adam chose that moment to give a little cry.

"Can I see my baby before I go?" Penny asked, a catch in her voice as she realised this would be her only chance to see her baby before she left.
"Of course," Ezekiel responded. He waved his hand and unknowingly, Jake turned to one side, showing Adam to his now deceased mother.
"Oh, he's beautiful," Penny said, with tears streaming down her cheeks.

She reached out to touch him, and the infant must have felt some connection as a smile spread across his face.

"It is time," Ezekiel told Penny.

I looked over and saw a tunnel of light appear.

"We're losing her!" one of the paramedics shouted.
"Take care of my baby boy," Penny begged me.
"I will," I told her. "I will look after him with the whole of my soul."
"Thank you," she whispered. "Live well my son."

She turned and moved towards the tunnel.

"You did well today, Protector Joseph," Ezekiel told me. "You were never meant to save the mother so do not despair on this. You saved the child and also set another on the path of his destiny."
"What of Adam's dad?" I asked.
"It is not yet his time to depart this plane," Ezekiel told me. "Adam's father will survive physically but, emotionally, this will damage him. Prepare yourself and your charge for the time ahead."

The Angel held out his hand and I took it, shaking it in farewell. The light vanished from the ambulance and they were gone.

"She's gone!" I heard the paramedic say with a sigh. "Note time of death is, err, nine thirty seven am."

I heard a sob from Jake, and looked over at the youngster, holding my charge. I reached out with my thoughts and reassured him that he, himself, had done a good job in saving Adam's father and keeping Penny alive long enough to deliver Adam into the world. His shoulders straightened and he cradled the young baby closer to him, with a look on his face that I am sure most people have whenever they look at a newborn child.

I felt the vehicle slow down and stop as we arrived at the hospital.

Chapter Four

For the next five years I watched as Adam grew from a baby to a toddler and then a young child. Throughout it all, his father John was distant. Don't get me wrong, he provided for Adam, everything that was needed for the child to live and grow physically. However, emotionally, he had withdrawn from his son, whom he blamed for the loss of his wife.

No matter how much empathy and love I poured into the man, I just couldn't break through the barrier of hate he had built around his heart. I spent my time between trying to knock down that barrier, and building a protective barrier of love around Adam's heart, ensuring that he grew to love his father unconditionally. Having lost my own father's love, I was determined that Adam would not lose his, even if it killed me. I often chuckled to myself at the absurdity of that statement.

As Adam grew, I could see why, at times, his father steeled himself against his son. Adam had the same dark brown hair, the same dark blue eyes, and even the same features as his dead mother. It must be extremely painful to have loved someone deeply, have them taken from you and then to have a child grow up reminding you so much of what you have lost.

John often hired nannies, or au pairs, to come and look after Adam as he grew, but as with all hired staff, the love so desperately needed by a child was missing. I often found myself phasing into Adam's sight when we were alone so that he could feel love and safety. I knew that I could not do this for much longer, as memories start to embed themselves after the age of five and my appearance would no longer be remembered as the imaginary friend that he thought he had. That was one of the rules set down in stone that Adam was not allowed to know of our existence. Heck, most humans in fact were not capable of admitting our existence, let alone being willing to see us.

I was also surprised that, during this period, I didn't see Yeqon at all. Not one appearance, not one vision, not one horn. This worried me greatly at first but, as the months turned into years and time rolled on, I guess I got used to it. After all, the agreement was that Adam would be at most risk as he turned thirteen. I guess the demon had better things to do than hang around for all those years waiting for the battle to start.

Me? I had all the time in the world. I had been consigned to Earth on this mission. I had no entry to Heaven and I certainly wasn't about to visit Hell, so I contented myself with observing my young charge, watching him grow, showering him with love and affection where I could.

The day came when Adam was to start school. Sure he had been to nurseries before, but John never seemed to remember to keep up payments to them and so he was moved from one to another, never able to settle, never able to create a young friendship that could last more than a couple of months. As such, even at a young age, Adam was slightly withdrawn, unable to have the confidence to make the first step and go and make friends. Fortunately, whenever he was away from the cold emotions of his father, Adam had an easy going attitude and a ready smile. This made him approachable and I did my best to nudge potential young friends in his direction at every opportunity.

As Helen, the latest in the line of nannies, dressed Adam in his school uniform, which basically consisted of a pale yellow polo shirt, and had the school badge and name embroidered on to it, and a pair of grey shorts, I sensed John as he looked into his son's room.

"Daddy!" Adam shouted in glee, spotting his father. "Look at me! I'm all growed up now!"

I saw a faint smile flicker across the man's face as he looked at his son with affection, before the familiar stony expression reasserted itself.

"Yes you are Adam," he said simply. "Time for school."

He turned to Helen and asked her if she had her car keys, which she did, and we were soon off on the short journey to King Edward VI Primary School, just six roads away. I had thought about planting a suggestion to walk in her mind, but one look at the storm clouds outside changed my mind. I was not about to let my little man get wet on his first day of school. The journey took next to no time and, as we approached the school gates, I felt apprehension flowing from Adam. I looked at him and saw a look of concern on his face.

"Don't worry Adam," I whispered in his ear. "You'll have fun here and make friends with boys and girls just like you."

A smile spread across his face and he literally jumped out of the back seat into Helen's arms once his seatbelt had been removed.

"Easy my little tiger cub!" Helen teased him. "Let's get you into class."

Adam took her hand and walked into the playground, which was crowded with small children running here, there and everywhere. There were a couple of impromptu football matches, if you can call a dozen boys under the age of eight running around after a ball a football match. Several climbing frames and swings were covered in young children and three poor adults trying desperately to make sure that the children were no danger to themselves or others.

I remembered when I was studying for my exams thinking that it would be great to go into teaching and had formulated what A-Levels I wanted to do to pursue that chosen career path. Looking at the harassed members of staff, I almost gave silent thanks that I did not achieve my goal. Of course, my alternative path was one that I had no idea I was going to choose instead! Trust me when I say that the harassed life of a teacher would have been infinitely more desirable than the path that I had chosen to follow.

At some point, Helen had ushered Adam into the reception hall and stood with a few of the parents, who had stayed to make sure their children were safely into the school system.

The Headmistress of the school stood in front of the forty odd five year olds and welcomed them to the school. She told them not to worry, that they would soon make friends with the other children and that if they have any problems to see their teacher. She then called a list of names out and the first sixteen children left the room with two middle aged women. The next sixteen children were called and again, off they went with their teachers and finally the names of the last set of fifteen children, including Adam were read out.

"Children, this is Mrs Jackson and Mr Williams, and they will be your teachers for the first year. If you would follow them to your classroom where you can settle down and start the day." The Headmistress finished off and after a quick hello and goodbye to some of the parents that she obviously knew from previous pupils, she disappeared into an office.

I followed the line of children into their classroom and saw four tables that each could sit four children, two on each side. A feeling of worry came over me, which was confirmed as Mrs Jackson began seating the children in alphabetical order. Adam's surname was Zegers and my young charge was seated with two other boys, but on the side of the table on his own.

I saw Adam's smile falter as the two boys opposite began to talk quietly to each other and Adam had just an empty seat next to him. I moved over to where the two adults were quietly looking at Adam's table.

"Did you hear about the horrible accident that happened to the Wilson boy last week?" Mrs Jackson asked Mr Williams.

A look of sadness came across his face as he nodded. "It was awful, the parents must be beside themselves, but still, who lets a five year old wander that close to a cliff top?"

"They weren't to know that there was going to be such a sudden storm though, Phil," the female teacher said. "It came out of nowhere and the poor boy was blown completely off the cliff into the sea below."

"And there was no way that a five year old could survive in the currents off Beachy Head Point," Phil agreed.

I was getting a feeling that this may not have been such an accident. After all, the school only took forty eight pupils in each age group each year to ensure that classes are not overcrowded and each pupil can spend quality time with the two teachers during the early learning stages, and for one child out of forty eight to meet with a sudden fatal accident, just days before term was due to start, and for that one child to be the one who would have sat next to Adam was too much of a coincidence. Silently I cursed Yeqon under my breath and turned my attention to the two boys sitting opposite my charge.

One boy was a blonde haired, blue eyed cherub. Freckles adorned his nose and when he smiled, the gaps in his teeth made his impish grin even more adorable. The other was a ginger haired podgy boy. His face seemed to naturally gravitate to a frown and I got an uneasy feeling from him. However, willing to give him the benefit of doubt, I touched each of their minds and gave them a small nudge of friendship towards Adam. They both stopped their conversation and looked at Adam.

"Hi, I'm Gawy," the blonde haired boy said, showing signs of a slight speech impediment.

"I'm Adam," my little man announced. "I like your necklace," pointing to a silver chain around Gary's thin neck. I spotted a small crucifix on the chain, and smiled as he was obviously from a family that at least acknowledged the existence of God.

"I'm Darren," the ginger haired boy told Adam.

After these initial introductions, the boys settled into a conversation regarding cowboys and dinosaurs. How the two topics got merged I have no idea, but who knows the workings of the five year old male mind? All I was concerned with was that Adam seemed to be getting along with the two boys and, hopefully, this was the start of friendships. From what I had learned, he was going to need friends around him later in life when the true tests started.

After a few more minutes of allowing the children to talk amongst themselves, the two teachers called the class to order and quickly outlined what they were going to be doing. It mainly consisted of reading, copy writing, speaking and basic times tables. Work books were handed out, along with pencils, rulers and erasers. Each child had a removable drawer from a cupboard where they were to store their equipment when not using it so that they didn't have to carry it back and forth from school.

The bell for break time rang and all the children, under the supervision of Mrs Jackson, walked calmly outside, back into the playground. I watched in amusement as Adam, with his two new friends, ran around the grass dodging imaginary dinosaurs, well I hope they were imaginary! I opened my mind up to the surroundings to cast a net of awareness across the school. I had been taught this trick as a way of detecting any threat to Adam, or myself. I was satisfied that there currently was no danger and allowed myself a few moments to relax.

Before too long, the bell rang again and the children headed inside for the rest of the morning's classes. The remainder of the day passed without incident, except for an unfortunate accident involving Gary's dinner tray, a bowl of chicken soup and Darren's polo shirt. I swear I had nothing to do with it!

As the afternoon passed, I sat perched on a cupboard, listening to the lessons, remembering from my own childhood the story that Mr Williams was telling. He had started with 'The Cat in the Hat', and I found myself getting lost in the story, let alone the younger children who sat, enthralled, with rapt expressions on their faces. I could see why the man had gone into teaching, as he kept the kids spellbound with his narrative, and his voice changed as each character came into the story.

I have to say, it had been one of the most enjoyable school days that I could remember, even if I wasn't strictly there as a pupil. Dark memories threatened to overwhelm me for a moment as the last two years of my own schooling came back to haunt me. To pull myself out of the depression that was beginning to settle over me, I concentrated on my little charge.

I looked over at Adam as he was carefully placing his pencils back into his drawer and I watched in horror as I saw an older, bigger boy appear from nowhere to push him headfirst into the cupboard. Adam's screams rang out as blood began to pour freely from his mouth, through the small delicate fingers that now cupped his wounded face. I saw white on the floor next to him and saw that small baby teeth were lying on the carpeted surface. Anger flashed through me and I felt myself grow powerful as adrenaline surged in my mind and I looked around for Adam's attacker.

The final bell rang to announce home time, shocking me and making me jump. I clenched my fists and looked once more to where I thought I had seen the older boy run. All I saw was Adam's class mates noisily getting up out of their chairs and placing them on the tables, readying themselves to go home. I couldn't believe that no-one was reacting to the attack on Adam, and helplessly looked at my young charge to see him calmly placing his own chair on the table. There wasn't a hair out of place, no injury visible.

I heard a demonic laugh and was instantly on my guard. However, I could see no sign of the beast. I pulled my thoughts together and cleansed my mind of his influence. I concentrated on looking at Adam and felt the darkness lift from my mind as the innocence of the child shone through.

I guess Yeqon wasn't being as absent and unconcerned about Adam as I had thought earlier in the day. I mentally kicked myself for becoming complacent and vowed to be more on my guard.

With farewells and goodbyes to the two teachers and his new classmates, Adam waited calmly by the school entrance, sheltering from the slight wind that had picked up. I looked around for Helen, but could see no sign of her. Where was she?

I whispered into Adam's ear to remain where he was. I left him to have a look outside the school gates to see if I could spot her. I could see a log jam of traffic at the top of the road, where the turning was to come down to the school. Casting my mind's eye, I spotted Helen in her small blue Ford Focus, battling to try to get past some idiots that had parked illegally on her side of the road, while a flow of traffic kept her pinned so she could not drive past.

A tug on my mind made me turn back to the school and to where Adam was, the link between us serving as a safety system. I could see a man that I didn't recognise talking to my dark haired charge and I willed myself back to his side.

"Come on Adam," the man said. "Daddy sent me to pick you up."

"Uh uh," Adam insisted, shaking his head. "I don't know who you are and Joe says not to go off with anyone I don't know."

"It's okay Adam," the man tried to reassure him. "Your Uncle Joe said it's okay as well. I live next door to him."

I felt anger surge through my being as the man was trying every trick to get Adam to go with him. Somehow Adam picked up on my feelings as he pulled away from the man.

"Joe isn't my uncle, he's my friend and he lives at my house," Adam shouted. "Get away from me!"

Adam's shouts brought Mr Williams from inside the school and as he approached the strange man, I could see a look of anger on his face.

"Who are you and what do you want with our pupil?" he demanded.

"I'm here to pick the boy up," the man said. "His Dad can't make it so he asked me to make sure he got home."

"Uh uh!" Adam protested. "Helen is picking me up!"

I could see Mr Williams taking in Adam's statement as I appeared next to the teacher. I whispered into his ear to believe Adam and that Helen was indeed just down the road. I saw his shoulders straighten.

"Look here pal," he started. "If you don't hop it, I will call the police and have you arrested for attempted kidnapping!"

The man looked the teacher over, and I saw his own demeanour change to one of greater confidence.

"What if I just take the kid anyway," he sneered. "Who's going to stop me? You?" He laughed, and as he did, I saw that he did outweigh Adam's teacher quite dramatically. Not only that, but the guy was built with muscles.

I cast my mind out, searching for help. I touched three of the female teachers inside, watching from the window, and Mrs Henderson, the Headmistress came striding out of the front door, mobile phone in hand.

"That's correct Sergeant Moore, there is a man in his thirties here trying to abduct one of my pupils," she said loudly into the mouth piece.

Faint sirens could be heard a few streets away and the man took a look around, just as Helen's car pulled into the car park. A glazed look came across his face and he stumbled forward before collapsing on the ground. Mr Williams bent over him, checking his vitals as two police cars screamed into the school yard, narrowly avoiding Helen who was rushing through the gate to Adam.

Upon seeing his nanny, a smile spread across Adam's face and, with a shout of glee, he took three huge strides and jumped into her outstretched arms.

As Helen repeatedly apologised to both Adam and Mrs Henderson for getting held up in the traffic jam, I once again cast my mind to the surrounding area. Something didn't quite sit right with me and, off in a corner of the yard, I sensed a malevolent presence. It wasn't Yeqon, I could tell that immediately. I think I had got used to the feel of his mind. It was an evil presence, but I was sure it was a lesser being than the likes of my opponent. I strode across to the shaded area.

"Show yourself to me," I commanded, pulling in the inner strength that Saint Michael had shown me in my training.

Wind gathered around us and I heard a snarl. I forced my mind outwards and felt the shape of a small being, crouched against the wall.

"In the name of the Lord, Our Father, I command you to show yourself to me and only me!" I bellowed.

Suddenly a small blue being popped into my vision. It could only have been around two foot tall, was fairly thin, but had the telltale small horns on the top of its head. It cast me a look of pure hatred with its yellow eyes.

"Who are you to interfere with my charge?" I demanded, anger surging through my being.

"I am not yours to command," the small demonic figure hissed at me.

"I am the agent of Our Heavenly Father, and I command you to answer my questions, starting with your name," I told the cowering form as I raised myself a few inches from the floor to show I had power.

I forced my mind into his and ignited the pain receptors, causing a burning sensation from within. The creature cried out in agony, causing my resolve to falter slightly as, even though it was a demon in front of me, I still did not truly believe in inflicting pain on other beings.

"Stop the pain, O Heavenly One and I will tell," the creature cried pitifully.

I lessened the effects of my assault, keeping just enough pain to cause discomfort and to remind the creature that I could inflict the suffering it had felt a few moments before.

"I am called Durchial, Master" the small demon told me.
"What were you doing here?" I asked.
"I was here to cause mischief," Durchial replied.
"How?" I enquired.
"By making that man take a child, I would cause his soul to be open for nourishment," Durchial responded.
"Nourishment?" I asked, not really wanting to hear that demons can feed on our souls!
"Yes Master, when a soul commits sin, it allows those of daemonkin to gain energy from it," the little blue creature told me with a grin, showing a mouth full of sharp teeth.
"So you were not here to harm Adam specifically?" I pushed, wondering that if he was, did that break the terms of the agreement? If it did, who could I ask?
"Adam? Who is he, Master?" Durchial asked.
"The little boy who the man was trying to kidnap," I told him. "My charge."
"Your charge!" he squeaked out. "You're a Guardian? But I see no wings, Master."
"I'm a Protector, and I just choose not to show my wings at the moment," I replied, hoping that a small bluff would work.
"No Master, I was not here for the boy, just to feed," Durchial said. "It's been so long since I have."

With that, the little demonic form sat down heavily on the concrete and sighed pitifully to himself. I almost felt sorry for him, but had to remind myself this was a demon that I was dealing with. At least he was just here randomly and not here at Yeqon's command. One thing was intriguing me though, and I had to find out the answer.

"Durchial, why do you keep calling me Master?" I asked.

The blue figure turned his face to look at me, questioningly. "You commanded my name from me, and now have power over me, Master," he

FOR THE LOST SOUL

said. "You can banish me back to the Second Realm or take me into servitude."

Servitude? As in a servant? Was that allowed? Did I want a demon servant?

"Master, I beg and implore thee not to banish me back to the Second Realm." The little demon was almost on his knees, as though praying.

"What would happen to you if I did?" I asked, wanting to know what would scare a demon into wanting to serve one whom he considered an Angel rather than go back to his home realm.

"I am not strong enough yet to survive the Second Realm," Durchial replied. "Unless I strike lucky, I must nourish for at least a further score of years before I can enter the Realm safe in the knowledge that I have the power to survive."

"If I accept your servitude," I started, seeing his eyes light up at the faint hope of remaining on this plane, "what can you do for me?"

"Anything you wish Master," Durchial almost stumbled over his words in eagerness. "I can influence the weak willed, or the already corrupt. I can inflict pain and suffering on those who have already lost their acceptance to Heaven."

I shook my head as this was certainly not what I wanted. I thought for a few moments and had inspiration. I'm sure a Muse must have wandered past! I would need to check that later.

"Can you sense other demons?" I asked.

"Oh easily Master," Durchial informed me. "We are linked by energy. It is how we hunt each other."

I shuddered at the thought, but passed over it.

"Is there any other way for you to find nourishment?" I queried. "If I accept your service, I cannot allow you to inflict pain and suffering."

A look of distress came over the little blue demon's face.

"It is rumoured we can be sustained from happiness and laughter, but no self-respecting demon would demean itself to be the source of joy to humans!" Durchial said, almost spitting the words of joy and happiness.

"Okay, here is what we will agree to," I started, thinking on my feet. "Firstly, you will work for me, cause no pain to any human unless I command you to, and you will receive nourishment from the laughter of the children we will be around."

I saw the demon begin to speak, and held my hand up to interrupt.

"Secondly, you will watch out for any demonic presence coming near my charge. I need a warning system, and you are going to be it. You will help me protect my charge from any demon interference."

"May I ask why you expect demonic interest in your charge?" Durchial asked.

"Yeqon wants his soul and I am here to stop him," I answered honestly, thinking it was the best and easiest strategy. Maybe I shouldn't have because as soon as I mentioned Yeqon's name, the little demon curled into a ball, looking around fearfully.

"You're 'The' Protector Joseph?" Durchial's voice quivered out. "Even in the depths of Hell, your name is cursed."

Okay, that worried me a bit. My name is known in Hell already. I just hope it isn't on a name plate for a room!

"Yes, I'm Protector Joseph and it is my job to protect that little boy's soul from Yeqon, and by all of God's Strength I will." I told him, injecting as much confidence into my voice as I could.

"Then Master Joseph, I am your servant to command," Durchial said, changing position to kneel in subjection. "If I can help bring down such a mighty being as Yeqon, my place in the hierarchy of the Second Realm will be secured."

That wasn't exactly what I was hoping for, but if it bought his loyalty to me, I would accept it. I sensed that Helen and Adam were getting ready to leave the school grounds, the police having finished questioning them. I looked around and saw the man that Durchial had commandeered earlier being loaded into the back of one of the police cars.

"Master, do not concern yourself about the man," Durchial told me. "He has a history of violence and abuse which is why I chose him."

I scanned the man quickly, and to my disgust found that my new helper was correct. It had not taken Durchial a great deal of pushing to plant the idea of kidnapping a child into his mind.

"We are going back to the house now, and then we are going to have a long conversation about the rights and wrongs of your new role," I told him. "You are not a demon anymore and cannot act like one in my presence."

I saw the little figure give a shrug, and with that, I placed my hand on his shoulder and willed my new companion and myself back to the house.

Chapter Five

For the next few months, I kept a close eye on my new little helper. I was unsure how the whole servitude aspect worked so, while Adam was asleep at night and Durchial was monitoring the house from the rooftop, I spent my time accessing John's internet. One of the other tricks that the Angel Forcas had taught me was how to use a computer without having to switch it on. I could simply lay my hand upon it, and with concentration I could connect to the World Wide Web.

I remember asking Forcas how it was that Angels knew about computers and he simply laughed and asked me who it was that came up with the idea. I struggled to recall the name of the bloke, until a Muse called Inspiral giggled her way into the training area and told me the story of the time she had spent with a guy called Charles Babbage, firstly at a school in South Devon, strangely enough called King Edward VI, and then later at Trinity College in Cambridge. He was the first to come up with, and design, a working mechanical mathematics machine in the Nineteenth Century and laid the foundations for modern computers to be created in the Twentieth Century. Other little hints and nudges followed the greater minds and here we are today with a fully connected world network and information at our fingertips.

I was desperate to find out everything I could about my somewhat reluctant ally and so I opened my mind to a search of demons, demon lore and prophecy. I was stunned at the sheer scale of information, both accurate and wildly inaccurate if Durchial was to be believed. There are unfathomable millions of demons across various realms of Hell and Earth. I kept coming across the name of what sounded like an important figure in demon lore, that of Horrodeon. He seemed to be regarded by researchers as anything from a minor demon, a demon prophet, general and finally a demon prince.

I found that there seemed to be an agreement in place between demons and Those That Fell, which I assumed to be Lucifer, Yeqon and the other angels that were cast down. This agreement seemed to centre on the demons helping the Fallen to reclaim Heaven in return for their release from the lower realms. That was a bit scary to think that demons could have free reign on Earth.

One thing that did please me though, was that Durchial did seem to be telling me the truth about him having to serve me until I either banished him, released him or devoured his essence. That last part sort of revolted me, but intrigued me at the same time. With a mental call, I summoned my little blue servant to my side.

"Yes my Master," Durchial said as way of greeting as he popped into the room beside me.

"I've been doing some research into your kin, and I've read that one way to make you disappear is to devour your essence," I said, as calmly and friendly as possible, not wanting him to think that I was in fact going to eat him! I saw his skin ripple in fear and he began to cower away from me.

"Anything but that Master, I plead of you," he begged.

"No, no, no, Durchial, I'm not going to 'cos I don't know how to for a start," I tried to reassure him with a chuckle at the end. "I just wanted to know what it meant, and how it could affect you."

"Master, it means that if one of my kin should appear, a battle can be fought between us and the victor can, if strong enough, absorb the essence of the defeated demon," Durchial explained.

"So it is like when you nourish on the energy of a human, you feed on the demon?" I asked, intrigued.

"No Master, when we nourish from humans, we simply sustain ourselves and grow slowly," the little demon told me. "When we feast on another demon, we absorb everything the other has gained previously, including powers. It is the quickest way to grow stronger, but the most dangerous."

"Well, I give you permission to feed on any demon who tries to attack Adam or us," I told my little helper, who grinned viciously and nodded his head in acceptance.

As I continued my mind read of the internet, I found myself unconsciously stroking Durchial's head, as if he were a pet. I only realised I was doing it when I heard a low growling noise from his throat. I pulled my hand away quickly, hoping I hadn't offended the demon, for as small that he was, he did still possess powers I was not able to replicate myself.

"Sorry Durch," I apologised to the blue figure beside me.

"Master, I am unsure what the feeling was you were causing me to have," Durchial said, looking up at me with an odd expression on his face.

"What did it feel like?" I asked.

"There was a feeling in my stomach, like I had devoured a swarm of moths, and it caused my throat to rumble on its own," Durchial replied. "It was like nothing I have felt, except maybe when I absorbed the remaining lava in my spawning pit after my elder brethren had left."

I sat, perched on the edge of the chair, looking down at Durchial in wonder. Is it possible that demons can feel joy and happiness? I know that they can achieve some level of satisfaction upon tormenting humans, but this was obviously as alien to my little companion as it was to me. I reached out and stroked his head a few more times and was rewarded with the same low noise emanating from his throat. It was definitely not a growl, more like the purr of a cat, but coming from vocal chords that can't replicate it.

As for my little charge, Adam, he was growing quickly. It was a good thing that his dad, John, was in investment banking and he earned a lot of money as Adam's need for new clothing would test a lot of people on a lower income. He was constantly exploring the large back garden of the Zegers' property, finding new games and adventures as he clambered up and down the many trees, round the bushes and generally playing around the sprawling lawn. Clothes were dirtied and ripped and, despite Helen's best attempts at repairs, his wardrobe was constantly being replaced and updated.

To my surprise, Durchial also seemed to enjoy himself, copying and shadowing the antics of the dark haired boy. I was naturally concerned to begin with, thinking he was just waiting for my back to turn so he could cause injury to my little man but, as time progressed, it became evident that the rumours of demons being able to feed of the joy of humans, as well as the suffering were proving accurate.

Gary and Darren also became regular visitors, much to my own delight. I could almost see a psychic bond forming between Adam and the blonde haired bundle of fun that was Gary. The red headed Darren seemed more reserved, distancing himself at times from Adam, but nothing that most people would notice. I suppose I only noticed as I was constantly scrutinising everything that any human did when they came in contact with my charge. The fright that I had received during the attempted abduction had raised my levels of concentration and, with Durchial taking some of the pressure off of me at night, I was more alert whilst Adam was out and about. There was still something that concerned me about Darren, something in his features that reminded me of something from my past. I couldn't quite put my finger on it and it annoyed the heck out of me.

School continued to play a major role in Adam's day. Mr Williams and Mrs Jackson were excellent teachers and Adam revelled in the challenge of learning. He was constantly volunteering to help others, and was fast becoming the popular boy of the class. I did everything I could to encourage this, leaning on people where necessary to ensure that their feelings towards my treasure was positive, not that he needed too much help. His easy going attitude and ready smile was more than enough to master it all on his own.

At the centre of his life was Helen. She was fast becoming a replacement mother to him and, as much as I thought I would become jealous of her myself, I found myself admiring her dedication and love for the little boy. She was the first face that Adam saw when he awoke in the mornings, and was the last one he saw after she tucked him into bed at night. Her patience was rarely tested and I started to wonder why she hadn't had children of her own.

One day, close to the end of the school year, Adam was in class and Durchial and I were sitting to one side watching the class. We were discussing Helen. I could sense that the little demon was getting better with his understanding of humans, so I had started to ask his advice on certain matters. It did cross my mind that a demon who thought like a human may be a bad idea as, if I released him back to being his natural self, he would have knowledge that could damage mankind, more than the current level of demonic human awareness. However, the more time we spent together looking after Adam, the less I saw him as a demon and more as a friend.

"Master, you have explained how a human mother nurtures and protects her young, and how the father protects and provides for the human family," Durchial started. "Yet the Helen woman is not Adam's mother so why does she nurture him?"

"It started as her job, her duty," I explained, knowing that he would understand the concepts of that. "However, humans have the capabilities of love."

I saw his blue face scrunch into an unasked question so I continued on.

"We can love on many scales. There is the love of a friend, where you would do almost anything to help them," I said, my voice getting slightly sad as I thought briefly about Jimmy. I made a mental note to myself to look him up when I had a bit of spare time.

"Then there is the love of a partner, a husband or wife, boyfriend or girlfriend. This is the most exciting love as it will be a rollercoaster of emotions. Then there is the unconditional love between a child and a parent. This is the purest form of love as there should be no limitations, no rules, nothing that stops you caring for your offspring."

I could feel myself beginning to get a little depressed as the memories of my own experience of family love had been totally conditional. With one sentence, I had ended all love that I received from my family. A shout and giggles brought my attention back to the present and I saw Adam and Gary exchanging high fives at some comment that had been made between them. Darren sat scowling at Adam and I put myself back on high alert for my little man's protection.

"So Master, why does the Helen lady love Adam?" Durchial asked me.

"Well, I guess as she doesn't have her own children and she has spent her time caring for Adam, watching him grow and blossom, I guess she has adopted him as her own," I suggested. "It's a dangerous thing to do because if Mr Zegers were to fire her, then it would hurt both Helen and Adam."

"Mr Zegers possesses the incendiary gene?" Durchial squeaked out, surprised. I chuckled and had to remind myself that he did sometimes take statements too literally.

"No Durchie, it means that he would tell her to leave the home and not come back," I explained. "It would mean she wouldn't be able to look after Adam any longer."

"So why does the Helen lady not love Mr Zegers as well?" he asked me.

"Because love doesn't work like that sometimes," I said.

"Well the Helen lady should be made to love Mr Zegers then she would be able to stay and look after Adam," Durchial said bluntly.

"No Durch, you can't just make someone fall in love with someone else," I tried to reason.

"Why not?" he countered. "You can make humans do things can't you?"

I sat back against the wall, stunned that the little blue demon had seen straight to the heart of a problem and come up with a solution so simple in its hypothesis. Could I make Helen and John fall in love with each other? If they did, maybe John would start opening his heart to Adam. Was I allowed to play around with the feelings of humans at such a high level? I mean, I knew I was allowed to give little nudges here and there, but God is huge on the whole free will thing, so I'm going to have to tread carefully if I do try to nudge them together.

"You're brilliant Durchial," I praised. "If we can get the two of them together, Adam should have a stable and loving home. Yeqon will struggle to upset him then!"

The end of the day came around and, with Helen in prompt attendance to pick him up, Adam was soon at home, changing out of his school uniform and going out into the back garden to play. I decided to try to put our plan into action and sent Durchial outside to watch Adam play while I started working on Helen's feelings. I touched her mind, sifting through her memories and came across those concerned with John. I discovered that she already considered him to be handsome, generous with his money, but not his emotions and, after the six months or so of her employment, she was becoming attracted to him.

I quickly re-ran a montage of her memories of John, finding the part of her mind associated with emotions and gently gave her a nudge towards love. I felt the feeling blossom inside her and saw her suddenly flush as she came to an understanding that she wanted to be more than just Adam's nanny. Happy that part one of my plan was in place, I willed myself outside to see what mischief Adam and Durchial were getting themselves into.

Adam was in the process of climbing one of the many trees, giving his best Tarzan impressions as he did so. I started to get a little concerned the higher he went and was on the verge of going to give Helen a nudge to come outside when I felt a chill wind whip around the garden. My inner instincts told me that this was not good and I saw Durchial spin around from watching Adam and crouch defensively, ready to strike out in protection.

"Well, well, well," a familiar voice said. "It looks like someone has been poaching players from the opposition team."

I would have jumped a mile in surprise if I hadn't been prepared but, as the youthful form of Yeqon appeared at my side, I nodded at him and smiled.

"It says nothing in the agreement about me getting help from non-Heavenly beings," I stated. "I bested Durchial and took him as a servant."

"Oh yes, I am well aware of his misguided attempt at having the boy kidnapped," Yeqon replied confidently. "It is one of the reasons that the creature has never amounted to more than a second rate foot soldier."

I bristled at his insult to my little companion.

"At least I know that Durchial will do as I ask, and come up with ideas to help out as well," I shot back.

"Oh yes, he is helping out isn't he," Yeqon said. "Quite the idea about getting the father to fall in love. Just a shame he's already gone and fallen for someone else."

"What?" I almost shouted in surprise. When did this happen and why didn't I know?

"Yes, I think the new woman in his life will surprise you," Yeqon said, brushing his hair back out of his eyes with his hand. "You may want to catch him."

"Catch who?" I asked. "John?"

"No," he said. "The boy."

I spun around just in time to see Adam lose his grip on a branch as a gust of wind caught him unaware. Durchial made a grab for him but was too late as the dark haired boy plunged downwards on a fall of around twenty feet. Not far enough to be a fatal injury, but still far enough to break something if he landed wrong.

I had to make a decision in a split second. I knew that to stop him from hurting himself, I would have to reveal my presence to him, and he was now at the age where I couldn't be explained away as an imaginary friend. This was now strictly forbidden as part of the rules of the wager. However, if I let him fall to the ground, he could really hurt himself.

Desperately I looked around, and in relief spotted an inflatable crocodile that had been bought at Helen's insistence on the last holiday that they had taken. You know the type of thing I mean? One of those inflatables that you can use as a paddling aid in a swimming pool. I caught one of the swirling breezes and with a flick of my wrist, I bounced it off the wall of the garden shed and it rebounded onto the green toy causing it to lift off and travel the short distance to position itself underneath the falling boy. Adam hit the body of the inflatable and, with a giggle, bounced a couple of feet into the air to land on the grass, fortunately with just a couple of scrapes from the branch which he slipped from.

"Hmm, nice flick there Protector," Yeqon said graciously to me.

"Yeah, well, I know I'm not allowed to appear to him anymore so I needed to do something otherwise he'd have gotten hurt," I replied.

"Next time, there may not be a toy to break his fall and we will see how you cope then," the eternally youthful being warned me.

"Bring it on," I challenged. "Whatever you throw at me, I'll be ready for you. I've countered all your attempts to hurt Adam so far, and I will continue to do so until the wager is over."

I stared confidently into his red and black eyes, watching his nostrils flare in anger as he struggled to maintain his composure. I had read that provoking the Fallen can sometimes lead them to losing control and phasing into humanity's visible range. This would certainly help me if I could get Yeqon to do it in front of Adam as it would at least give me a free pass to do the same at a stage where I may need to.

"Let's see how you cope with this!" Yeqon snarled, and with a burst of flames, he disappeared.

I looked back at Adam, who was picking himself up gingerly, rubbing his arm where a small trickle of blood was running down his bare arm. He saw it, scrunched his nose and started to walk slowly back into the house.

"Helen!" the little lad shouted, his brown hair sticking out at all angles, and tears finally beginning to leak from his blue eyes.

"What's wrong Adam?" the nanny said, walking into the kitchen.

Upon seeing the distressed state of the youngster, she rushed over to him, grabbing a cloth on the way. She pulled him into a hug, letting him have a brief cry into her chest before wiping his face with the cloth.

"Blow," Helen said, holding the cloth to his nose, and in true boy fashion, now recovering from his shock, Adam opened his mouth and blew into the cloth.

"No silly billy, let's blow your nose and then get you cleaned up," Helen chided.

She picked him up and placed him on the table top, turning to the sink and wetting another cloth to take care of the blood marks on his arm. A little cry came from the child as she applied some anti-septic cream to the cuts and, with a final inspection, she proceeded to reach for her ever present brush. I swear I do not know how she keeps one so close to hand but, then again, when your charge is as unruly as Adam can be, I suppose it becomes second nature.

As she started to fix Adam a get well snack, the blue form of Durchial reappeared at my side, looking worried.

"What's wrong Durch?" I asked the little demon.

"Master, you should not provoke the Fallen One as you do." He advised me.

"Well I was getting a little fed up of him always being the big I am, showing off what he can do," I replied. "I thought I should give him something to think about for a change and, by being confident, that should do it. After all, Adam is okay, and nothing he has tried has hurt him yet."

"But still, he is the Chosen one of Lucifer, and one of his generals and closest advisors," Durchial told me. "He has power unlike any Daemonkin and would best even most Archangels. It took a battle with the Archangel Michael to finally banish him to the lower Realm."

"Well, Saint Michael has trained me, so I know a thing or two that he may not," I confided to my little helper. I could see he was about to continue, so I held up a hand. "I will take things more cautiously around him though, and we better be extra vigilant for the next few weeks. He promised me that I wouldn't be ready for his next attack."

We heard the growl of an engine as John's car announced his arrival home, and Adam jumped off the kitchen table and ran to the front door to greet his father. As normal, John simply gave his son a cursory pat on the head, the only real sign of affection that Adam had received from his father, and the man strode into the kitchen.

"Helen, I'm sorry for the short notice, but I am going out for a meal this evening and won't be back until late," he announced. "I'll need you to watch Adam for me."

"Of course I'll watch him," Helen said smiling at the boy. "Is it a late business meeting again?"

"No, I've actually taken the advice that everyone, including you, has been giving me, and I'm going out on a date," John said.

I could see the smile on Helen's face waver for a moment, before returning in a fake smile, noticeable only to myself. I felt around in both their heads, as I could start to see the plan I wanted to put in place unravel before my eyes. I could sense the pain in Helen, and felt guilty after prodding her already growing feelings over the edge into full blown love.

I touched John's mind and found a sense of anticipation and excitement about meeting a woman. I held some hope for my plan when I discovered it was a blind date that had been set up by a work colleague.

John walked out of the kitchen, humming to himself and went upstairs to get himself ready. I saw Helen's demeanour slump slightly before she perked herself back up as Adam came up to her with a drawing that he had done at school. It was after Durchial had come up with the idea of getting Helen and John together, and when Mr Williams had asked the children to draw something from their home, I gave Adam a nudge to draw a picture of John and Helen, with himself in the middle holding both their hands.

"Oh Adam, that's a lovely picture," Helen gushed, looking at it as though it was a piece by Da Vinci or Rembrandt. "Come on, let's go and stick it up on the refrigerator."

The fridge was the boy's official art gallery. It was almost full of his drawings that had subject matters as varied as dragons and dinosaurs to flowers and footballers. One did catch my attention that I hadn't seen before. It was a small part of a larger picture, based around the house. I could easily tell the three figures that were detailed to be John, Helen and Adam, but then I could see a black figure in a cloak off to one side. Horns came out of the top of hood and a chill ran through me.

"Come here for a minute Durchial," I said.

"What is wrong Master?" the little demon asked me.

"Do you recognise this figure at all?" I queried, pointing at the drawing. "Is it a demon?"

"Yes Master," Durchial replied. "That is a demon. What is it doing on this drawing?"

"That's what I was about to ask you," I told him. "This is one of Adam's, which means Adam must have seen it."

"Master, that could be problematic," the blue figure by the side of me warned, a shiver flowing over his skin.

"Why? Do you know which demon it is?" I asked.

"Yes my Master," Durchial responded. "It looks very much like it is Horrodeon, Prince of Daemonkin."

"Horrodeon?" I quivered. "As in the one who made those prophecies?"

"You know of the Prophecy, Master?" Durchial asked me in surprise.

"Well not all of it, just something about a Soul Key being needed to free your kind from the Low."

"Master, here is the full Prophecy," he said, holding his hand out. A bound scroll appeared, which he passed to me.

I took it nervously, my shaking hands untying the deep red ribbon. I unravelled the scroll to see a gothic type of text written on the parchment. The writing was in red ink, well I hoped it was ink anyway. Knowing the history of demons, it was probably blood!

As I started to study the passage, I could almost hear a demonic voice in my head, saying the words as I read.

"Hear me, it is I, Horrodeon, thy leader and Prince,
As our demise was stopped, our kin were bound since,
We have one way out, listen to me,
We must be released by the Soul Key.

The Highest Disciple of those fallen so low,
Will do battle as he is quick not slow,
To defeat the lowest of those most high,
Allowing Daemonkin to be free to fly.

The Soul Key shalt unlock our prison,
To guard him closely is our mission,
The hands of the Fallen are open and waiting,
Deliver the Key and be freedom creating,
Release us from the Lowest Kingdom,
Raise us to Exultance so be free there with them.

IF the Soul Key be given willingly,
So Daemonkin be released from eternity,
The one who delivered will be revered above all,
But the Soul Key denied passage once more, the fool.

YET, lest the Soul Key be delivered without Daemon aid,
Bound to the Second Kingdom we will be forever and a day,
Harken to me, Horrodeon, thy Prince, or pay."

I read the passage twice, trying to take in what I had read. Was this the battle that I was involved in? If I was, then it meant that Adam must be the Soul Key. So not only was I fighting against Yeqon, but the whole of Daemon kind as well, each with their own agenda.

"Durchial, you knew about this and you have said nothing over the last few months," I accused him.

"Master, it did not occur to me that the Adam boy could be the Soul Key," the little demon replied.

"But now that you know, are you going to turn on me?" I asked, knowing he wouldn't tell me if he was.

"Master, I am your servant. By besting me, this ties my essence to yours and overrides my previous loyalties," Durchial explained. "Until you release me, I must do your bidding."

"And if my bidding means ensuring that the Fallen don't get their hands on Adam's soul?" I queried.

"Then I will place my essence in front of any threat to the Adam boy to protect him," Durchial replied.

I studied the blue figure in front of me, and despite my misgivings of him still being a demon, my inner feelings told me that I could trust the little guy.

I heard John coming back down the stairs, looking extremely smartly dressed for his date. He was obviously out to impress. In a way, I was pleased that he was going out, even if it wasn't with Helen because it showed me that he could still hope to find love in his life. If I could nurture that love, maybe it could grow and flow to Adam.

I was sorely tempted to follow John, to see who the woman was, but the shock I had just received about Adam being at the centre of a demonic prophecy was too much for me and I felt that I needed to stay close to my little charge, to protect him if anything came up.

John said his farewells and was out of the front door and away on his date as Helen settled into preparing dinner.

MICHAEL ANDREWS

Chapter Six

School had finished for the summer and it was with a sad farewell that Mrs Jackson said her goodbyes to the children as she was moving away from the area. Her husband had accepted a job offer abroad which consisted of a promotion and the salary package to back that up, so amidst many tears, not just from the fifteen children in her class, she left the school gates for the last time.

I was concerned that this could be the start of Yeqon's next attack on Adam as it had been several weeks since his appearance at the house, but so far nothing out of the ordinary had happened to my young charge. I wondered if he could have arranged for the Jacksons to move away so he could install a teacher who would not be as nice to the children as she had been, but all my enquiries showed that the job offer was genuine.

As for the new teacher, I had lifted the name and face of her replacement from the mind of Mrs Henderson, and was pleasantly surprised to see it was a young teacher called Louise Yeates. Leaving Durchial to look after Adam, I had stolen into Mrs Henderson's office while she was taking the morning assembly and had reviewed the interview file, including her c.v. and application. Louise looked like a fine candidate for the job of a primary school teacher. She was only twenty two, so this would be her first appointment coming straight from university and a one year placement. I realised, as I was reading her file, that she shared my birthday. Not only the day, but the year as well. This depressed me a little, thinking about what I could have done with my life if I hadn't chosen the option that I had. Would I have become a teacher? I mean, looking back over the last five years or so, watching out for Adam whom I had come to love dearly as I guess I would a younger brother, I could see that I would have had the patience to deal with children in that way. However, I guess I will never know as, with the two slices of the razor blade, I chose an option never given to me by my careers advisor.

Everything else seemed to be moving along nicely in Adam's life as well. Gary seemed to be permanently attached to the dark haired young boy, and even the flame haired Darren was mellowing. Helen was as loving as ever, although I could sense her growing concern with John's budding relationship with his mystery woman. In a way, that concerned me but, currently, the benefits were definitely outweighing any downsides.

As his relationship with the woman continued, he seemed to be opening up more and more to Adam. No longer did he greet his son with just a pat on the head, but he was now frequently giving the boy affectionate hugs and smiles, and took the time to ask how his day had been and what he had done. My only concern was that, no matter how hard I pushed into John's mind, I could not get a clear image of the woman from his memories. The best I could decipher was an image of a dark haired woman who looked a little younger than John, maybe in her mid-twenties, and the initials GH.

However, as long as it was having a positive effect on John's attitude towards Adam, then it was all good. I concentrated my efforts on researching more into the prophecy that had me so troubled. It seemed that, no matter where I looked, it kept coming back to the fact that not only were Yeqon and I battling for Adam's soul, but a whole multitude of heavenly and not so heavenly beings were also interested. I couldn't understand why Our Father, who surely knew what would happen if Adam were lost, had put me in charge. I mean, there are gamblers who like to stake small amounts on long shots in the hope of winning big, but this was huge. Not only all the souls of the kids who had committed suicide before me, and those still to choose that option, but we are also talking about releasing all of the demons onto an unsuspecting human race.

As the summer drew on, Helen made sure that Adam was as active as he could be. She ensured his boundaries were expanded, so frequent trips were made while John was at work. In a way, it was also a learning curve for me as I got to follow them to places I had never been before. Working museums that showed what it was like to live in the nineteenth century, the Natural History Museum and other places of learning which Adam ate up, despite his young age. He loved looking at the various models and statues.

Helen, although not particularly religious herself, also enjoyed architecture and took my little nudge to heart and made sure that Adam visited various cathedrals and churches. I felt that the more I could impress on Adam about the beauty of God, the less likely he would be to stray from the path that I needed him to follow.

One sunny day, Helen had taken Adam to visit St Paul's Cathedral. The building, re-designed by Sir Christopher Wren in the late Seventeenth Century after it had been damaged in the Great Fire of London, holds a special place in the minds of most of the British population. Helen was no different and her enthusiasm for the history of the building was infectious to Adam. As she was explaining about how famous figures, such as Admiral Nelson were buried here, and that the wedding of Prince Charles to Lady Diana was held here, I couldn't help but notice an elderly woman, sitting on a visitor's bench, staring at Adam. No, scrub that, more correctly, staring at me.

I double checked in my mind that I hadn't phased by accident and assured myself that I hadn't, so I let myself wander to near to where she was sitting.

"I can sense that you are nearby, even though my eyes cannot see you," she said softly. "Make yourself known, spirit from beyond, as you are confusing poor Edith."

"How can you know I'm here?" I whispered into her ear, startling her slightly.

I allowed her to gather herself, standing up slowly, gripping her walking sticking to aid her movement. She picked up her black handbag, looping it through her right arm, which contrasted nicely with her knee-length light grey dress. She started walking away from the bench towards the Chapel of Saint Michael and Saint George, which I thought was a very appropriate place for me to go and hold a conversation.

I followed her, wishing that I could call Durchial to ask him to watch out for Adam, but as he is Daemonkin, any step onto consecrated ground would be extremely painful for him and could even wound his essence.

"So, poor old Edith here cannot figure you out spirit, for I sense the taint of demons upon you, yet you are here in one of the holiest places in the Anglican Church," the old woman said in my general direction.

I looked around and saw that we were in a secluded corner, so with a deep breath, I phased myself into her vision. I saw her eyes widen slightly as my youthful form became visible to her.

"Hello Edith," I greeted her. "My name is Joe, and I'm one of the good guys."

"Well, you would hardly introduce yourself as a bad guy now would you?" she tittered.

"I'm guessing you are a sensitive," I said to her, remembering my lessons from Jackson, as she sat down in a pew. I looked up at the wall and there was a mural of Saint Michael and Saint George, flaming swords drawn standing over slain demons. I gave the figures a brief nod of salute as I took a seat next to the old lady.

"Yes my young one, I have always known of the spirits that roam our plane," she told me. "Some I can hear, some I do not want to hear for they are the devil's accomplices, and sometimes I hear the cry of a soul as it departs for a higher realm."

She looked at me, her face showing a brief sign of sadness before returning to a smile.

"You however are different," she continued. "I have the sense that you are in judgement, and in battle."

I felt a brief touch as she lifted her hand to touch my face. I took her hand in mine, and for the first time in nearly a decade of years, I felt compassion flowing towards me from a human being. Tears welled in my eyes and I couldn't stop myself from being drawn into her embrace.

"There now dear, tell Edith what is wrong, what your purpose is on this realm," the old lady soothed.

I briefly explained what had happened to me when I was alive. I started to skip parts that I didn't think she would like or accept but, when she sensed I was missing details, she frowned at me, telling me that if she could accept that her female friend and neighbour of eighty years liked women in that certain way, then she had no problem with a boy of my age liking boys. I flashed her a grin at her straightforwardness and continued with the full story.

"So there is a demon sitting outside the Cathedral, doing who knows what?" she chided me. "You've left him alone and he could be feasting on the souls of the young?"
"No, Durchie isn't like that anymore," I argued. "He's changed since I bested him. I would trust him with Adam's life."
"Durchie?" she asked. "That is a strange name for a demon."
"Well, he's actually called Durchial, but I like the sound of Durchie better," I told her. "It makes him sound less, um, demony."
"So he is a full blown demon, yet you trust him?" Edith asked me.
"Implacably," I replied. "He has had many opportunities to betray me, if that is what he wanted, and yet he has remained loyal. He can sense other demonic presences and so he is a great bodyguard for Adam."
"And this boy Adam," she started. "He is important how?"
"Well, Our Father and Lucifer have had a bet for the souls of the Lost Youth, as they call them," I explained. "If Adam lives through to his thirteenth birthday, God wins back all the Lost Souls."
"And if he doesn't?" Edith asked.
"We're condemned to Purgatory for eternity and Yeqon gets my soul as a plaything," I whispered softly.

I shivered at the memory, as I always do, of Yeqon holding his double pointed spike on the day that I first met him. No matter how hard I try to forget it, something constantly reminds me of that vision.
I saw a look of concern cross the elderly woman's face at my announcement and, once again, she reached forth her hand to gently pat my knee.

"Well then my young spirit, we will have to see what old Edith here can do to help you," she said to me.
"No offence ma'am," I said respectfully, "but what would you be able to do against Yeqon and the like?"

"I have seen many things in my time, young Joseph," the old lady started. "I know things about the spiritual world that many humans are not aware of. Ever since I realised that I could commune with the ethereal planes, I have researched every piece of information that I could find and spoken with every friendly spirit that would commune with me, to better understand my place in God's scheme for the universe."

I was impressed at the dedication of the woman, and wondered if I could use her knowledge to help me in any way. I opened my mind to hers to see if I could pick any knowledge, but a frown spread across her face.

"That's not very polite young man," she scolded me, though a small smile on her lips told me that she wasn't too upset. "If you need any help or advice, you just need to ask."

"Sorry Edith," I apologised, hanging my head slightly at being caught. "I've gotten so used to having to work that way that it has become natural for me to sift people's thoughts."

"Why not just ask them like you have me?" the old lady queried.

"I'm not supposed to let my presence be known," I replied. "As you're already aware of the spirits, I am allowed to become known to you with no consequence."

Edith opened her mouth and started to say something when suddenly, she stiffened and cursed at a spot just behind me. I turned to see the blue form of Durchial just a few feet behind me.

"Durchial, what are you doing?" I asked my little helper. "I thought it hurt you to come in here?"

"It does Master," the demon hissed at me, pain showing across his features. "Please ask the Communer to stop cursing me."

I turned back to Edith who was still muttering curses under her breath, and took hold of her hand, bringing her back from her trance.

"Edith, please stop, you're hurting Durchie," I pleaded with the old lady.

"Durchie? You mean your pet demon?" she queried. "It is he who is in here?"

"Yes and he wouldn't be unless he needs to tell me something important, so please let him be," I asked her.

With an upturned nose at the thought of allowing a demon to be inside the Cathedral, Edith turned and looked up at the mural of Saint Michael, crossing herself as if to ward off the evil she perceived to be in her place of worship.

I turned back to Durchial, who looked a little more comfortable but I could still see a look of discomfort in his features.

"Okay, what's wrong?" I asked.

"Master, there is a threat to the Adam boy," Durchial announced.

"What! Here?" I asked, looking around, opening my mind immediately and allowing it to sweep through the area. Linked into Adam's soul, I found him immediately and was pleased to find that the little boy was happily laughing as Helen was taking full advantage of the acoustics of the dome and was exploring the joys of the Whispering Gallery. I tried widening my search, but with the amount of people and the size of the building, it was just too large to cast my mind net over it all.

Edith had turned back to us in concern at the little demon's announcement and, with a resolved look upon her face, approached Durchial.

"There is only one demon present in this holy place Joseph," Edith started, "and that is your servant."

"Nether the less Master, I sense danger to our charge," Durchial insisted. "I would not risk the wrath of Prince Horrodeon for entering sacred ground if I was not certain."

"Edith, I trust Durchial, so I am going to check on Adam," I told the old lady. "Can I come and see you at another time?"

"Young spirit, you are always welcome to seek my advice if you need it," she replied fondly, taking my hand once more. "Go and protect your charge."

She leaned in and gave me a grandmotherly kiss on my forehead, and I felt a warm sensation on my skin. I raised my hand to the area of my face, and saw a hint of amusement in her eyes.

"That is to remember old Edith by," she said. "Think of that and you will always be able to find me. Now go!"

With her stern command ringing in my ears, I phased myself back out of the visible spectrum and willed myself back to the side of Adam, whose dark hair was flowing as he ran around the circle passageway, giggling as he avoided the outstretched hands of his nanny, Helen.

"Adam, stop running," Helen said, slight frustration showing in her voice for one of the first times that I could remember. "You could hurt yourself."

"Nah!" came the response from the boy, as he weaved in and out of the other visitors. Some looked on in irritation, while others had a smile on their faces delighting in the enjoyment of the young boy.

I managed to catch up with the dark haired bullet and, with a suggested whisper in his ear, the near six year old pulled up, puffing as he tried to catch his breath, allowing the harassed nanny to reach him.

She quietly chided the young boy for running off, and after the sorrowful look on his face at being told off had wormed its way back through Helen's defensive façade, she couldn't help but pull Adam into a hug letting him know that everything was alright once more.

With Adam back in the safe clasp of his nanny, I looked around using my inner vision to spot the demonic attack that Durchial had come to warn me about. As I filtered out the field of human presence, I was surprised to find two angelic forms off to one side, observing Adam. I looked over at them, taking note of their appearance. There was a tall male, dressed in a shining silver breastplate, white robes masking the remainder of his appearance. His platinum blonde hair swept back severely showing what looked to be a haughty face that I am sure I would have found attractive if there was a hint of a smile anywhere nearby. The female was slightly shorter, her long flowing, dark auburn hair contrasting with her own white robes. Dark eyes followed my little charge and his nanny.

"Durch, we're ok," I said to my little helper. "There's no danger here."

"But Master, I sense hatred and anger directed towards the Adam boy," he argued.

"That may be the case, but there is no sign of Yeqon or his kind here," I told him. "Go back outside and keep watch. There are a couple of angels in here and I want to go talk to them but I don't think they would appreciate you being in here."

"Yes my Master," Durchial bowed submissively and disappeared from my view.

I cast my mind out and found him back outside, perched on the roof muttering curses under his breath. Even I wasn't sure what some of the words meant, and I'm probably pleased that I didn't. I turned back to where I saw the heavenly beings a few moments ago and was pleased to see that they were still there. I willed myself over to them, allowing myself to be visible to them.

"Greetings Heavenly Ones," I bowed reverently to the pair of angels. I didn't recognise them as they had not been involved in my training but I still knew the presence of higher angels when I felt them.

"Protector Joseph," the taller of the two greeted me.

"May I be of any assistance?" I asked politely, wondering what they were doing here, watching my charge.

"We have been assigned to monitor the progress of the Innocent," the female told me, almost looking down her nose at me, an impressive feat bearing in mind I was perhaps two inches taller than her.

"And we are concerned about the being that you have recruited to assist you," the male added. "His kind are the foot soldiers of Lucifer, and yet you willingly allow him access to the Innocent."

I riled at the disdain in his voice, and at the expressions on their faces, as I started to defend Durchial for the second time that afternoon. The male angel held up a hand to interrupt me as I was getting into full flow about the servitude aspect of a demon's personality.

"Daemons are not part of Our Heavenly Father's plan for Earth so they are not worthy of our attention," he told me, condescendingly.

"The very fact that you have allied yourself with one such being proves once again how far your soul has fallen," the female added.

I really was getting the sense that these two did not care very much for me.

"Look, I will do anything to ensure that Adam is protected and gets through to his thirteenth birthday so that we win this battle," I stated. "I would have thought that you would be offering advice or help if you want us to beat Yeqon and Lucifer!"

"The Innocent would have a better chance of survival if he was not being protected by one such as you," the male angel sneered out at me.

"One such as me?" I queried, the penny finally beginning to drop in my knowledge as to who these two angels actually represented. "You must have been in the section that didn't want me to have this chance at redemption."

"Your continued existence is an insult to Our Lord," the female angel almost spat at me.

A growl came from the side of me as the air shimmered and the blue figure of Durchial appeared.

"You dare appear in Our Father's House demon!" the male angel hissed.

"When it comes to protecting my Master, I have no barriers set by your kind," replied Durchial. "I will not allow you to interfere with his mission."

"Not allow?" the female laughed. "Do you have any idea who we are and what we can do to your kind?"

"I recognise that you are from the Seraphim, those closest to your Father, and I am sure that you believe you can command me," Durchial replied. "However as my essence belongs to the Protector, you will have to best him before you can command me."

I saw the confident and self-important look disappear for a moment on the faces of the two angels and, picking up on his bravery in light of the revelation that the two figures in front of me are supposed to be the highest of God's angels, I took a gamble to push home the advantage that Durchial had cracked open.

"That's right, Durchial is mine to command and mine alone," I told them. "If you want to battle me for control of him, let's rumble."

The pair backed off slightly so I pressed further.

"Oh, I suppose though that this would upset Our Father wouldn't it," I said. "After all, I am his chosen tool in this battle against Lucifer, and it wouldn't be good for you to be seen trying to disrupt God's plans now would it."

"You know nothing, Protector," the female snarled at me. "Once you lose the battle and are consigned to Purgatory, where your kind belongs, order will once again be restored in Heaven."

Not giving me a chance to reply, the pair vanished in a blaze of light that I was sure would disturb the people around us, but no-one seemed to be giving us a second glance.

"Durchial, what the hell, um I mean heck was that all about?" I asked, slightly intimidated now that it seemed I was not just battling Lucifer's angels.

"There are those of the Second Realm who believe that the War of Heaven was not finished by the Casting of the Fallen," the little demon explained to me. "Some believe that forces still exist within the Light, working to bring the Fallen back into their Father's Kingdom."

"Oh great, so not only am I battling with Yeqon and his angels and allies, then the demons who want Adam's soul to release themselves back to Earth," I whined, "but now I've got to watch those who are supposed to be on my side as well."

"Master, we should get the Adam boy back to the safety of the Home," Durchial advised.

"Yeah, at least we can keep a closer eye on him there," I agreed.

Durchial looked at me in surprise.

"Master, do you not know about the protection boundary?" he asked me.

"Protection boundary? What's that?" I said perplexed.

"There is a psychic barrier that surrounds the living complex," Durchial replied. "I am not aware who installed it, but it does not allow in anyone who wishes the Adam boy ill, unless invited by a member of the Home."

"Wait, so you are telling me that Adam is completely safe at home?" I wanted to double check.

"No-one who wishes the Adam boy harm can enter the premise unless invited," he re-emphasised.

"Let's get them home then," I urged.

Spotting that Adam and Helen had not moved from the spot where the nanny had caught hold of the errant child, I looked at Durchial.

"Your discussion with the Seraphim was conducted in a crack in time to allow no harm to befall the Adam child," he explained.

"Who did that?" I asked, wondering if I wanted to find out who had that type of power.

"It could have been a number of beings, my Master, but it is one of my former master's favourite tricks," the demon replied.

"And just who was your former master?" I queried.

"I thought you already knew, my Master," Durchial replied. "I was the hand messenger for Prince Horrodeon."

"This is why you know so much about the prophecies?" I asked him.

"Yes Master," he answered.

The noise of the Cathedral visitors filled my ears again as I felt us slip back into the normal flow of time, and I knew that I would have to save any further investigation until I got Adam back to safety now that I knew not even holy ground was a safe haven for him. I reached out and gave Helen the impression that Adam was tiring and she, with a glance at her watch, announced that it was time to head home.

A short half hour journey later, and they were arriving home. As the small car pulled into the driveway, Helen had to swerve to avoid the speeding blue blur of a Porsche as it left the house. I saw a glimpse of a dark haired woman behind the wheel, arrogantly taking more than her fair share of the road. A seldom heard curse escaped the lips of the nanny as Helen took evasive action, mounting the curb to make sure that the near collision remained just that, a near one.

I had a prickly feeling run through my spirit as I watched the Porsche pull away and I let my mind drift towards to offending car. This must be the mysterious woman that John was dating, and now was my ideal opportunity to introduce my mind to hers. However, as my psychic eye approached the car, there was a blur in my vision, as though I was looking at a photograph where the subject was out of focus. I concentrated and pushed all my power into the vision and for a moment I saw inside the car with clarity. A shock of recognition ran through me as I took into view the shoulder length dark hair, the fine bone structure of a face that I had seen before, and the narrow brown eyes that I had looked into so many times during my life on Earth.

The initials, GH. They represented the name of the person who had hated me more than anyone else during my life. The cause of all my suffering. The person who had outed me to my school, to my friends, to my parents. The person who had taunted me as I went to my death.

Gillian Harris.

My sister.

Chapter Seven

Having watched Helen ensure that Adam was safely tucked up in bed, I whispered into his ear for him to fall asleep and have sweet dreams. I have never found out if my quiet suggestions about his sleep ever worked, but he didn't seem to have any nightmares when I did, so I kept whispering. Once I was confident that Adam was in a deep sleep, I sent a call out to Durchial.

"Yes, my Master," the little demon said as he popped into my vision as I sat, watching the boy sleep.

"I need to find out if someone is under the control of Yeqon," I told him. "How can I do it?"

"That is difficult, Master," the blue figure replied. "Yeqon is second only to Lord Lucifer in the Underworld, and his powers of deceit are legendary. If he can touch a weak willed human, or one already on its way into darkness, then it is simple for the General to turn the human into his tool."

"But Edith said that she could sense that I had been in contact with you," I mentioned. "Surely there has to be some way to see if Gill has been touched by Yeqon?"

"Gill?" Durchial asked.

"Yeah, that's the name of lady that John has been seeing," I replied.

"You know her?" he asked me.

"Unfortunately yes, I do," I replied. "She's my sister, well was my sister."

"Then you should be aware if she has been turned," Durchial told me confidently. "She will be different, once turned."

"Unless she was already a dark soul as you said," I reminded him. "She wasn't very nice to me and was behind most of my pain when I was alive."

Durchial paused for a moment as if in thought, which I assume he was. Suddenly a sly grin came across his face.

"Why not appear to her and see what her reaction is?" the little demon asked. "If she is surprised to see you, then she is not Yeqon's willing pawn."

"But if she is surprised to see me, then I have broken the rules set out by Our Father and by Lucifer," I told him.

"What would happen if you did?" he asked.

"I'm not actually sure, but I don't think it can be good for me," I answered.

"Is there no-one you can ask?" Durchial enquired.

I pondered that question and racked my brain, wondering if Edith would know. As she wasn't aware of the wager for our souls, I guessed not. I am supposed to be on my own as well, so I can't appeal to Heaven for help, not that some of the Angels up there would want to help me anyway.

"No, I don't think there is anyone, unless you know someone?" I said to my little helper.

"I can try to find out, Master," he told me and, with a pop, disappeared from my view.

I sat on the edge of Adam's bed, looking down at the sleeping figure of my young charge. His face was a mask of peacefulness. I thought back through his first six years of life and realised that, other than losing Penny on the day he was born, I had managed to keep him safe from harm and from the pain and suffering that had been predicted for his life.

Feeling better about myself, I let my mind drift and my thoughts went back to my own pain and suffering. The shock of Gillian suddenly re-appearing into my life, if I can call it that, brought back memories that I had long since thought banished. I tried to recall the good in her, before she turned on me, and struggled to think before her twelfth birthday, when I would have been ten. All of the close times that we had spent together, the little secrets between us, all of them were to keep her out of trouble with my parents and with other adults. Everything she did seemed to be manipulating me into being the one to take the blame when things went wrong.

Then when I came out to her, how had I not seen what her reaction would have been. I guess I had been blinded by a sibling love and had ignored some obvious pointers. Looking back, it was Gill who was the one who told my parents in such a way that they could not help but be disgusted by me. It was Gill who had poisoned my parents thoughts from their previously liberal views, to the bigoted ideas that so hurt me during my last two years of life.

For the first time since my death, I thought of my parents. Were they still alive? They must be as it has only been seven years since my death, and they would only be in their early forties, having had Gill when they were twenty, and I came along two years later. I had made my mind up in an instant that I wanted to go and see them, to see how my death had affected them, if it had.

"Master, there is a way," Durchial said, making me jump by suddenly re-appearing at my side.

"Jeez!" I exclaimed, gathering myself.

"Who's there?" a small voice came from the bed.

I looked over and saw a pair of blue eyes peeking over the top of a duvet, casting glances in all directions at the sudden noise in his room. Crap! The shock of Durchie's entry must have over-ridden my normal control and I allowed my voice to become audible. I slowly walked over to his bed and reached out to stroke his shoulder length hair. He really needs to have it cut, I thought.

"Shush Adam, everything is okay," I whispered into his ear, trying to soothe him back into slumber.
"Is that you Joe?" the little boy said.

Crap again! He's not supposed to remember me! Oh well, there's only one quick way to get him back to sleep and if I have to bend the rule slightly, so be it.

"Yes it is, Adam," I whispered. "You're safe because I'm watching over you as I promised I would."
"Forever?" came the sleepy response.
"Forever and then a day past it," I replied, watching him succumb to my suggestion to sleep. Forever and a day past it. It was a reply that came so natural to me as it was the statement of friendship between Jimmy and myself so long ago.

My memories flooded back once again, and I could take no more. With a signal to Durchial to watch over Adam, I willed myself away from the room, not wanting my grief to overflow onto my young charge. My sub-conscious must have kicked in as I found myself flying through the air. Within seconds I found myself standing in a room. A bedroom. One that broke my spirit and I collapsed onto my bed, onto the same dark blue duvet that had covered my bed on the day I took my life.
Tears streamed down my face as I remembered happier days in this very room. I clutched a pillow to my chest as I glanced around at the walls. My bookcases were still in place, filled with the collections of science fiction and fantasy that I had so adored during my life. My CD collection was neatly stacked within their holders. Sobs broke loudly from my very core as I wondered why my room was still as I remembered it.
I heard light footsteps outside the door, and suddenly the dark room was cast into light as the door opened. I could see the shadowed outline of a woman and I felt my soul yearn to reach out to her. I watched as my mother came into the room, pausing at various sections, straightening a book on the bookcase, moving a ruler on my desk.
The way she moved, slowly drinking in the atmosphere within my bedroom, it became obvious to me that this was a regular journey for her. I willed myself

off the bed as I saw her come over to sit on the duvet, ready to stare at the picture on my bedside table. It was one from happier times, a holiday, where my father had persuaded a fellow holiday-maker to take a photo of the four of us. I looked at my mother and saw that time had not treated her well. She had tied her hair up into a bun, making her appearance more severe. Her face, once so beautiful, was now drawn and tired, dark bags beneath her eyes. It was her eyes though that were the major difference from the last time I saw her. Her hazel eyes were full of regret and sorrow.

As she sat down on the bed, she bumped into the pillow that I had grabbed to cry into. I could see her look around the room, as if searching for an intruder. She lifted the pillow, ready to put back in place, but hesitated and lifted it to her face and took a breath.

"Joseph?" she whispered out loud. "Oh my poor boy, I'm so sorry for what we forced you to do."

Tears streamed down her face as she smelled the pillow once more. To my surprise, I realised that my essence must have left a smell of myself on the pillow which she could pick up. I reached out, towards the mother who had rejected me in my life and lightly touched her shoulder. She clasped her hand up towards mine but I pulled away before she could take my hand in hers.

"Arthur!" she shouted out suddenly. "He's been here!"

My mother ran through the door and down the stairs, repeating over and over the fact that she believed I was there. I had to follow. I had to see him. I had to see my father, the last person I saw alive.

As I made my way downstairs, I noticed that the stairway wall was devoid of the pictures of my sister that used to hang there. In fact, as I entered the lounge, not a picture of my sister was in sight. I edged myself into the room, taking in the full scene. The layout hadn't changed at all. There was still the same flowery sofa and easy chair, along with the high backed chair that belonged to my father. I studied the room and was surprised to see photographs of me, as a child, adorning the walls and mantelpiece. When I was still alive, virtually all of the pictures of me had been removed as they did not want to be reminded of my presence in the household.

"Who's been here Sally?" a shaky male voice replied.

I saw the head of the figure turn in the chair and I laid eyes on the man who was my father. I couldn't help but let out a gasp as I took in the vision of a shadow of a man. My father should have been forty four. However, in his place was a man who looked to be in his late sixties at best. His hair had thinned and his skin sagged around his face. A look of profound sorrow was etched in his dark eyes. The man I had so feared during the last two years of my life was a living shell of a man.

"Arthur, here, take this," my mother said handing the pillow to him. "Smell it, I can smell our boy."

He reached out his hands, the arms trembling at the effort and took the pillow from my mother and lifted it to his face. As he took a breath, I let my mind open to touch his, to see what drastic changes had taken place. I could sense the tears begin to fall down his face and his memories flooded with all the good times we had shared. The football matches we had attended, the kickabouts in the back garden, the television programmes we used to watch and all the fun we had, before I was outed to them by Gillian.

Something fundamental had changed since my death. I could feel the love flowing from them at my memory. Slightly confused, I let my mind open to include my mother as well and found a place inside her full of sorrow and regret at my passing, and also anger and hatred. However, as I explored this, I found it was aimed at my sister and not me. As I probed deeper, I discovered that my parents felt that my sister was different to how she had been as a child, how she had turned darker and more secretive as she became a teenager. I guess they must have put it down the change into adolescence but looking back, something drastic changed in her behaviour.

Even after my death, my sister continued to manipulate my parents, and burrowing into my parents memories showed me that they had eventually disowned her after she had tricked them out of their savings, turned them against their friends and nearly cost them our home. After they had come out of her control, my parents came to realise that they had treated me badly and set to atone for it. They replaced the simple headstone at my grave, which gave me a chill as I watched my mother's memory like a repeat of a television programme, and a beautiful marble statue took its place. They also looked into the prospect of fostering, but then illness struck my father.

I turned to look at the shell of the man I feared so much from the age of fourteen. I didn't need to probe to see the illness that ravaged his once healthy body.

"It's cancer I'm afraid, Protector," a voice said from beside me, startling me.

"Ezekiel!" I gasped, taking into view the Angel that I had last seen at Penny's death.

"Long have I watched your family, from the first cry of help of your young troubled soul, through your death and beyond," he told me.

"Is he going to die?" I asked, my voice strained at the thought of my father dying.

"Of course, all men die Protector, it is the nature of Our Father's Will," Ezekiel replied.

"No, I meant now," I pushed. "Is that why you are here?"

The Angel of Death looked at me, studying me. He reached out to touch my tear stained face. My body, so nearly recovered from my earlier bout of depression threatened to open up once more. Pulling me into an embrace, he let comfort flow into me, calming me down.

"It is not yet his turn to meet Saint Peter, young one," he reassured me. "It is you I came for."

"Me?" I squeaked. "But I'm already dead, and you can't take me yet 'cos I've still got to protect Adam and stop Yeqon."

"I am not here to interfere with your mission, Protector, but to offer my apologies," Ezekiel soothed. "I tried to stop your parents from falling under the spell of the Fallen and turning against you, but I did not realise that Yeqon himself was behind the turning."

"Yeqon? Why was he after my parents?" I asked, shocked that my enemy knew of my family.

"It was not your parents he wanted, but" he started.

"Gill! He wanted Gill," I interrupted, pieces beginning to fall into place.

"That is correct, he turned her when you were young, allowing her to gain powers of persuasion and seductiveness," Ezekiel confirmed.

"So how have my parents got out from under her control?" I queried.

"For years I had been trying to counter her influence, but your death was the hammer blow that smashed her control," he replied.

"So are they truly good again?" I asked, forgiving them in my heart, knowing now that they were manipulated by a force greater than they could have battled.

"Not truly," the Angel answered, "but enough that Our Father will forgive them, now that you have."

Satisfied that my parents would at least make it to Heaven, I opened my mind to them, to give them a touch of my forgiveness for their treatment of me. I saw their expressions change to sorrow, joy, happiness and regret all mixed in together.

"Is there anything you can do to help him?" I asked. "If they have changed for the better, then my Mum shouldn't lose him as well as my sister and me."

Ezekiel looked at me and at my parents for a moment and his expression went blank. His head cocked to one side, as if listening and with a nod of his head, his eyes refocused upon me.

"A chance will be presented to prove that they have indeed changed for the better," the Angel told me. "If they can both grasp this chance, then the onset of the disease will be delayed."

"What chance?" I asked. "Can I help?"

"You already are," he replied.

I looked again at my parents. My father still clasped the pillow as if, by holding it, he was holding on to the memory of me. The winged figure by my side touched my shoulder.

"Come, we must talk," Ezekiel told me.

"Okay," I replied and let him put a hand on my shoulder and suddenly we were high above the city.

I gazed at the scene below me. It looked so peaceful, so beautiful. Away from the hustle and bustle of the ground, London had a serenity about it. Street lamps mapped out intricate patterns of light, twisting and turning across the canvas of the land.

"So, what is so important that you are allowed to talk to me?" I asked, looking at his face as he studied me. "I mean, I thought I wasn't allowed any help from you guys."

"I'm not here to help, as such," Ezekiel replied. "But to warn."

"Warn?" I said, surprised. "Warn about what?"

"You have done extremely well in your role as Protector so far," he started. "However, as the Innocent moves into his sixth year, the battle for his soul will intensify. Already the Fallen have moved their pawns into position to strike and you need to gather your allies around you to protect him."

"Allies? I don't have any," I replied quickly. "I'm on my own here you know."

"Really? What of your pet demon?" Ezekiel asked. "What of your Communer?"

"Edith? I only met her today and she's old," I retorted. "I don't think she would be up for a fight against Yeqon, do you?"

"You would be advised to learn the strengths, not only of your opponents but of your friends," the Angel advised me. "Communer Edith is known to Heaven. Seek her for advice and comfort when events spiral from your control."

"Who says they're going to?" I said, angrily shaking his grip on my shoulder. "I've managed fine without your help so far and, despite everything Yeqon has thrown at me, I've bested him every time."

"Then I pray for the soul of the Innocent that you continue to best him, for should thee fail, all will be condemned to Hell." Ezekiel released me and, with a burst of light in the sky, disappeared.

I thought about what he had said and, as my brain sifted through the information, I felt my feet touch back down on solid ground. The knowledge that my sister had given herself over to Yeqon, even before I had come out to her, rankled me. I felt my anger grow as I thought of the evil she had done, not just to me, but to my parents as well. I looked around and saw that I wasn't in the best of neighbourhoods. There were windows and doors boarded up, litter scattered across the street and the general hum of noise seemed quieter here.

"I'm sure I saw the little runt come this way," I heard a deep voice say.
"Well he won't get far as it's a dead end," a second voice sneered.

I cast my mind open and saw two men, common thugs by the look of them, walking slowly up the alleyway, stopping to open skips and peer into darkened doorways. They were obviously looking for someone and my thought was confirmed when I heard a whimper and a squeal. I saw the bigger of the two, a guy who looked to be about six foot tall and maybe just as wide, grab at a bundle of clothes I had thought were rags. The face of a boy, who looked to be around twelve, was uncovered from the scraggy hoodie.

"Please Jerry, I'm sorry I ran," cried the boy.
"Too late for sorries kid," the smaller of the two men replied. "You know that you belong to Mr Mackay and if he rents you out for the night, then you damn well go where you're told to, and you do whatever the client wants."
"But I've heard some of the others talking about that guy, and they say he's really mean," the boy sobbed, tears freely flowing from eyes that had been rubbed red.

As the bigger man shook the boy, his hood fell away showing a head full of curly blonde hair. The solitary streetlamp cast its light towards them and, as they moved further into the alley, I could see bruises on the young boy's face.

"Now then Petey, you have embarrassed Mr Mackay with one of his most important customers and he just won't have that," the man called Jerry said.
"Look, I'll go back, I'll be good and do everything he says," Petey begged. "I promise."
"Not this time, kid," Jerry said. "After you wouldn't perform at the party last week, and now this."

I saw the man shrug his shoulders and as he pulled his hand out of his coat pocket, I saw a flash of metal and realised that they weren't just going to slap the kid about as punishment. The anger that had been building up in me began to boil over. Despite this, my over-riding acknowledgement of the Sixth Commandment meant that I didn't feel like I could be the one to take a life, but with Ezekiel's advice still ringing in my ears, I sent a call out for Durchial.

"Yes Master?" the blue figure said, appearing at my side.
"Protect the boy," I commanded.
"But the Adam boy is at the home," Durchial asked, confused.
"No, not Adam," I replied. "Him."

I pointed at the boy who, realising that the remainder of his life was being counted in mere minutes, had lost his self-control. I saw his eyes dart around, looking for any help that he could get as he struggled to free himself from the gorilla grip of the still unnamed thug. I sensed the fight go out of him as his body sagged in the tight grip and Jerry approached him, the knife held low.

"Now kid, don't struggle and I'll make it quick and clean," the knife wielding thug told him.

"Look Jerry, spare me and I'll be your boy," Pete begged, offering anything to save his life. "I know that you liked it that time."

"Well, you were good Pete," Jerry mused, moving his free hand to stroke the blonde hair.

I saw hope glimmer in the young boy's sad eyes before widening as the man raised the knife towards the exposed throat.

"Stop!" I commanded, allowing myself to become visible.

"What the fuck?" Jerry exclaimed, jumping away slightly from where I had appeared at Pete's side.

"Leave him be and you shall be saved," I said, in my most authoritative voice.

"Who's gonna stop me kid," Jerry sneered. "You?"

"No mate, not me," I replied. "Him."

Durchial materialised by the side of the smaller man and, with a swipe of his talon, slashed the knife out of his hand. Jerry cried out in pain, clutching the shredded flesh to his chest. The taller, fat thug released Pete and made a move towards my little demon. That was the mistake which almost cost him his life as, with a twirl of his body, Durchial spun and raked his claws across the fat gut hanging out over his belt. The man collapsed to the pavement, groaning and holding his now blood stained shirt.

"Durchie, don't kill them," I shouted.

"Master? It's what we do," he said turning towards me.

"It's not what I do, I'm not comfortable taking a life," I told him. "Can you do something to them that will stop them doing this type of thing without killing them?"

"Yes Master," Durchial replied.

"Do it and I will look after Pete," I commanded.

I turned toward the shaking boy who was now curled in a ball against the side of the skip that he was previously being held against. I reached out with my mind to calm him down, or at least to allay his fears of me.

"Pete is it?" I asked, offering my hand to him. "My name is Joseph and I'm here to help you."

"Why?" the boy whimpered, hotching himself backwards, trying to put further distance between us.

"Because I can," I replied, deciding not to try bullshitting the kid. "You're safe from those two guys now, Durchial will see to that."

"Durchial?" he asked. "You mean, that monster?"

Now that was unfair. Okay, Durchie was a demon, but he was hardly a monster anymore.

"Durchie is a friend and he helped save you from those guys," I said gently to him. I had used the conversation and Durchial as a distraction so that I could cover the gap between us and, before he could react, I slipped my arm around his thin body.

"No, get away!" he whimpered again, trying to pull away. I held firmly to him, whispering softly that he could trust me. I didn't really want to use my suggestive powers, but I needed to get the kid to trust me.

Two screams filled the alley way, making the pair of us jump in surprise and I glanced over to see the two thugs running down and out of the mucky dead end. I threw the returning Durchial a questioning glance and he shrugged at me.

"I have given them time to think about their sins, Master," he explained. "I set up mirrors in their minds so that it reflects their memories back at their thoughts."

"How long will it last?" I asked.

"Until I remove it, or they die," he said simply.

"Am I really safe from them?" whispered the little voice of the youngster I was cradling.

"Yes Pete, you are," I replied. "Now, do you want to tell me what happened?"

"Do I have to?" he muttered, his face dropping to his chest.

"Well no, not if you don't want to," I told him. "But if I'm to help you, I need to know what it is you were running from."

"It's just that you won't want to help me if I tell you what I was doing," he replied sadly.

"Pete, have you murdered anyone?" I asked. A shake of his head was his reply.

"Have you raised a false idol?" I continued.

"Huh?" was the response.

"Look Pete, I swear by Our Heavenly Father that, no matter what you tell me, I will help you," I promised him, allowing my mind once again to touch his in reassurance.

He looked at me, his blue eyes locked onto mine and for a moment, I could see everything that he had been through. An unknown father who had used his drug addled mother, who's only means of support was to whore herself out. The mother who, when the child was old enough, brought him to the attention of her pimp who, in turn, used him for his own and his clients' pleasures. No wonder the kid didn't want to tell me these things.

"It's okay Peter, you don't need to say anything," I told him softly, gently stroking his side as his situation overcame him and he sobbed quietly into my side.

"Master, we should leave this place," Durchial told me, bringing me back to the present.

"Okay, let's go," I said, willing the three of us to nicer surroundings; the garden at the back of my parents' house.

"Where are we?" Pete asked.

"My parents' place," I said. "How about you stay with them for a while?"

"Why would they let me?" he asked.

"Because they need a son once more to look after," I replied. "I think you could fit the bill."

Hope sprang in his mind, before his despair re-emerged.

"What would they want me to do?" he demanded. "I'd prefer to kill myself rather than carry on doing that stuff."

"Pete, please don't ever think that," I whispered, his threat piercing my heart. "You have no idea what that would mean to you. Besides, they won't make you do that stuff anymore, they will protect you and raise you properly."

I stood him up and brushed him down to make him appear a little more respectable. Thinking on how to get my parents to recognise a chance of redemption, I removed the coral chain that I had been given as a present by Jimmy on my thirteenth birthday, and had worn every day since.

"Here, wear this for me," I said, fixing it around his slender neck.

"What is it?" he asked.

"A little something to remind you of me," I replied, as I ushered him towards the back door.

"Aren't you coming with me, Joe?" Pete asked.

"I can't," I answered. "I'm not really here."

With that, I pushed him towards the door and knocked. I waited until I saw the kitchen light come on. Pete was looking back at me and I gave him a wave and a smile and phased myself slowly out of his view. The door opened, surprising the boy who spun around.

"Hello, what do we have here?" asked my mother.

"Um, I'm Pete, and I was told that you would be able to help me," the twelve year old said, a bit of confidence in his voice.

"Help you how?" Mother asked.

"Joe said that you needed a new son to look after, and he said that I could be the one," Pete stammered, looking worried at the surprise on her face.

"Joe? Which Joe?" she questioned, putting her arm around Pete to lead him inside.

"Your son, well he said he was anyway," Pete replied. "He gave me this."

Pete held out the chain to show her my present. Tears streamed down her face as she looked out into the garden, obviously looking for signs of me. Was I allowed? If I made an appearance, would it seal her taking Pete in?

"Master, we must go," Durchial said from beside me.

"I know," I replied. I sighed, knowing that my parents needed to take care of Pete with faith in their hearts, not with my appearance.

I took hold of Durchial's arm and willed ourselves back to the Zegers' home and to Adam's bedroom. I was pleased to see my little charge was fast asleep and a touch of his mind showed he was untroubled.

"Master, with regards to finding out if the Gill lady has been turned, I think I know someone who can help," my helper advised.

"Don't worry Durch," I replied. "She was turned a long time ago."

"Are you sure Master?" Durchial asked.

"Ezekiel confirmed it, along with a few other things," I said sadly, wondering what happened to the good Gillian that I would have grown up with. "I've been told that the attacks will start to intensify, so we need to prepare ourselves."

"Yeqon musters his forces?" the demon asked and, upon receiving my nodded reply, added, "Then let him come, for we shall ready our own."

Chapter Eight

The next few months saw Durchial and me investigate every little incident where anything untoward happened within the Zegers' household. While I sent Durchial off chasing down the demonic prophecy and more information about it and how it would affect Adam, I concentrated my efforts on trying to break through the barriers in John's mind so I could try to break the grip that Gillian had on his affection. I regularly touched Helen's, trying to keep her focused on winning John herself, as well as watching my sister like a hawk every time she set foot anywhere near my boy.

When she wasn't around, I relaxed slightly and allowed Durchial to watch Adam while I spirited myself off to confer with Edith. The old woman was an absolute revelation when it came to her knowledge of the Bible, Satanic Prophecies and the creatures of the Netherworld. I spent hours listening to her, questioning her and garnering as much knowledge as I could on the topics that I thought would help me protect Adam. She introduced me to several friendly and unfriendly spirits, those that have yet to make the Passover into either Heaven or Hell, and I learned some of the deceit that the Fallen Ones can contrive. I began to look upon Edith almost like a grandmother, or at least a very elderly aunt, and I think she also was enjoying the interaction with me.

As the new school year started, while Adam cemented his friendships with Gary and Darren, I introduced myself to the mind of Adam's new teacher, Louise. I gave her a little prod to open her heart to my little dark haired charge, not that I really needed to. I was extremely pleased to see that she was completely devoted to the children in her care, her heart seemed to have endless love for them. My own heart soon went out to her though, when I stumbled into a conversation between her and Mrs Henderson one rainy Friday afternoon while I watched Helen usher Adam, Gary and Darren into her car so that she could drop them off on her way home.

"So Louise, is there a special man in your life at the moment?" the older Headmistress enquired.

"No, I'm still single," Louise replied "and, to be honest I'll probably stay that way."

"Oh, why is that dear?" the motherly Mrs Henderson asked, concern showing on her face at her young teacher's sombre expression.

"I suffer from endometriosis, diagnosed when I was fifteen, which means that I can't have children," the young teacher replied sadly. "I don't think there are many men my age who are looking for a partner who wouldn't be able to give them a child."

"I am so sorry to have brought it up, dear," Mrs Henderson said regretfully, putting her arm around the brown haired teacher. "I'm sure that not every guy is looking for that, so there is still going to be someone who will see past that and find out what a wonderful woman you are."

"I hope so," Louise responded, "but anyway, I have more than enough children to look after now with the fifteen in my class."

I saw the beautiful smile, that I had seen when she first entered the classroom, reappear on her face as she thought of the children in her class. I could sense the affection flowing from her and I knew in my heart that Louise was definitely one of the good guys, or should that be gals? Remembering a trick from Saint Michael, I fixed a protective barrier around her. It wouldn't totally protect her if a force of similar power to me, or stronger, tried to attack her, but I would feel the attack and could quickly arrive at her side to try to help her.

Satisfied that I had done enough to keep her as safe as I could, I willed myself alongside Helen in her car and listened to the inane chatter of the three eight, or soon to be eight, year olds in the back seat. The absolute most important topic of conversation was the forthcoming party to celebrate Darren's birthday. He seemed very eager to make sure that Gary and Adam were both definitely attending, almost to the point where he was not at all bothered if no-one else showed up.

"Everyone will come, Darren," Adam reassured him. "No-one wants to miss a party."

"Yeah, don't worry Dazza," Gary added. "I think that Tracey really likes you."

I saw a smile spread across the ginger boy's face as he took that information in. I had hoped that we would have a couple more years before the terror of girlfriends started, especially as I am totally unprepared for dealing with girls! Thinking about who was around to give me advice, I found my options extremely limited. Okay, Edith was female but, come on, she must be in her nineties or something! I wondered if Cupid, or Eros, or whatever he was called in real life actually existed. If he did, maybe I could put a shout out to try and get some advice.

As I was musing, Helen pulled the car up a small driveway to a fairly large detached house. The lawn was immaculate and there was a brand new, sleek, black BMW parked in the driveway. A shiver passed through my being as I read the personalised number plate.

'TY13R'

The front door opened, and a well-built, red headed man stood in the doorway.

"DADDY!" Darren shouted in glee as he jumped out of the car and, as his little legs pumped, carrying him through the puddles, I saw a smile light up the man's handsome face. A face that looked so familiar to me, even if it was now a few years older. The child leaped and was caught by strong arms as the man pulled his son to his chest.

"Yuck Darren, you've got me all wet!" a deep voice announced. Even though it was deeper than I remember, I recognised it all the same.

"Thanks for bringing him home Helen," the man said. "It's really appreciated."

"It's no problem Mr Walford," Helen replied. "It's not far out of our way, especially when we drop Gary off as well."

"Well, thank you all the same," the man added. "So are you still okay for next weekend?"

"Of course I am," the nanny answered. "I wouldn't miss this little one's eighth birthday for the world."

"You don't mind staying and helping out?" he queried, flashing his trademark smile at her, a smile that had melted my hatred for him on many occasions.

"Of course not, Mr Walford," she replied. "I enjoy watching the children have fun and enjoying themselves."

"That's great then, we'll see you next Saturday morning," he said.

"Bye Helen, thanks for the ride," Darren said, turning to her and smiling an identical smile to his father's.

"See you next week Darren, and see you soon Mr Walford," she said in farewell.

"Thanks again Helen, and how many times have I told you not to call me Mr Walford?" the man queried.

"Okay, okay," she replied. "Until next Saturday, Tyler."

She got back into her car and, after making sure that the two boys in the back were still strapped in, she took a long look back at the man. I didn't like the look she cast in his direction; a look of longing and of want, but I suppose I couldn't fault her as it was an expression I am sure was on my young face many times as I had gazed at my first crush. How could I have missed all the signs? Darren's red hair, his looks and build, his strength of character. All of them now reminded me of Tyler when we were younger.

As Helen started the car and drove off in the direction of Gary's home, I was standing on the driveway, contemplating this new development. I remembered my initial dislike of Darren when he had first met Adam, but over the last three years or so, his friendship with my charge had allowed me to forget that feeling and I had become fond of the ginger haired boy. To find out that he was the son of one of my worst tormentors had caught me completely unawares.

I had to investigate the now adult Tyler, the man who had grown up from the teenager whom I had last seen as he removed himself from my mouth, his taunts ringing in my ears almost as much as his punches to my face had done on that fateful day when I took my life. I willed myself into the Walford residence, feeling a prickly sensation as I passed over the threshold, something I had never experienced before. I made a mental note to check it out with Durchial later, as my little demon friend had warned me that the beings from the Underworld are just as adept as those from Heaven with regards to setting up protective barriers and warning glyphs. That concerned me as if I had just passed through one, not only would it alert whomever, or whatever, had set it to my presence, but it could also mean that the Walfords were under demonic influence.

As I phased through the front door, I saw a hallway that was cluttered with shoes, trainers, bags and varying items of sporting equipment. It reminded me so much of Jimmy's house when we were kids, my best friend never getting out of his habit of leaving items of clothing or equipment where he shed them, much to the dismay of his mother. I felt an ache thinking of Jimmy. For a fleeting moment, I allowed myself to wonder what his life had become. Was he married, or career minded? Was he still in Japan or had he moved back to the UK? Did he know I'd died?

My musing was interrupted when a laughing Darren ran past me shirtless and up the stairs. A smiling Tyler followed him, calling for him to take a bath. This would give me some time to look around and, as I did, I noticed that there were photographs everywhere. Most were of Darren throughout all of his ages, some I recognised were of Tyler's parents and there were a couple of Tyler at what looked like presentation evenings. I had to admit, seeing him dressed in a tuxedo, he looked very sharp and all the feelings that I had for him resurfaced for a moment, before I mentally kicked myself and reminded myself that he was a major influence in my death.

I was surprised to see no pictures of a wife and, looking around the lounge and kitchen, it was easy to spot that the place needed a woman's touch. I moved myself upstairs and found Tyler watching his son take his bath, asking him about his day. I filtered out the conversation as I tried to touch Tyler's mind to sift his memories.

The first surprise was that there were no barriers to block me. I had full access to him, should I desire it, and although I had two initial thoughts, one of causing him pain in revenge for all the pain he caused me, and the second of a temptation to seek out all of his sexual activities, I concentrated on gaining just the information that I needed. The second surprise was an underlying sense of guilt. Guilt that he believed he had caused my death, but it was also tinged with a sense of fulfilment. I delved deeper and found that, just as he had begun to consider his own sexuality, my sister had come along and trapped him into dating her. As captain of the football team, this gave him a perfect cover and, after sleeping with her for the first time, he cast aside all doubts in his mind and began his homophobic attitude. I saw all the insinuations she had made about me to him, about my feelings and attractions and how she had, slowly but surely, built up the hatred in him for me, to the point where he had attacked me that first time. Then, for the next six months, she continued attacking his private insecurities with comments to make him doubt himself, she pointed out opportunities for him to prove his manliness by bullying weaker boys who, even if they weren't gay, gave an impression of being so. Of course, I was the main focus of my sister's and Tyler's attentions. Once Gill was happy that the foundations were in place, she left him for another boy, and his hatred for our family increased. As a school captain, it was not the done thing to vent his frustrations on a girl, so my pain just increased as he concentrated on me.

His life changed shortly after signing professional terms for one of the Premiership football clubs. The prospect of a comfortable life lay ahead, but a drunken night out with friends, celebrating, ended in a car crash and a smashed knee that would never heal properly, thus ending a promising career before it started. His girlfriend promptly left, seeing her future of a comfortable life, being a footballer's wife disappear and he was left literally holding the baby, Darren.

I found myself filled with sympathy for him and, for the second time in a matter of months, I was willing to forgive a major influence in my demise. That feeling was short lived though, as I heard his next comment.

"I don't know why you want that pansy boy at your party, Darren," the deep voice complained.

"But Adam is my friend," the little boy responded. "And he isn't a pansy."

"I know one when I see one, and I'm telling you he is," Tyler told him. "I don't like you hanging around with him as it could rub off on you."

Oh please! I thought. Tell me he's not so thick as to still think you can be influenced so heavily. You're either gay, straight or bisexual. Nothing that anyone can do can change that. Anyway, there was nothing that Adam had done that would mark him as gay. He's only eight for God's sake!! Oops, sorry Father!

Not wanting to hear any more, sensing that his attitude hadn't changed anyway, I willed myself back to the Zegers' just in time to see Helen's car pulling away and Adam happily bouncing into the house, looking for John to tell him about the upcoming party. He found him on the phone talking to someone, who I discovered very quickly to be Gillian.

"Daddy, when are you taking me shopping to get Darren's pressie?" the young boy questioned, interrupting John in mid-sentence.

"Not now, Adam," John scowled. "Can't you see I'm on the phone?"

"But you told me to ask you when I got back from school," Adam complained.

"Well you'll have to wait until I'm finished," his father told him shortly, returning to his conversation with my sister.

Adam waited patiently for a few minutes but, with John showing no signs of ending his conversation, Adam tried again.

"Daddy, you said we would go tonight," Adam said quietly, tugging on his father's shirt. "The shop shuts soon."

"Be quiet boy," John hissed at him.

"But you promised!" Adam cried and, in a rare show of defiance, the young boy reached forward and pressed his finger on the call end button on the phone.

A hand shot out before I could react, not that I was supposed to be allowed to, and Adam stood, stunned into silence, clutching his cheek as the pain of the first ever smack delivered by his father raced through his nerves.

"Oowww!" cried the young boy, tears welling in his eyes.

"I told you not to interrupt, now go to your room!" John snarled, the expression on his face unlike anything I had seen from him before.

"But what about Darren's pressie?" Adam asked, his voice stuttering in short gasps as he tried to keep himself from crying.

"You can forget that now," John snapped back. He picked up the phone and started redialling Gill, ignoring the boy at his side.

"I hate you!" Adam yelled out, stamping his way up the stairs.

"Oh, you didn't just shout that at me?" John shouted back, slamming the phone down and storming after Adam, who had now picked his own pace up, running up the stairs and to the supposed safety of his bedroom, shutting the door behind him.

"Master, should we stop the John man?" Durchial asked, suddenly appearing at my side.

"We can't," I told him, much to my sorrow. "Unless he puts Adam in mortal peril, we have to let things play out."

"But Master, the John man means to hurt the Adam boy," the demon told me.

"Well, sort of," I said. "I'm guessing he will spank him, which will be a first for Adam but not for other children. I'm more worried about why he won't keep his promise to Adam."

As much as I wanted to be with Adam and stop John from spanking him, this was definitely not in my realm of responsibility and would seriously break my secrecy instructions. Knowing I couldn't do anything until it was over, I stayed outside Adam's bedroom, half closing my ears to the sound of flesh upon flesh and the yelps of pain from the eight year old. Finally, after what seemed an eternity to me but in reality was only less than a minute, I saw John re-emerge from Adam's room, a satisfied smile on his face. Anger flared inside me.

"Master, no!" I heard Durchial hiss at me, bringing me back to my senses as I realised I was building up a physic shock. I took in a deep breath, well I would have if I could breath, and slowly released my pent up energy.

Concentrating instead on the quiet sobs coming from Adam's room, I willed myself to the side of his bed. Looking down, I saw the small boy lying face down, his head buried in his pillow, his trousers still pulled down. I could see the prints of John's hands on his flesh and my anger welled up again, only to be replaced with a healing focus as I took the pain away. Adam's sobs turned to sniffles and finally he quietened completely. Finally, I heard the little snore that I had fallen in love with as my charge descended into sleep.

"Master, why did the John man not keep his word?" Durchial asked me as I sat on Adam's bed, gently stroking his brown hair, soothing his way into a dreamless rest.

"I'm not sure, but I'd bet my soul that my sister had something to do with it," I replied.

"Master, that would be a problem," my little demon friend responded.

"I know. If Gill has gotten into John's mind, we could be in all sorts of bother," I told him.

"No Master, well yes, that would cause trouble," Durchial said. "But I meant that you currently do not own your soul so how can you gamble it?"

I stopped in mid flow of my calming strokes to Adams' head to look at the small blue figure. I had learned a lot of Durchial's expressions in the three years we had been together, even though some were lost in human explanation, but the look on his face was one I hadn't seen before. His eyes were narrowed and his lips curled back slightly showing his sharp fangs. Suddenly a snort escaped his mouth and his body shook slightly.

"Durch, are you laughing?" I asked in wonder.

"I made one of your human jokes, Master," he told me.

"A joke? Durchie, that's brilliant," I enthused and reached over to pat my little helper on the shoulder.

Thoughts careered through my mind as the impact of the change in my demon friend hit me. If he could learn humour, and by that I meant good humour and not the pleasure they receive from causing mischief or worse, then maybe there was hope that they could change for the better. I still worried greatly about the fact that, if I lost Adam, demons would be freed upon the Earth.

The remainder of the night passed without incident. It was only when Helen was getting the sullen boy ready for school that John's actions came to light.

"So you didn't get to go shopping for Darren's present last night?" the nanny asked Adam.

"No! Daddy wouldn't take me," he grumbled.

"Why ever not?" Helen asked, her face frowning.

"He was on the phone to Her again!" Adam whined, his face screwing up in distaste. At least he had the correct impression of my beloved sister!

"So why wouldn't he take you afterwards?" she asked, pulling Adam's jumper over his brown locks.

"'Cos he's a meanie and he shouted at me and then, and then," Adam paused, his face a mask of sadness. "And then he spanked me for being an ungrateful pest."

I sensed the gasp from Helen without even having to hear it as she heard the news that John had raised his hand to his son for the very first time. She drew Adam into a hug.

"Oh sweetie, you must have caught him at a bad moment," she soothed. "I'll tell you what, how about we go shopping for Darren's present straight after school?"

"Can we?" Adam bubbled, a smile coming back to his face.

"Sure we can," Helen reassured him.

"Let me go get my money I saved!" Adam yelled in joy as he dashed back up the stairs, reappearing moments later holding some coins in his little hands.

"Do you want me to hold that for you while you're at school?" the nanny asked him.

"No, it's okay," Adam replied, putting the money in his pocket. "I'll take real good care not to lose it. It's for my friend so I won't lose it."

Proud of himself for saving up his pocket money to buy Darren a present, Adam took Helen's hand and walked out of the door, babbling to her about what he was going to buy the red headed boy, a boy who was suddenly back on my 'to watch' list. I felt I needed some advice and, remembering Ezekiel's own advice about using my allies, I told Durchial to watch over Adam while I went in search of Edith.

Now, being an ethereal being, I could quite easily pop straight to any location where I would find the old physic. However, the first time I appeared next to her in her kitchen while she was making herself a pot of tea, I was quickly reprimanded for scaring 'the beejezus' out of her but she forgave me almost as soon as I had 'acquired' an identical ceramic teapot from the South Coast, decorated with the Cornwall landscape, to replace the one she had dropped.

So, naturally, I always make sure she sees me coming, which unfortunately, is getting harder to do with her fading eyesight.

I cast my mind's eye out and found Edith sitting alone, as usual, in St Paul's Cathedral, watching the steady stream of visitors file past her taking in the architecture and murals of the magnificent building. I willed myself to a safe distance from her and slowly walked up to her, taking a seat in the empty pew by her side.

"Good morning Joseph," she said in greeting.

"Morning Edith," I replied. "How do you know that I'm there before I've said anything or made myself visible?"

"I have my ways, young one," she chuckled.

"You'll have to tell me one day, just in case someone else figures it out as well," I asked her, more in hope than expectation. Edith always closely guarded how her abilities worked.

"We'll see! Come, walk with me so I don't look like an old crazy sitting here, talking to myself," she announced getting slowly to her feet. I reached out to help her, only to be shooed away. "I'm old but I'm not ready for the knackers' yard just yet!"

I giggled, as that was one of her favourite comebacks to any hint of an indication of her age. She started off in the direction of the Chapel of Saint Michael, where we had had our first introduction. I quickly scanned the Cathedral for other non-human beings and, once I was happy I was here alone, I phased myself into view. To any person looking on, we were now just a normal couple of visitors, a teenage boy spending time with his grandmother. Or maybe that should be great-grandmother? I did check myself over to make sure I had clothed myself properly as I did make the mistake once, a few months ago, of phasing in to Edith's view having shed my normal grey robe, that had been placed on me by the Powers That Be, and I had forgotten that I needed to replace it. Let's just say that it was the only time I was pleased that the old lady's eyesight wasn't as good as it used to be.

"So what is troubling you Joseph?" Edith asked me.

"Why do you think something is wrong?" I countered.

"These days, you never come just to visit old Edith," she chided me, making me hang my head slightly. She placed an arm around me. "Old Edith knows that the time is coming where you will be tested, so fear not about keeping an old woman company. You have to protect the boy. All of Heaven, and those poor Lost Souls, are depending on you."

"Well, most of Heaven," I muttered, thinking back to the encounter with the two Seraphim in this very Cathedral.

Edith's expression told me that her hearing was never better, but she chose to ignore my comment and pressed on.

"What help do you require from me?" she asked.

"I need to break my sister's hold on Adam's father," I explained. "I've tried to break through but, for some reason, her grip on him is too strong."

"But if love is involved then, surely, goodness must shine through?" Edith questioned.

"There is no goodness within my sister," I said through gritted teeth. "Ezekiel told me she is Yeqon's creature, and has been for years before I died."

"Hope surely exists for redemption for every soul," the old lady mused.

"Not hers!" I retorted.

Edith's face drew into a sorrowful frown, and I immediately apologised for snapping at her. I went on to explain how John was now blindly following Gillian's lead in things, starting to ignore Adam once more, and how he had struck his son for the first time.

"It's only going to get worse, unless I can break her grip," I explained. "Adam is going to get hurt and I can't allow that, but I cannot directly intervene between Adam and his father."

"Oh, the silly laws that our Father agrees to with his silly bets with Him!" Edith cursed. "Let me think."

We sat there in silence, Edith deep in thought, me looking at the passing strangers. For once, people could actually see me and think I was just a normal kid once more. It ached in my heart, remembering life and how it could be so beautiful. I was brought out of my musing by a whack on the shin from Edith's walking stick.

"Ow!" Despite the shock of pain running through my shin, I grinned at her as she knew exactly what she was doing. It felt good to have a feeling like that, something I don't normally experience while I'm in my spiritual form.

"I have an idea, but we must leave holy ground to explore it," the old lady told me.

"Why?" I queried.

"Our Father probably wouldn't appreciate my summoning a fallen soul into His House," she smiled.

"Oookkaaaayy!" I drew out in a breath.

Getting my revenge for the blow to my shin, I loudly suggested 'Grandma Edith' take my arm to steady her steps, as we got up to leave. Edith flashed me a grin in acknowledgement of my one-upmanship and handed me her handbag to carry, something I hadn't thought of. It seemed no matter how hard I try to get ahead, heck not get ahead, just draw even on points with our jokes, she still managed to get the upper hand. We took a slow walk out of the Cathedral and, as we crossed the threshold, I felt the now familiar warm sensation of the barrier, put in place by the Church when it consecrated the land.

We crossed the paved area in front of the building, and I followed as Edith led me up some steps into a square garden. We took a seat on one of the benches surrounding the grassy centre.

"I like it here," Edith told me. "I can watch the world pass by, everyone so busy, busy, busy, yet they still stop and take the time to look at God's handiwork."

I looked back toward the building we had just left, and couldn't help but be awed by the stunning structure. The dome, a replica of the Basilica of St Peter in Rome, was magnificent, shining white against the backdrop of the clear blue skies that we had this morning.

"So who is it you are going to ask for help?" I quizzed, wondering who I was about to meet.

"An old acquaintance, a spirit that has yet to cross to the other side, but has intimate knowledge of things that can happen, let's say not strictly by the book," Edith replied.

"Should I phase out?" I asked.

"No, I think he'll find you interesting," she replied.

"In what way?" I wondered aloud.

"You're a special case, young one," Edith responded, patting my knee. "He may want certain information, or favours, in return for the information we want from him."

"Favours?" my voice quivered, now wanting to know what she was setting me up for.

"Oh nothing like that silly boy," Edith scolded me. "There are skills that you have that he may ask about."

"I'm not teaching any fallen spirit anything that will harm a human, or an Angel," I said firmly.

"Don't worry, that's the last thing he would want," Edith replied. "Now hush while I try to call him."

Once again we sat in silence, although I could see the old lady's pink lips moving as she silently whispered whatever calling she needed to attract the attention of this soul who was going to help. I watched her, fascinated, as her expression changed along with her body posture as she seemed to be in the middle of an intense discussion when, suddenly, she smiled and relaxed onto the back of the bench.

"So come on then, you old crow," a male voice said from the side of us, startling me. "What do you want now?"

"Advice Benjamin, that's all," Edith replied, turning to look at the figure that had materialised on the pathway in front of us.

"Ah advice eh? Never cheap that, you know!" the figure said before he seemed to realise that I was there. "You seem to have an apprentice."

"Not quite," Edith chuckled. "Meet Joseph, he's the one who needs the advice."

The man looked me over and I found myself doing the same. He certainly wasn't what I had pictured when Edith told me we were meeting up with a less than savoury character. He seemed to be a man in his late twenties, dark hair, dark eyes. He was dressed in casual clothes, but his casual appearance looked more put on than his demeanour suggested.

"Ah, young fellow me lad, nice to meet you," he said, offering a hand. "Benjamin Grover esquire at your service. Call me Ben."

"Joe, um, Joe Harris," I introduced myself, taking his hand, which proved to be a mistake as a flash of insight hit me as soon as I took it. I sensed a great confidence in himself, but also fear. Without meaning to, my mind searched his and I discovered that he had been a budding entrepreneur, struggling to make ends meet when he shared a table in a busy bar with a stranger. A stranger who offered him the means to set his business running and introduce him to the right people to enable him to move in social circles he could previously only have dreamed of.

"You're not who you seem to be, young Joe," the man said, pulling his hand from mine.

"That's never happened before, I'm sorry," I quickly apologised, not wanting to upset the man before I could see what he could say to help me.

"I sense now that you are one like me, almost," he smiled. "A spirit yet to pass."

"Not by choice," I replied.

"Meaning?" he queried.

"Meaning I killed myself but, instead of being damned, I've been given a second chance," I said with a deep breath of hope. "If I complete my mission successfully, I will hopefully get let into Heaven."

"Ooh a mission? A secret mission?" Ben cooed.

"Not really a secret one, as everyone seems to know about it," I sighed. "Who was that stranger?" I asked trying to deflect any further questions.

"Who do you think it was?" Ben replied with a grin. "Why do you think I'm picky about who I see?"

"That man, that was?" I stumbled over my words, my instinct kicking in.

"Yup, that was the main guy from below," Ben replied. "I made a deal with him for a successful life but, as always, he managed to find a way to twist it to his own needs and, one marriage, three mistresses and one nasty accident later, he came knocking for payment."

"Your soul?" I guessed.

"Well, I didn't feel like he had kept up his end of the bargain, so I decided to default on payment," Ben laughed. "So here I am, on the run."

I smiled as his wry humour over his situation infected me. Edith, obviously having heard the story before seemed to have nodded off next to us. I saw him look at her, almost with affection, before his gaze returned to me. All traces of his good humour vanished as he took me in.

"So, why do you need my help so badly that Edith would risk my soul by consorting with you, Protector?" he asked with a low voice.

"You know me?" I asked, surprised.

"Of course, every spiritual being knows of you," he replied. "Tell me quickly, for your presence is a beacon to the Underworld and there is someone whom I would prefer to remain oblivious to my whereabouts."

I explained quickly about my sister, her corruption by Yeqon and how she was now turning John against his son.

"So why is this boy so important?" Ben asked.

"He is an innocent," I replied. "Isn't that enough?"

"No," the man replied shortly. "The upstairs crowd wouldn't send a Protector for just any soul."

"Okay, look, there is a wager between Our Father and Lucifer. Adam is the gamble," I started to explain. "If I keep him safe, I free all the Lost Souls of the Youth from Hell."

"And if you don't?" Ben queried.

"Then Satan gets to keep all the souls, and he gets mine and Adam's as well," I replied softly.

I heard Edith's breath shorten, as I knew that the thought of Adam and me being condemned to Hell upset her. I looked at her, dabbing her eyes with a white lace handkerchief and sent her a comforting emotion burst. As I saw her expression brighten slightly, I turned back to the form in front of me, one that I was getting a real feel that he was a con man of the worst kind. As I turned back to him, I felt myself freeze. I tried to move, but couldn't. I was being held in place by some unseen force.

"So what's to stop me from holding you, trading your soul and that of this boy for my own release?" Ben said suddenly, circling me, showing me that he was the one who had taken control of my essence.

"You wouldn't do that Ben," I snapped back, trying to instil a confidence in my voice that I didn't feel.

"You could be the key to release me from my agreement," Ben murmured, placing a hand on my shoulder. "If I can keep you trapped, that would give Yeqon free rein on your boy."

He stepped away from me, a smile on his lips and a pensive expression on his face.

Chapter Nine

"Benjamin Grover, you stop teasing Joe now!" Edith barked, a harsh edge to her voice that I hadn't heard before.

"Well, there could have been the chance the He would trade," Ben replied. "But then again, I'm not the one to take His word anymore."

He waved a hand at me and I felt my essence released. I turned on him, my anger building. I felt energy flow into me as I pulled it from the surrounding area, readying a psychic blow to the spirit.

"Now hold on laddie," Ben said to me, holding up a hand. "You need my help, and I've just given you a demonstration of what I can do."

"Yeah, now let me give you one!" I hissed.

"Joseph Patrick Andrew Harris!" Edith scowled. "You release that energy now, or I'll take you over my knee."

My full name. No-one ever uses my full name unless I'm in really big trouble! Automatically I reacted to the command in her voice and let the energy build up seep back out of my being and turned to the old lady, who suddenly appeared to be seven foot tall and two hundred pounds. She wasn't of course, but in my mind's eye she was a titan.

"Sorry Edith," both Ben and I said in unison, both of us breaking into a smile at the thought of her punishing the pair of us.

"Look Joseph," Ben started. "Can I call you Joe?"

I nodded.

"Edith said you've got a problem and that she thought I could help," he continued. "I owe the old crow a couple of favours after she has hidden my existence, in the past, from those looking for me so, let's see what you need and what I can do to help."

"And in return, what do you want from me?" I asked, surprised at his sudden acquiesce.

"Well, I understand that you have a certain something helping you," he replied. "Something that has powers of its own."

"Durchial?" I queried. "What do you want from him?"

"It has a defensive ability that warns the creature when other Underworld beings are close," Ben told me, something that I already knew. "I would like that ability."

"I'm not sure if it is something that can be taught," I confessed. "I would have to ask him."

"Well, ask him then," he said.

"He's looking after Adam at the moment," I answered. "I'm not leaving Adam unprotected at any time."

"The demon can instruct you," Edith piped up. "There are countless instances in the past of humans gaining knowledge and powers through interaction with demonic beings."

"You are sure?" Ben quizzed the old lady. "If I give him what he wants, that is my price."

"I am sure Durchie will agree, especially if I instruct him to," I said confidently.

"Fine, agreed," the man replied, spitting on his hand and holding it out towards me.

I cringed slightly at the thought of that, but then remembered that we don't actually produce saliva so it was just for show. Grinning to myself, I copied his actions and shook his hand to seal the deal.

"Okay then, I'll need to do some checking around on this bitch of a sister of yours," he said, watching me intently as he spoke.

"How soon do you think you can help?" I asked, ignoring his attempted rile of me. Well, I do think she is a bitch as well, don't I!

"Depends on how far you are willing to go," Ben replied. "If you want her out of the way permanently, I can arrange that fairly quickly, but if it is just to remove her influence from this John bloke, then that will take time."

"Permanent? What exactly do you mean by that?" I asked.

"Permanent as in no longer on this Earth," came the simple reply.

Was I ready to do that? After all, even though she was the major influence in my suffering, she was still my sister. Could I sign her death warrant?

"Look, for now, just see about getting rid of her influence," I told the guy. "If things get out of hand, I may ask you to move things up, but I'm still operating under the Ten Commandments here."

"Pah! What a waste!" Ben answered. "Don't you think that they're a bit out of date?"

"Maybe but, with no update from Him, that's what I'm working to," I responded. "I chucked away my pass into Heaven once, I'm not going to do it again."

"I hear you kiddo," Ben said softly, his demeanour changing from the cocky, happy go lucky, shifty character to one of regret. He pulled me into a one armed hug. "I'll do what I can to help you get your goal and, maybe, when you meet Saint Peter and he looks through that damn Book of his, he might see some side notes explaining how I helped you."

"I'll tell you what Ben," I started. "Help me keep Adam alive, and I'll pull in whatever favours I can to get you away from that agreement."

He pushed me away slightly, placed both hands on my arms to look at me deeply in the eyes and, with a nod to Edith, he vanished. I turned back to Edith.

"Can we trust him?" I asked her.

"About as far as you can piss into a hurricane," she replied, making my mouth drop open in shock. "Oh come on, us old 'uns were using swear words while you were just a twinkle in your granddaddy's underpants."

"Now that's a thought I'd prefer not to explore," I giggled. "Seriously though Edith, thanks again for your help."

"Well it took you long enough to figure out I'm not just some crazy old lady who talks to herself," she smiled. "Now, why don't you go and check on your boy."

I bent forward and pecked her cheek and willed myself away.

Confusion settled in my mind as, instead of appearing directly in Adam's classroom, I found myself in the assembly hall. It was filled with children and parents. A chill passed over me as I saw two uniformed policemen, along with half a dozen men and women who, while they were in suits, also carried themselves as officers of the law. Panicking I scanned the room quickly and breathed a sigh of relief as I saw the brown haired figure of my little charge. However, his shoulders were shaking and I could see Helen with her arm around her, whispering into his ear.

"Durch, where are you?" I mentally shouted.

"Here Master," the blue figure replied, materialising beside me.

"What's happening?" I asked.

"A boy has been taken," he replied.

"Who?" I started to ask before I saw Mrs Henderson and a man in his forties walk onto the stage calling for order.

"If I may have your attention, children and parents," the Headmistress called out.

The room quietened immediately, showing to me once again that the situation was serious.

"As some of you are aware from the phone calls you have received, one of our pupils has been abducted and we have called the police to resolve this as quickly as possible," the motherly lady said, a tear rolling down her cheek. "This is Detective Inspector Dands who would like to address you."

The broad man moved forward, a note pad in his hand. A cough to clear his throat and he looked up, slowly scanning the hall, looking at the anxious faces of pupils and adults alike.

"We received a phone call from Mrs Henderson thirty minutes ago informing us that one of the pupils, an eight year old male, was seen by a teacher, a Miss Yeates, being forced into a black Audi on the pavement just outside the school gates. The gates were locked but, upon investigation, the fencing to the left had been cut away, allowing access.

At this moment in time, we are reviewing the partial registration plate given by Miss Yeates and we are checking all CCTV cameras along the routes away from the school.

As soon as we have any further information, we will let you know. In the meantime, please do not be afraid for your children. We are convinced that this is a one off opportunist. However, we will be stationing a uniformed policeman at the gates for the next few days, for added security and safety.

Thank you."

The man stepped away from the centre of the stage, conferred for a few moments with Mrs Henderson before leaving the hall with a couple of the plain clothed officers in tow. Voices erupted in a volcano of noise as the impact of the missing child, and the thought it could have been their own, hit the parents.

I moved myself over to Helen, who was still comforting the sobbing Adam. I saw the tall figure of Tyler, his hands on Darren's shoulders, as the red head struggled to keep his own emotions in check. I glanced around, looking for Gary's mother but failed to see her. Fear shot up my spine as I realised I also could not see Gary.

"Durch, is Gary the boy who has been taken?" I gasped.

"Yes Master, the Gary friend boy was the one removed," the daemon replied.

"Did you see what happened?" I asked. Getting a nodded response, I continued. "Did you get a look at who took him?"

"Not really Master but," Durchial paused. "But I did sense non-human interference."

"I don't understand," I complained out loud. "If they figured that I wasn't here, why not take Adam? Why take Gary?"

"Maybe they did not know you were absent, Master," my little helper pointed out.

"But then, why Gary?" I asked.

"This may have nothing to do with the Adam boy," Durchial suggested. "It could be just another human turned bad taking a child."

"Well, whoever it is, I'm going to go and get Gary back," I promised myself.

Just as I was about to will myself away, I caught a glimpse of Adam's tear stained face as he was being carried out of the hall. My heart constricted and I knew that, as much as I wanted to go and find the missing boy, I couldn't leave Adam in his moment of need.

"Durch, I want you to go and see if you can find anything out about who has taken Gary," I commanded. "I'm staying with Adam. He needs me."

"Yes Master," Durchial bowed and vanished to wherever it is he goes to when he is off researching information for me.

Despite the little Daemon's thoughts that this isn't connected to us, I knew in my heart that Yeqon was behind it. Call me paranoid maybe, but just because I see Yeqon's hand in everything untoward, it doesn't mean that he isn't behind this. However, I needed Durchial to investigate as it was taking all of Helen's nannying skills to try to calm down Adam. As I made my way past the crowded assembly hall, I heard the Walfords in conversation.

"Now you see what I mean, Darren?" Tyler was saying to his son.

"Not really Daddy." The young boy replied.

"Look at how the pansy is crying over his boyfriend going missing," the man hissed.

"He's just upset 'cos Gary's been taken," Darren argued.

"Well you're Gary's friend aren't you?" his father argued. Receiving a nod from his son he continued, "and you're not crying like that."

"Well, no," he agreed.

"Trust me, he's a pansy boy and you will do well to avoid him, otherwise it could be you he infects next," Tyler finished.

Anger and frustration surged in equal amounts within me as I heard the pathetic arguments put forth by the older Walford and, to my distress I sensed them seeping into Darren's mind. I reached my own mind forward to cleanse him of the thoughts, but found my way blocked.

"Oh dear Protector, can't you break through?" a familiar voice said in a low chuckle.

"Yeqon!" I hissed, turning on the demon, only to be confronted by his angelic form.

"You know, it would be a lot easier on you, and them, if you just jumped sides and came to work for me," he smiled. "You have performed heroically over these last eight years, and even my Lord Lucifer has started to take notice of your skills."

"You can go do one!" I snapped back. "I'm going to save Adam and piss all over your bonfire!"

"Don't be too hasty my worthy young opponent," Yeqon whispered, circling me. I cringed as he put a hand on my arm. "My Lord can reward you with pleasures that you could never dream of, more than anything that He up there can offer. Whatever your heart desires can be yours. A new turn on the Wheel of Life, money, power, love, whatever you wish, my Lord would give you."

"And in return?" I asked. "What would he want in return?"

"Just your service and loyalty," the angel replied. "Do my Lord's bidding and you would be rewarded."

"And if I don't?" I responded.

"Then you will continue your with losing battle, and ultimately face judgement," Yeqon said, a hint of longing in his voice. "After all, you must remember this?"

He held forth his hand and the dual pronged spear appeared, glowing white hot at the fork. I felt the physic energy emanating from it as it rolled towards me, causing my essence to shrink away as it touched me.

"You can't win against me, Joe," he whispered into my ear. "You can't even break through a simple mind barrier I have set up around the ginger brat."

"Why? Why involve Darren?" I asked. "And Gary?"

"Darren is a second generation capture. He will be useful as I torture your charge," Yeqon laughed. "And the blonde? Well, if you can find him and save him, I'm sure he will be a crucial ally for your boy."

"And if I don't?" I queried, not really wanting to know the answer.

"Then his pain and suffering will be on your hands. You put the two together, and now he has to suffer the consequence of your wish for your charge to be happy," he replied.

"I'm going to find Gary. I'm going to save him." I hissed. "And when I find him, if so much as one hair on his body is harmed, I will, I will..."

"You'll what?" Yeqon laughed. "You'll pit your puny Protector powers against that of Lord Lucifer's Most Chosen? My offer lasts one lunar turn. After that, you will feel the full force of the power of the Underworld."

He disappeared from my view and I looked around, noting that the people close by had pulled on coats or buttoned up jackets. I guess that there must be a cold flow from the Fallen, so I touched the air around them to warm it back to normal for the time of year. I quickly made it to Adam and Helen's side and laid a hand on the young boy's shoulder and muttered a calming cantrap, taking the edge off his sorrow, allowing Helen to guide him out of the school and into her car.

Their journey home was one of silence. My own thoughts were going ten to the dozen following the words of Yeqon, and the abduction of Gary. Guilt ripped through my core as I pondered his words. Was it my fault? I had prodded the young boy towards friendship with Adam, but with the human free will, he must have been inclined to be friendly anyway. Darren had needed a good push but, with Gary, just a guiding hand was required. I desperately needed Durchial to uncover something, anything, that would help but now knowing that the abduction was at the hands of Yeqon, I dare not call my little helper in case it alerted the Fallen to him.

As the car pulled up on the driveway, I saw with disgust that my sister's blue Porsche was parked alongside John's car. I pushed myself into the house ahead of Adam and could hear sounds that I didn't want to hear echoing from upstairs. I quickly reached out to Helen's mind, distracting her with the thought that a trip to the back garden to feed the goldfish would be in order, and also help keep Adam calm. It had been an idea from Durchial which we had used to distract Adam, and Helen, on numerous occasions when we needed to ensure that they were not walking into anything upsetting in the household.

Not wanting Adam to be outside too long, I increased the sound of their conversation so that it resonated into the bedroom. I heard John's voice cursing, and my sister's telling him to remain in bed.

"Not while my son is at home," I heard John say. "I told you I'm not comfortable with that."

"Well at some stage you're going to have to be," Gill replied.

"What? Why?" he asked.

"Well, sooner or later, we are going to be living together," I heard my sister explain. "He's going to have to get used to the noise then."

I heard a sigh.

"You're not thinking about changing your mind are you?" Gill asked, a hint of steel in her voice.

"No, no, of course not dear," John quickly replied. "Look, let's just play things by ear for now and find out what they are doing home at this time of the day."

With dark muttering under her breath, I heard movement and saw the couple, now fully dressed, exit the bedroom and make their way downstairs.

They entered the kitchen just as the dejected form of my charge and Helen came in from the garden.

"You're back early," John complained.
"What happened? The kid get kicked out of class?" Gill sneered.

Adam shot my sister a hateful look and ran from the kitchen. A quick touch of his mind showed him holding back his emotions to keep them from spilling out in front of her. Helen shadowed his look before turning her attention back to John.

"No, unfortunately Adam's friend, Gary, has been abducted from the school," the nanny explained. She cast a glance at Gill before continuing, "Adam is obviously very upset, so it would be nice to show him a little support."
"Well these little things do come to test us now and then," Gill said, her voice dripping with laced honey.
"Little?" Helen retorted, her voice going up a few notes. "Gary has been Adam's best friend since they started school, and for him to be taken by a stranger..."
"Who says it was a stranger?" Gill answered back. "Maybe it was a family friend."
"Then why would he be struggling to get away?" Helen asked, standing her ground.
"Now then ladies, let's not fight," John interjected, earning a reproachful look from both. "I'm sure there's a reasonable explanation behind this."
"Yes, I'm sure it's all a big misunderstanding and Adam's friend will be fine," Gill agreed.

I saw Helen stiffen as my sister reached forward to pat her condescendingly on her arm.

"I'm going to go and check on Adam to make sure he's fine," Helen said, obviously wanting to get away from Gill.
"No, it's okay dear," Gill interrupted her. "I'll go and look in on him."
"You?" the nanny asked incredulously.
"Yes, me," Gill replied. "After all, when I move in, I'm going to be a lot more involved in taking care of him, so this is a good starting place for him to get used to me."

Gill turned and left the kitchen, heading in the direction of the stairs. This certainly wasn't good. I was torn between going with her to make sure Adam was okay or staying with John and Helen to try to limit Gill's damage between them. Helen had turned back to John, a sorrowful look on her face.

"So when is this happening?" she asked.

"In the next few weeks," John replied softly. "We've been discussing it for some time, and we feel that Adam is old enough now to understand and also, it is something we both want."

"What will happen to me?" Helen asked, a catch in her voice. "Will you still need my services?"

"Gill works from home and is willing to take Adam to and from school, and obviously will be here for when he is at home," John started. "Also, Adam is getting to the age soon where he won't need a nanny any longer."

"I thought I was more than that," Helen whispered more to herself. "So how much notice will I receive?"

"Don't worry about that," he replied. "I'll make sure that you have enough to tide you by until you find another position."

I felt a pain in my arm and Durchial appeared at my side.

"Master, come upstairs," he hissed at me.

I willed myself to Adam's bedroom to see that Gill had taken hold of his arms and was shaking him slightly. I could sense the dislike and fear spilling from him, along with his efforts not to cry in front of her.

"What's wrong with you? Pull yourself together," Gill snapped quietly at him, making sure that she couldn't be heard by the pair downstairs.

"But Gary is in danger," Adam's voice croaked.

"Well, just thank your lucky stars it wasn't you, Adam," she said gently, her voice lowering all of a sudden into a more concerned one. "After all, you're a little cutie and you would tickle the fancy of any random pervert."

"What do you mean?" Adam asked, confused over her new tone, and her comments.

"Well, I'm sure that whoever has taken Gary is enjoying himself immensely at the moment," she sneered, her true intentions shining back through. "I just hope you don't mind damaged goods if you ever see your friend again."

She pushed Adam back onto the bed and with a triumphant smirk on her face at Adam's shocked comprehension of her words, she turned and swept back out and down the stairs, leaving my little charge staring into space. I saw a tear trickle down his smooth cheek and I reached my mind out to comfort his, to deflect his thoughts away from contemplating what my sister had inferred but I ran across a block as I touched him. This was new and unusual. I probed at it, finding that I could easily bypass it without any effort on my part, but I wanted to investigate it before I removed it.

As I did, I saw a wall of pure white light shining around the figure of a small eight year old being that looked a lot like Adam, but with small variances. I quickly realised that this was how Adam saw himself, and the white wall was a barrier he, himself, had built to protect him from the cruel comments of my sister. Deciding to leave it in place, I pushed through it and reached the small figure, wrapping it in love and comfort. Immediately, Adam calmed down and pulled out his school book from his satchel and concentrated on his homework that he had received in the morning session before the abduction.

"Durch, I need you to look after Adam for a while," I asked my Daemon helper.

"Yes Master," he replied, moving into a position between the child and the door. "Can I appear if the Gillian bitch woman tries to hurt the Adam boy again?"

"As tempting as that is, unfortunately not," I told him. "Just call me, and I'll come back."

"You will be trying to find the Gary boy?" he asked.

"Yeah, it's my fault that he's been taken, so I need to get him back before he's hurt," I said, my earlier guilt resurfacing.

"Master, no matter who the Adam boy was friends with, someone would have been taken to hurt him," Durchial told me. "The nature of the Fallen is to find something dear and hurt it rather than the target as it causes the target more pain and anguish than hurting the target itself."

"I think I'm getting that," I agreed. "Nothing hurts me more than seeing Adam suffering."

"Go find the Gary child, and I will protect the Adam boy," Durchial told me, a hint of command in his voice.

"I may need help," I told him. That reminded me of my deal with Ben. "Um, Durch, you know how you can sense other demons and the Fallen?"

"Yes Master, it is most useful," he agreed.

"Are you able to teach it to someone?" I asked.

"You need it not, Master," Durchial replied, a little confused. "You have your mind net that can sense non-Humans."

"It's not for me," I said, and told him about the agreement I'd made. I apologised for not asking him first, which he waved away.

"To look after the Adam boy, you must do what you need," he said simply. "I am yours to command, and if you command me to teach this spirit, I will."

"I'd prefer not to have to command you, Durch," I replied softly. "I'd like to think that we are friends, working together, rather than a Master and Servant."

The little daemon paused, studying me. He moved over to me and laid his claw on my arm. "Master, I too am finding that you are more than a Master to me," he said. "You do not treat me as a slave, and seek advice from me. You are knowledgeable, yet seek help from the Edith lady and now this Ben spirit."

"So we're friends?" I asked. It had been so long since I'd had a friend that I found myself beginning to get a little emotional.

"Yes Master, friends," Durchial agreed. "However, you must remain my Master so that others cannot command me to do their own desires."

"I can live with that," I smiled.

"Master, you cannot," the daemon responded, that same expression on his face from earlier. "You are already dead."

I laughed, rubbed his shoulder and willed myself away from the Zegers' and went high above the city. I wasn't exactly sure how to start looking for Gary, and hoped that, by taking a bird's eye view of things, inspiration would hit me. I thought of my time with Inspiral and wished that there was some way of spending a little time with one of the Muses. After all, their job was inspiration!

I opened my mind and cast it downwards, but was overwhelmed by the sheer size of the thought field coming back at me from the population of London. Normally, if I was casting around looking for threats, I could filter out human thought, but this time I was looking for a human. Hopefully two I thought to myself because, if Gary's abductor wasn't human, all sorts of issues would rear their head.

After trying various smaller filters in different sections of the city, I gave up on that idea and directed myself down towards the police station, where I had sensed the aura of Detective Dands. Sliding into his office, I saw the man hunched over his desk studying reports, flicking from one to another. I reached forward to touch his mind but found my way blocked. A prickly feeling went up my back and the air shimmered in front of me to reveal the form of an Archangel that I did not recognise. I did sense that he was from Heaven, and not a Fallen, so I relaxed slightly.

"Protector, your involvement here is forbidden," the deep voice of the winged figure told me.

"Who are you, sir?" I asked politely, underneath, my mind seething at being thwarted in my effort to try to find Gary.

"I am Halaliel, Archangel of Karma and Destiny and you are forbidden to intercede in this destiny," the Angel replied.

"But there is a little boy in danger," I told him. "I have been told, by Yeqon himself, that Gary is going to be hurt and I need to get him back to safety."

"Your mission is not to save that young boy, but to prevent Adam Zegers from following your own path of self-assassination," Halaliel responded. "If Gary Wilcox is to be recovered, it must be done at the hands of humans."

"But that may be too late," I complained. "If I can get inside this policeman's mind, I can see what information he has and then can start looking from there. I can save Gary before it's too late."

"It is too late," a second deep voice intoned from behind me.

I recognised it but did not want to acknowledge his presence, as the child inside me wished and hoped that, by not seeing him, he wouldn't really be there. Tears started to leak from my eyes as I looked at Halaliel, sadness showing in his face. An arm was laid across my shoulder and I was turned to face him.

"Ezekiel," I sobbed in greeting.

"Protector, it is not your mission to save all the children, just your charge," the second Angel consoled me.

"He's dead isn't he?" I asked, my breath getting shorter in emotion.

"Not yet," Ezekiel said raising hope inside me, only to banish it. "However, I am about to go to him to take him up to Our Father's Kingdom."

"Can I still have a chance of saving him?" I begged.

"This is a fixed point nexus," Halaliel interrupted as Ezekiel was about to answer. "Destiny cannot be altered."

"Can I at least be there with him?" I asked.

Receiving a nod from Halaliel, Ezekiel laid his hand one my shoulder and I found myself in a dingy room. Thick curtains blocked out any hope of sunlight making it through the windows, the only source of light was a single uncovered bulb, hanging bare from the ceiling. The walls showed signs of disrepair, flaking paint and peeling wallpaper. I saw a computer on top of a desk in the corner, images flashing across the screen that turned my stomach. Clothes littered the floor and, to my great distress, I saw those that would fit a young boy. An eight year old. A cry of pain caught my attention.

"Do not look Protector, for you shall be tainted with his evil," Ezekiel commanded me.

"Why is this happening?" I asked, wanting to know why God would allow this.

"Unfortunately we cannot win every battle for the happiness and fulfilment of every soul," he replied sadly. "Sometimes evil things happen to those we would prefer not, but their suffering on this plane is short, whereas their place in Our Father's Paradise is eternal."

"If he's going to die, can we make it now so he has to suffer no longer?" I begged.

Ezekiel studied me for a moment, pondering my request and, maybe, seeking advice from elsewhere, before he turned swiftly and moved to the bed. He reached forth a hand and laid it on a mess of blonde hair. I saw the small body stiffen suddenly before going limp. Muttered curses from the beast of the man who had taken him filled the room but I now only had eyes for the small, shining figure that now stood at the side of Ezekiel.

"Who are you?" Gary asked. "Are you here to save me?"

"In a way child, yes," Ezekiel said softly, kneeling down to look him in the eyes. He let his wings unfurl and they took the boy into an embrace. "You will no longer hurt now, my child."

"But that man, he will get angry and hurt us," Gary sobbed in warning.

"He can't see us Gary," I told him. "You're safe from him forever."

"You're Angels aren't you?" Gary gasped.

"He is," I replied, pointing to Ezekiel. "I'm still hoping to be."

"But why can I see you?" Gary asked.

"You've been badly hurt I'm afraid," Ezekiel explained. "Hurt so much that your body couldn't cope."

"You mean, I've died?" Gary cried, pulling away from the Angel. He turned to me and I dropped to my knees, motioning for him to come to me.

"I'm so sorry Gary, I tried to save you but I couldn't find you," I whimpered as he ran and hugged me, my hands rubbing his back in an effort to soothe him.

"What about my parents? What about Adam?" he sobbed. "I'm not ready to leave them."

"Your parents will draw strength from your memory and work tirelessly with other children who are in danger, saving hundreds and thousands of children through the GW Foundation that they will set up in your name," Halaliel announced, appearing in the room. "Your mortal life may have been short upon this plane, but your legacy will touch countless others. That has been your destiny, little one."

A smile touched Gary's lips for the first time since we arrived. "But what of Adam?"

"Adam is my responsibility," I told him. "I know he was very worried about you and he will miss you for the rest of his life."

"Are you Joe?" Gary asked, suddenly pulling back slightly so he could look at me. "You are, aren't you?"

I looked guiltily at the pair of Angels, as Adam is not supposed to have memories of me. The pair of them just smiled.

"Yeah, I'm Joe," I admitted.

"Adam told me about you once, he said you were like his guardian angel," Gary enthused.

"I'm not an Angel, but I am his guardian," I explained. "Durchie and me try to make sure bad things don't happen to him."

"Could I be a Guardian?" he asked, his face shining in hope.

"I don't know, but I'm sure if you ask Saint Peter, he will be able to tell you," I told him.

"It is time," Ezekiel announced.

I released Gary, who walked over and took the Angel's hand. Another curse from the man who had abducted Gary caught my attention.

"Wait, what about him?" I asked, pointing to the vile aspect of humanity.

"He will be dealt with by the human police, or not," Halaliel said.

"Not good enough for me," I retorted angrily. "If you won't do anything about him, I will."

"Protector, you cannot break The Sixth Commandment," Ezekiel warned me.

"I don't have to," I replied, a little hotly. "I have Durchial."

"There is another way," Halaliel said. "Think Protector, it will come to you and Gary can have his retribution."

"Uriel!" I shouted in realisation of his hidden meaning.

The red haired figure of the Angel of Retribution appeared in the room. Resplendent in shining silver armour, his wings held back, a sword in a scabbard hanging by his side.

"Took you long enough!" Uriel grouched. "I thought I was going to have to wait for the paperwork to come through on this one for a moment!"

"Paperwork?" I asked.

"Protector Joseph," Uriel said, turning to me. He held out a hand. "It's a pleasure to meet you. Angel Jackson speaks very highly of you."

I blushed at the compliment and muttered something back about it being nice to meet him too.

"Now, to deal with this scum," he announced. "Ezekiel, are you taking the young one before or after?"

"Gary, I think it would be best if we left before," Ezekiel explained. "You can learn about this as part of your Guardian training when your teachers believe that you are ready."

"Okay sir," the little boy replied. "Will you say bye to Adam for me please Joe?"

"Of course I will, little one," I told him, drawing him back into a hug. "You learn everything you can up there, and be the best guardian ever, ok?"

"I will," he promised. He leaned forward and gave me a kiss on my cheek, which I returned with a peck to his forehead.

As he returned to Ezekiel's side, I felt the air shift around us and I took in a breath as I realised we had become visible to the man.

"What the fuck?" he stuttered. "What are you doing over there brat? And who the fuck are you others?"

"We are judgement and you are guilty. Divine Justice will be served." Uriel announced.

"The fuck? What the fuck are you on?" he cussed at us.

"You killed me and these Angels are going to make you pay for it," Gary piped up.

"We are now due at the Gates," Ezekiel said. Raising a hand in farewell to me, I watched as he took Gary and phased out of view along with Halaliel, leaving just Uriel and me with the man.

"Jesus H. Christ where did they go?" the man spluttered.

"Our Father's Son does not have a middle name, scum," Uriel spat at him. "And if He did, you are unworthy of saying his name."

"Look, I dunno what the kid said, but he's making it up," the man lied.

Rage boiled up in me and I didn't even bother pulling in any energy as I swung a fist and connected with his face, knocking him backwards. I heard a steely scrape and turned to see Uriel raising his sword.

"You have been judged and you have been found wanting, your soul is cursed and tainted by the Fallen. You accepted their gifts with no thought of the suffering it caused. You are condemned," he announced and with a single swing, his sword passed through the body of the man.

I fully expected to see blood, guts, gore, the usual stuff that you see in the movies, but was surprised that his body remained intact as it toppled forward. However, still standing upright was the ghostly form of his spirit, a shocked expression on his face.

"What's this?" he cried, as he watched his body fall forward.

"Judgement," Uriel replied.

I felt a cold chill in the room, and looked on in horror as first one, then four, then six forms appeared around the man's soul. All were skeletal figures, chains in their hands, evil grins on their faces. A final figure appeared... Yeqon.

"Well, well, well," the Fallen one said. "Looks like someone's fun has come to an end."

"You! You said I would have the boy for the rest of my life!" the man accused.

"And the rest of your life was what you achieved," he laughed. "Now is the time for payment. Your soul, for eternity in the depths of despair. Take him."

The six figures acted as one flurry, casting chains around the man until he could stand no more. Collapsing on the floor, his eyes pleaded with us for forgiveness.

"It's too late for that, scum," Uriel said. "Take him, we're done."

"Always a pleasure, Uriel," Yeqon mocked. "Protector, I see you found your missing child."

"He's in a better place, and will do so much good that you still end up losing, Yeqon," I replied calmly, not allowing him to tarnish Gary's memory. "You just don't realise what love for another can accomplish."

I turned to Uriel.

"Can we make sure that someone is told where Gary's body is so that he gets a proper funeral?" I asked.

"That has already been taken care of, Protector," he replied.

"Then we can go," I suggested.

Uriel nodded, placed a hand on my shoulder and we disappeared from the room.

Chapter Ten

Tears streamed down the face of my young charge as, for the second time in less than a week, he said goodbye to someone he cared deeply about. After the sadness of Gary's funeral, where Helen held him closely throughout the service with John being absent, the nanny quite firmly voiced her opinion of the lack of comfort and support that the man was giving his son after the death of his best friend. Words became heated and Adam's carer was shocked by John announcing that Gill would now be taking over the responsibility for his son with immediate effect.

I could see my sister beaming in evil delight as she watched Adam's tearful hugs of farewell, and the promises that Helen was giving him about coming back to see him.

"I don't think that will be necessary Helen," Gill told the nanny, taking her arm away from Adam's shoulders.

"What do you mean?" Helen asked.

"I don't want the child confused as to who he will answering to from now on," Gill explained. "So it is in the best interests of all of us for you to have no further contact with him at all."

"You can't ask that!" the nanny gasped, looking at Adam, who's own face was showing signs of distress.

"It's not a request," my sister grinned sadistically. "I knew that you wouldn't obey a simple request, finding some reason to keep coming back to see him, so my good friend who just happens to be a High Court judge, has already signed this restraining order."

She produced an envelope from the pocket of her coat and handed it over to the dumbstruck Helen.

"When you read it, you should take note of the phrasing 'the subject shall not approach within two hundred yards of the child, and no contact through any means of communication shall be allowed.'" Gill smiled sweetly at the nanny.

"Basically you're out of his life and if you have any type of contact with him, I'll have you arrested and jailed."

She pushed Helen away from them and, with a strong arm around Adam's shoulders, forced him to turn around and half walked, half dragged him back into the house. Once inside, she instructed Adam to go to his room. Relieved to be getting away from my sister, Adam turned and fled, throwing himself face down on his bed as he cried tears for the loss of Helen. Not for the first time this week, I reached out to comfort him but, as I did, I came across the shining white barrier once more in place. This time I had to work to get through it, but once past I eased peaceful thoughts into Adam's mind, allowing him to become calm. I felt the pain of his losses, both Gary and now Helen, eating at his heart and I knew that I would need to do something to replace them.

I pondered how I could replace Gary without over-riding the memory of the friend who deserved to be remembered by Adam, and found myself thinking of Darren and his changing attitude. After the initial shock of their friend's abduction and murder, the ginger haired youngster was showing signs of becoming more and more like his father. He had started becoming more vocal in class and on the playground, belittling some of the less confident pupils. Somehow, he always escaped detection as there never seemed to be a teacher present when it happened. Adam, noticing the change in his friend's behaviour approached him about it one day, and was now on the receiving end of snide comments himself.

Miss Yeates, in a well-meaning effort to comfort the two boys who had grown close to Gary, had moved Adam's seat and placed the two next to each other. With no new intake in their year however, this meant that they were alone on the table meant for four, and allowed Darren plenty of opportunity to snipe at Adam. Adam in turn, not wanting to turn his back on his friend, took the insults without complaint and offered words of support back to his friend.

One sunny day, a few weeks after Gary's death, Adam learned of Darren's new found hatred for him. The children had eaten lunch and they were out in the newly reinforced, fenced in lawned area having an impromptu kick about with a football that one of the other Year 4 boys had brought in. Adam was becoming adept as a winger, his footwork and close ball control already belying his age and, as he picked up possession for his team, he easily beat the challenges of three of his opponents. I could see him smiling, maybe for the first time since that fateful day, when suddenly, he was upended by the ginger haired figure of Darren, who crudely chopped his legs from beneath him, and I saw Adam hit the ground hard.

I felt the shock of pain run through my head and I immediately willed myself to Adam's side, ready to heal anything that was too painful for him to cope with. I was pleased when I found that, other than a growing bump on his forehead, he was generally unharmed, just a little shaken. Even so, I could see dampness in his eyes as he fought to maintain a cool demeanour.

"What did you do that for Daz?" a dark haired boy called Phil asked.

"Hey, it was a good tackle!" Darren complained, protesting his innocence.

"No it weren't!" Phil retorted. "It was mean."

"It's a rough game," Darren told him. "If Adam don't like it, he shouldn't play."

"You okay Ad?" a second boy asked my charge, who shook his head, not yet trusting his voice.

"Oh jeez, look at him!" Darren whined. "He's gonna cry, the big pansy!"

"That's not fair Daz, you hurt him," Phil said, sticking up for the smaller boy, gaining nods of agreement from the other boys, including Darren's own teammates.

Sensing he was beginning to lose face, and possibly standing in the pecking order of the year, Darren turned and held a hand out to Adam to help him up. As Adam took it, I saw Darren's hand tighten, squeezing the dark haired boy's hand as he pulled him up off the floor. As their bodies came close, Darren leaned in.

"If you think this hurt, wait for later pansy boy," he hissed quietly in Adam's ear.

"Why are you being so mean?" Adam asked, his voice croaking slightly as he regained his composure.

"'Coz it's your fault that Gary's dead!" Darren hissed. "If he'd have stayed with me inside, rather than going out to play with you, he would still be alive!"

"It's not my fault that man took him!" Adam snapped back, his voice rising slightly. "It could have happened anytime!"

"I wish it had been you! My Dad says that its boys like you who attract men like that," Darren hit back, stunning both Adam and myself with the venom in his voice.

He pushed Adam away, turning back to the game, leaving Adam looking on. I could tell his words had stung my young charge as he moved away from the pack of boys, walking slowly over to the edge of the playground and took a seat on the kerb, by the fence where tributes had been laid in memory of Gary. He flicked through the different cards on the flowers and toys, his eyes finally resting on the little grey teddy bear that he had taken from his own collection. I felt an outpouring of sadness from him once again and, as much as I wanted to take away the hurt, I knew that he needed his grieving period.

I was now beginning to get more concerned over the hatred that was building within Darren. Remembering my own experiences of bullying, I needed to try to stop it before it started to get too much but, no matter how hard I tried to break through the barrier that protected his mind from my thoughts, Yeqon's skill was simply too great for me.

With no Helen for Adam to turn to either, I was running out of allies for Adam to confide in. Gillian was successfully taking over the household, having now moved in permanently, and her influence over John was complete. Everything that she wanted to happen, happened. After the initial period where the pair of them spent as much time together as possible, John's work now seemed to be taking up more and more of his time, leaving Adam alone in the house with my sister. Any hopes that I had had of her mellowing were dashed on the first day, when Adam was banished to his bedroom, leaving Gill free rein over the rest of the house.

Initially this wasn't a problem as Adam had his CD player, games console and television to keep him occupied. Today, however, was a turning point in her cruelness towards him as, when Adam made his way to his bedroom, I saw her move towards the fuse box where I noticed that some new switches had been installed. A flick of one switch and the power was cut to Adam's room.

"Gill, my telly doesn't work!" Adam complained as he came back down the stairs.

"I told you to go to your room, Adam!" Gill snapped at him as he entered the lounge.

"But there's something wrong 'cos my telly don't work and my CDs don't either," Adam explained.

"Well they wouldn't as the electric has been turned off," she smiled at him. "You shouldn't be wasting your time with that crap, go read a book instead."

"But I want to watch Spongebob!" Adam grumbled.

"I wanna watch Spongebob!" Gill taunted in a childish voice. "Come with me!"

She jumped up and grabbed him by his arm and dragged him into the kitchen. She threw open a cupboard and grabbed a pack of sponges and thrust them into Adam's chest.

"You want sponges, here! Take these and go get a bucket and I want you to clean the steps to the back door," she commanded. "If you are a good boy and get them as clean as I want them, then you will get your tea tonight."

"But, but," Adam started, before receiving a hard smack on his rear.

"That is the only butt I am interested in hearing about and, if you don't do as I say, then I will get a stick from down the garden and you won't be sitting on your butt for a week!"

Adam squeaked and grabbed the sponges, making his way to the garden. He ran to the shed and fetched a bucket. Heading back into the kitchen, he was stopped by Gill.

"I don't want a mess in my kitchen," she announced. "Use the garden tap."

"But it's cold," Adam complained.

"It will toughen you up," Gill smirked. "You've been allowed to grow up soft. You don't want the other boys calling you a pansy boy do you?"

"No!" Adam retorted, knowing that he was already being called that by Darren.

I watched on in despair and anger as he ran back out to the outside tap. He half-filled the bucket and struggled with it back to the kitchen door. Looking at the steps, I could see that, although they had some moss and mud on them, they weren't too bad. I let my mind touch the concrete and found that I could give the surface a little nudge to release the dirt easier so that Adam wouldn't find it too difficult to clean. Even with that help though, it still took him two and a half hours to clean the seven steps leading from the patio to the kitchen.

I gave him a light touch to tell him he'd done a great job as he stood up gingerly, his knees cramping slightly from kneeling down for the whole time. As he emptied the bucket of dirty water down the drain, I heard the back door open and saw Gill inspecting the steps, looking for faults. My pride in Adam swelled as I saw her expression turn from grinning malice to one of bitter disappointment as her chance to punish him disappeared when she saw what he had achieved from sheer hard work.

"Well, now we know that you are a good little scrubber boy, I think we'll let you clean the whole patio," Gill announced, her smirk returning as Adam approached her after stowing the cleaning equipment back into the shed.

"But it's huge!" Adam groaned. "Daddy normally gets a cleaning company in to do it."

"Well, Daddy isn't in charge of the finances anymore," Gill replied. "I'm looking after the spending and I don't think we need to pay all that money if you are capable of doing it."

"Do I get pocket money for doing it?" Adam asked, a light of hope shining in his eyes. "Daddy always says that if I do my chores, and then do some extra, he will give me my pocket money."

"Pocket money?" my sister asked, sounding aghast at the very idea. "Do I get pocket money for feeding you? For washing your dirty, smelly clothes?"

"But, but, that's your job now Helen isn't here, isn't it?" Adam asked innocently.

"So I'm to become your slave? I don't think so boy!" Gill spat, grabbing his arm and pulling him up the steps. "I think you need a short, sharp lesson in how things work round here now."

"I'm sorry, I didn't mean it!" Adam cried out, as did I, as pain shot through my arm as Gill tightened her grip on him. Again, my essence linked into his in an effort to nullify any physical pain he may have to endure.

"I was going to reward you with a nice meal for you efforts but now, you rude little boy, can make do with this," she said as she pushed him onto a chair.

Gill spent the next few minutes slicing some cheese and placing it between some dry bread. A glass of water was pushed towards Adam, as he looked up at the woman, his eyes full of sorrow. For a hopeful moment, I thought I saw her expression soften at his sad face, but her mask of steel was soon restored with a flash of red in her eyes and she walked away from him, returning to the lounge.

"Make sure you clear up after you've finished and then go to your room," she shouted as she poured herself a glass of wine and settled back down to watch television.

I sat and watched Adam slowly eat his sandwiches, taking his time to chew each mouthful to get as much nutrition from each bite as possible. He sipped at the water, not wanting to risk incurring any further wrath of my sister by daring to get some juice from the cupboard to flavour it. I needed to do something but, for once, I was struggling.

I remembered back to a conversation I had had with Ezekiel, all those months ago on the night I had found Petey, and realised that this was what he had been warning me about. I replayed the conversation through my head, but all I could remember was my pig-headedness and my self-congratulatory attitude at the time. It was an attitude that had cost Gary his life.

Tears welled up in my eyes as, not for the first time in the last few months, I allowed guilt to rip through my soul. For the first time, I was suffering a succession of defeats to Yeqon, and I needed to stop the trend. I needed help. I thought about Ben, but he was off investigating how to break Gillian's influence over John, and Edith was more of a sounding board than a problem solver. Durchial, as great a help as he was in watching Adam, preferred his solutions to be at the end of his claws.

His claws! I still shuddered at the memory of the small man who had attacked Pete with the knife, crying out in shock as Durchial shredded his flesh. As I recalled that night, I felt a tug to my essence. I played it back through my mind and, each time I concentrated on Pete, I felt the tug. The image of the curly haired boy fixed itself in my mind and I just knew that something was intertwining his destiny with Adam's.

"Durch!" I called out, waiting for my little daemon to appear by my side. "Look after Adam. I need to go and see someone."

"Certainly Master," he complied.

I willed myself to my parents' house, appearing in the back garden not too far from where I had left Pete with my mother. I was pleased to see a miniature goal on the back lawn, a football in the net. A mountain bike was propped against the back wall of the house, leaning lazily and making the place look slightly untidy, something that would never have happened when I was younger. Well, alive anyway!

I tested the threshold, wanting to make sure that my parents were indeed free of all unworldly influences and was surprised to feel a glyph was in place but, instead of the harshness of Hell, I felt the warmth of Heaven. I moved through into the kitchen and immediately stumbled across my mother, humming to herself as she kneaded some dough. The smell of baked bread assaulted my nose and my memory flashed back to the happier times of my childhood. Mother always made her own bread, using a variety of ingredients so that we never just had plain. I touched her gently, gaining a sense of happiness from her. I felt her pause in her humming slightly, as if sensing my touch, so I quickly left her and moved into the hallway. Hearing voices in the lounge, I passed through the door and was concerned to hear the volume rising.

"But I want to help!" a teenage boy was arguing. "After everything I've been through, and now I'm in a great place, I want to give back."

"Peter, I understand that," my father replied in a strong voice. "But I'm not sure if you're ready for everything that can be associated with what you want to do."

"I know that you're concerned Poppa, but if I can survive what that man made me do, then I can survive any nasty comments made at school," Pete replied.

I stood back and studied them for a moment. Pete had grown, most definitely. He was now a sturdy young man, fifteen years old and showing signs of confidence in himself that he had sorely lacked that night. His blonde hair was now cut short and he was looking like fulfilling his potential of becoming a handsome young man. An aura of confidence shone from him, along with a deep affection for my parents.

The biggest shock to me was the difference in my father. No longer frail, he looked to be back to how I remembered him physically. Emotionally though, he was showing all the signs of being a loving carer for Pete. I shoved down the quick bout of jealously that reared itself, before seeing the strong bond that the two had formed.

I touched Pete's mind to see what had made him so worked up. There was a project being set up at his school, funnily enough the same school that I attended, to help mentor younger pupils. Sort of a Big Brother/Sister campaign where older pupils would be paired with the more vulnerable younger pupils. They would befriend them and help them with school work, bring them into social circles, and generally be there for the youngsters if they were having any problems that they felt they couldn't tell to an adult. My sense of pride in him swelled when I discovered he was one of the pupils driving the project past objections of his peers and some teachers, and I felt a sense of thrill knowing that, by saving him all those months ago, I was helping to improve the lives of others.

Somehow I needed him to be assigned to Adam, but the problem was that Adam was still at the King Edward VI School whereas Pete and the programme was at Northbrook Main School. Could I keep Adam safe on my own for the remainder of the year, or could I find another way?

"Of course you can, dummy!" a clear voice beside me laughed, startling me.

"Wha...?" I started, turning towards the noise, raising my arms in a defensive stance.

"Oh, you going to fight me now are you?" the purple robed figure asked. A figure that had wings. White wings.

"Zadkiel? What are you doing here?" I asked, stunned to see one of my many tutors. Of course I dropped my arms back to my side.

"You're not the only celestial being that has hands in many pots down here," the Angel of Freedom, Benevolence and Mercy told me.

"I know that, it was drilled into me often enough up there, or wherever I was!" I grumbled.

Despite Zadkiel being one of my tutors, he was also a friend, one with a wicked sense of humour that, at times, had me rolling on the floor while some of the stuffier, sorry make that more traditional, beings looked on down their noses.

"Well, I was wondering who had come through my glyph and when I saw it was you, I decided to pop down to say hello," the auburn haired Angel explained.

"That was your glyph?" I asked. "I knew it wasn't from Yeqon's lot."

"Glad to see you listened to Saint Michael!" Zadkiel joked. "Sometimes his lessons involve battering the information into your head with that damn great big sword of his."

We both chuckled as we remembered my training, Zadkiel being an observer on occasion. However, I turned serious as I heard my father finally give his reluctant acceptance of Pete's desire to press on with the 'Be A Friend' programme.

"So why have you got a glyph on my parents' house?" I asked.

"I keep a check on all of my human agents," he explained.

"Pete is one of yours?" I quizzed, receiving a nod. "Where were you when he was going to be killed?"

"He wasn't mine then," Zadkiel said. "He was due to die that night, but you and your little blue friend changed his destiny. Saint Peter was most put out as he had already read his Book and had found a place for him in the Lower Choir."

"So how did I change it?" I asked.

"Your demon," came the reply. "Demons operate outside Our Father's Plan for humanity, so the interaction with the creature changed Pete's destiny."

"I thought destiny couldn't be changed. Halaliel wouldn't let me save Gary as it was his destiny to die." I muttered in disgust. "You mean that I could have saved him if I'd have taken Durch along with me?"

"No my friend, Gary's destiny was different. It was a fixed point nexus within the Universe. Nothing you could have done would have altered his fate." Zadkiel placed an arm around my shoulder, allowing me a brief moment of comfort before he continued. "For Pete, on the other hand, his destiny had been tied to a certain tainted soul, and he had crossed him. Now, he is currently free of that taint and can fulfil another destiny, one that I have chosen for him."

"Yeah, this 'Be A Friend' project, it sounds really good," I concurred. "In fact, that's now why I want to call in the favour that he owes me from when I saved his life."

"To do what?" Zadkiel pondered, raising a questioning eyebrow.

"I want him to stretch the format and include the children from the final year of lower school," I told him.

"The point being, to befriend your charge and help him through the tough times ahead?" he guessed.

"Yeah," I confirmed. "I'm in a bad streak at the moment. I don't seem to be able to stop Yeqon in anything at the moment, and it's hurting Adam."

"Let's see what we can do then," Zadkiel said, reaching forward to touch Pete on the shoulder. I could almost see the idea forming behind his shiny eyes as they widened as he took in the flow of knowledge from his Angel mentor.

"Poppa, you know what would be even better?" Pete said suddenly, drawing my father's attention back from his newspaper.

"What's that Pete?" he replied.

"How about we start off with the younger schools as well?" Pete said. "If we befriend the kids in the last year of the primary schools, they can learn about the middle schools before they get there. This way, they will know other kids so that it isn't as scary for them when they start the new school."

"That's an ambitious plan son," Dad responded. "But one that makes sense. Why don't you go and see that Mr Johnson about it on Monday?"

"Cool! Thanks Poppa." Pete reached over and hugged my Father, who returned the embrace for a few moments before releasing the boy who bounded outside. Pete said a brief farewell to my mother before collecting his bike. I could hear his thoughts telling him not to wait until Monday, to go and plant the seeds of his idea now, while they were fresh in his own mind.

I watched as he pushed his bike out of the garden and decided that I wanted to go and see this teacher, this Mr Johnson, to make sure that he was receptive to the idea. Zadkiel bade me farewell and phased out of sight. I quickly followed the youngster, pedalling for all his worth. I cringed and nearly reached out on the two occasions that he swerved between oncoming cars, before he finally pulled up to a stop outside a small house that overlooked a church.

I felt a chill run through me as I looked over to the graveyard. Of course I recognised the church. It was the one that I used to attend occasionally, on the days my parents decided they wanted to show that they still had faith.

Somewhere in that graveyard my body was buried. I resisted the sudden urge I had to visit my grave, as I wasn't sure what would happen. I thought I saw movement between the yew trees, and I squinted my eyes against the sun to get a better look. I was shocked to see around a dozen ghostly spirits wandering along pathways, some following visitors who I could tell from the feelings I was getting, that they were the loved ones left behind.

Shaking off the vision, I turned my gaze back to Pete as he knocked on the red door of the house. I watched as he shifted his weight from one foot to the other, biting his bottom lip as he waited for the door to be answered. Nervously, he knocked again, this time hearing a shouted response that the occupier was on his way.

I quickly scanned the house for any glyphs or warnings and was pleased that it was clean. I waited, as patiently as the young teen in front of me, as the door finally opened.

"Oh, hello Pete, what are you doing here?" a man's voice said.

"Hi Mr Johnson," Pete replied brightly. "I hope you don't mind me coming round but I had another idea about 'Be A Friend' and wanted to tell you about it 'cos I think it's really big and important that we should do it and I hope you like it and agree to it and…"

"Pete, take a breath!" the now known Mr Johnson chuckled. "Come on in and we can talk."

Pete grinned at the man and walked into the house. I quickly followed, as I hate having to travel through walls or doors as it itches. I saw the back of the blonde haired man as he walked into the kitchen, where he opened the fridge, removed two cans of cola, passed one to Pete and then ushered him into the lounge. They took seats on the sofa beside each other and the man reached into a briefcase by the side of the small coffee table and pulled out a folder. He opened it and spread the contents onto the table.

"Okay then project leader, tell me what's on your mind," Mr Johnson said.

I half listened as Pete explained his latest idea, while I studied the teacher in front of me. My soul ached as I looked at him. All doubts I had had about whether the teacher would listen to him vanished. The man who sat in front of me, next to the boy I had saved, was in his mid-twenties. His face was so familiar to me, as it was the one that had comforted me for two years while the bullying intensified. It was the one that cried alongside me when the pain got so bad that I couldn't hold back tears any longer.

"Jimmy?" I whispered out loud, my voice thick with emotion. Something must have slipped through my phasing control as he looked up from the papers on the table and almost straight at me before returning his attention back to Pete.

All my questions about him could be answered by one touch of his mind. However, I owed him too much to invade him like that. I decided to find information out the old fashioned way by observing and listening. His enthusiasm for Pete's project was plain to see, and he was even expanding further the details about how to link in with the primary schools.

As they talked, I looked around the room, taking in the photographs and pictures on the tables and bookcases. I giggled to myself as I saw one of the bookcases full of text books and training manuals, with the exception of one shelf which was jammed full of comic books! I recognised some from our childhood, which reminded me of happier times.

I let my gaze run over the pictures on the sideboards, and saw his parents and younger versions of him in various tourist spots in Japan and China. I was surprised to see that, just like Tyler, there was no sign of a woman in any of the recent pictures and, as I moved along the fireplace, my eyes were drawn to a small seven inch by five inch frame. I reached out an unsteady hand and touched the glass frame as I gazed at Jimmy and myself in just shorts and trainers, sitting under a tree. A bottle of water was on the ground in front of us. I remembered complaining to Jimmy's mum after she had taken the picture, as I was going through a self-conscious stage having just been outed at school. Jimmy's parents had taken us away for the day, a rare treat. Jimmy's parents persuaded my parents to back down from their decision to keep me at home, and we had spent the day playing football with his dad, roughhousing and generally being two fourteen year old boys without a care in the world.

Again, my emotions must have played havoc with my essence as suddenly, I felt the picture frame push backwards and it toppled over onto the mantelpiece, startling not only myself but Jimmy and Pete. They both looked up as I moved quickly away to the other side of the room. Jimmy got up and walked over to the fallen frame. He picked it up and gazed at it, letting out a small sigh.

"Are you okay Mr Johnson?" Pete asked, concern in his voice at the sudden sadness in his teacher's demeanour.

"Yes, just remembering lost friends is all," my best friend replied. "He is one of the reasons why I am so proud of you for coming up with this idea, and why I am throwing my weight behind it."

"What happened?" Pete asked, getting up and walking slowly over the fireplace. "Who is it?"

"My best friend. He was bullied for years and no-one cared enough to stop it," Jimmy explained, his voice beginning to catch. "He killed himself on his sixteenth birthday."

"That's really sad," Pete murmured. "Do you miss him?"

"Forever and a day past it!" Jimmy replied, a wry smile on his face at the memory of our catchphrase.

Pete took the picture from his teacher and turned it over, making sure it wasn't damaged. I saw the young boy's blue eyes widen in recognition.

"That's Joe!" he gasped.

"What do you mean?" Jimmy asked, shocked at Pete's statement.

"There was this guy, I guess a little older than in this picture, and he was the one who saved me from two men who were gonna kill me," Pete rushed out. "Joe appeared with something else that looked like a monster but it talked, and he fought off the men and then took me to Momma and Poppa's."

"You're adopted?" Jimmy queried, wanting to know more about this new revelation from his favourite pupil.

"Um, yeah, Mr and Mrs Harris took me in after I showed them this." Pete leaned forward, pulled his t-shirt forward and fished out the multi-coloured coral chain necklace that I had given him.

"That was Joe's!" Jimmy exclaimed. "I gave it to him on his thirteenth birthday. What are you doing with it!"

"Joe gave it me, I promise!" Pete stammered.

"That's impossible Pete," Jimmy softly whispered. "Joe died ten years ago."

"But how would I know that this was Joe?" Pete asked, pointing at the photo. "I've never been here before, or nothing!"

"If you live at the Harris's house, you must have seen a photo of him," Jimmy accused.

Deciding I needed to diffuse this before Jimmy ended up carting him off to the police for stealing, I reached out and touched him. I let my love for him flow through and he immediately relaxed, a look of wonder on his face.

"Joe?" he asked the air.

"What?" Pete queried.

"I think that Joe is here," Jimmy replied. "I just felt, I don't know, wonderful for a moment, and I know in my heart that I can believe what you have told me."

Knowing my work here was done, I phased myself back to the Zegers' and into Adam's room where he was sound asleep, having tired himself out from scrubbing the steps. Nodding to Durchial that he could patrol outside, I settled myself by the side of the sleeping boy. He stirred slightly, muttering in his sleep and it sounded like he was encountering a bad dream. I stroked his hair gently, hushing him and pushing away the oncoming nightmare.

"Hush now, my sweet boy," I whispered. "Everything is going to be alright. You'll soon have Pete looking after you as well."

Adam's breathing settled down to a steady rhythm, and I watched as a small smile crept onto his face.

Chapter Eleven

"Okay class settle down. We have some visitors today." Miss Yeates announced loudly, trying to be heard over the humdrum of babbling nine year old voices.

"Who, Miss Yeates?" a blonde haired girl asked.

"There are some pupils coming in from Northbrook to talk about a new project they are running," the teacher replied.

"Project? So what's that to do with us?" Darren sneered.

"I think you'll all find it very helpful for when you leave here and go up to the Main School after the summer," Miss Yeates told him, and the rest of the class, ignoring the tone in the little bully's voice.

I saw Adam lean towards Darren, who automatically positioned his body further away from the brown haired boy.

"I wonder what it is that the Main schoolers want with us," he whispered to Darren.

"They're probably coming to check out who they can pick on next year!" Darren snapped back. "You'll be right up there, number one target."

"No! Miss Yeates and Mrs Henderson wouldn't allow that," Adam countered, his face dropping slightly at the prospect of having bigger kids picking on him, as well as Darren and his little gang.

I watched Darren glance slyly over at the three boys on a table on the far side of the classroom. I saw him nod to them and suddenly an argument broke out between them, drawing the teacher away from the area by the two boys.

"Look, once they know you're a fucking pansy boy, every boy is going to beat the shit out of you," Darren hissed. "Either that, or do what that bloke did to Gary!"

"How many times do I have to say?" Adam started, his voice dropping to a broken whisper. "I am not a pansy!"

"My Dad says you are, and he knows what pansies are like as he used to try to straighten them out when he was younger," the ginger bully retorted. "Don't worry Adam, I'll make sure all the kids at Northbrook know you're one!"

Adam looked helplessly at the boy who had been his friend. Since the bullying had started in earnest, with the pansy comments, the shoves in the corridors and the kicks on the football pitch, some of the boys in the year gravitated towards Darren's stronger character, while the rest drifted away from Adam, not wanting to become targets themselves. I could see his situation uncomfortably mirroring my own. The only difference was that Adam was still so young. It was almost laughable to suggest so if it wasn't for the fact it was now causing him pain.

I saw him turn away and felt the anguish pouring over him. He rubbed his eye with a fist before putting his head down and concentrating on his maths exercises that he was trying to do correctly. He cast frequent glances over at Darren's exercise book, wanting to help the struggling boy, but afraid of what else would come out of Darren's mouth.

There was a knock on the door and I saw Mrs Henderson, the Headmistress, walk into the room, calling everyone to attention.

"Okay then boys and girls, as Miss Yeates will have told you earlier, we have some boys and girls who have come from Northbrook, where you will be going next year," she started. "They have come to explain what the school is like, and what you can expect."

"Bigger guys to help me beat you up!" Darren whispered into Adam's ear as they watched Pete, two other boys and a girl enter the classroom.

"Why? Can't you do it on your own?" Adam snapped back in a rare moment of defiance.

Darren looked at him and smiled.

"Of course I can," he grinned. "After school, down the alley way between the corner shop and old man Grundel's garage!"

Again, I tried to break into Darren's mind but came up against the now familiar touch of Yeqon. In frustration, I turned to Miss Yeates, thinking that I could get her to intercede somehow. However, as I looked over at her, ready to touch her mind to persuade her to leave for home earlier than normal, I saw a look of wonder on her face.

I turned to see the destination of her stare and saw an identical expression on the face of the teacher who had accompanied the older children into the classroom. Of course, it was Jimmy! I could almost hear the twang of Cupid's bow, even though I knew he didn't exist, having asked Edith previously. I reached out and touched her mind and saw a picture of two halves of a soul coming together.

There were a few sniggers from the children who had noticed that their teacher had turned into a living, breathing statue, which brought Louise out of her trance and she smiled shyly at Jimmy, moving over towards the side of the room so that Pete and the other main schoolers could begin their presentation. As she positioned herself next to a cupboard, I saw Jimmy move alongside her.

"Hi guys, I'm Pete and this is Jack, Harry and Jessica and we're here to talk to you about the 'Be A Friend' project that we are running," Pete started. He and the other three older children went on to explain how it worked, telling the class a little about the school they would soon be attending, and how they were getting volunteers from Northbrook School to put their names forward as mentors for Adam's school year.

"So finally, if you are interested in having a mentor, please see Miss Yeates, who has a form for you to fill in listing your hobbies, likes and dislikes and she will pass them on to Mr Johnson," Jessica announced. "The committee will then match you with the best pupil from our school, who will be in touch and come and see you."

"Any questions?" Pete asked.

Seeing several hands go up, he pointed to a small girl at the front of the class.

"So the mentor will help us around the big school?" she asked, earning a couple of snorts of laughter from Darren's cronies at the back.

"That's right," Jessica replied. "Your mentor will be with you for the whole of the first week, making sure that you find your way around the school, get to the correct classrooms, be with you at breaks and lunch and generally answer any question you have."

"Cool!" the girl smiled.

"Can we change our mentor if we don't like them?" a dark haired boy sitting on the table next to Adam asked.

"Of course," Jack answered. "It's important that you get along with your mentor, as they are there to help you and, if you don't feel you can trust them, then they can't help."

"All you have to do is either ask your mentor, or come and see one of the committee members, which is made up of us four kids and three teachers," Pete added. "We will then re-assign you to another mentor."

"Are there enough mentors for everyone?" Adam asked.

"Good question," Harry said. "At the moment, we are still recruiting, but when we visited Blackthorn Road School," he paused as several of the boys booed their rival school, "a lot of them said they felt like they didn't need a mentor."

"It is voluntary and you will only get assigned a mentor if you want one," Jessica added.

MICHAEL ANDREWS

"Can I have you?" Darren asked loudly, with a now familiar sneer on his face. "You're pretty!"

"Well thanks, but we will be assigning mentors who are the same sex as you, as we think it will make it easier for you to talk about any problems," Jessica replied, a faint blush creeping up her cheeks. I could see the look that she shot her fellow students, which promised violence if they brought that comment back up.

"Hey, Adam, you might get lucky!" Darren said, raising his voice so that everyone could hear. "You might get a boy who's a fag like you!"

The boys who had been dragooned into Darren's clique all laughed at the latest insult to my charge, and, as Adam's head dropped in embarrassment, I saw Jimmy start to say something. Pete shook his head in disgust at Darren's comment.

"Well, I'm not sure if you are or not, and I'm sure you don't know either, but there is no problem either way," the teen announced. "There is a Gay Straight Alliance club at Northbrook, and the school operates a non-discrimination policy for any race, disability or sexual orientation."

"Oh great, the place is gonna be full of queers!" Darren sighed. He turned to his mates. "Backs to the walls lads!"

"What's your name?" Pete asked.

"Why? You gonna hit on me?" the ginger boy giggled.

"No, I just want to make sure that, if you do ask for a mentor, we give you the right person," he replied.

"Darren Walford! You apologise now!" Miss Yeates said sternly to the boy, who gave her a look that showed that, even if he did, there was going to be no sincerity behind it.

"Darren is it?" Pete asked, moving forward and dropping down on his haunches so that he was eye level with the bully. "Here is your first bit of advice from the mentoring team to help you fit in. We don't like bullies, and we definitely don't like bigots. There is nothing wrong with somebody being gay, straight or bisexual. I should know, I'm gay."

Darren pulled away from the teen with a look of horror in his eyes. Adam, however, perked up at the teen's statement and looked at Pete, staring him straight in the eyes. Pete moved past Darren and placed a hand on Adam's shoulder.

"If you want, I'll gladly be your mentor," the teen announced.

"You, like, run the project?" Adam asked, staring at the older boy with a slight trace of awe in his expression. "Would you have time to mentor me?"

"Pete is the leader of the set up committee, but he will be stepping down once it's up and running so he can concentrate on being a mentor," Jimmy announced.

"Yeah, this was my idea and I want to be involved in helping someone," Pete smiled.

I gave the teen, and the other three students a faint touch of congratulations and they bade their farewells to the class to go and talk to the other final year classes. I was pleased to see Louise hand Jimmy a piece of paper, that I easily sensed had her telephone number on it. Miss Yeates deserved to have someone nice to fall in love with, and in Jimmy, she certainly would have that. My only concern was that, with her inability to have children, Jimmy's skills as a father in the future would go to waste.

The children talked loudly for the rest of the class, Louise allowing them the free time to discuss the mentor programme. She was happy to hand out five of the mentoring questionnaires, one of which went to Adam. I watched as he neatly filled in the relevant questions, pleased that he did not need prodding to complete his answers, which I was sure would get him assigned to a good mentor. I still held out hope that Zadkiel would play nicely and let Pete mentor Adam, but even if the teen wasn't assigned to my charge, I was sure he would be okay. Not surprisingly, Darren didn't ask for a form.

As the bell rang to signify the end of class, I managed to get Louise to ask Adam to stay behind to help tidy up the classroom, something that she normally did herself. I saw Darren scowl as Adam accepted the request, and he shuffled out the door, muttering to his crowd of friends about Adam being chicken.

Adam, now free of any fear of insults from his peers, allowed himself to return to more of his old personality, chatting freely with his teacher, who was still concerned over the effects that Gary's death was having on him. Assuring her that he was coping, he waved goodbye and headed out into the rain for the thirty minute walk home. Now that Helen was no longer employed by John, and with Gill stubbornly refusing to chauffeur 'the brat' around, Adam had been forced to walk to and from school, no matter what the weather. Whispering a quick enchantment, I managed to slow the fall of rain around Adam so that, while he still got wet, the temperature was warm and he didn't get soaked to the skin. Suddenly Durchiel appeared at my side, as I walked alongside Adam.

"Master, the Darren boy is still waiting at the appointed place," he announced.

"What? Why hasn't he gone home?" I cursed under my breath, hoping that the time Adam had spent clearing the classroom would have put off the ginger bully. "Is there anyone with him?"

"No Master, the other boy childs left when the rain started," Durchial explained.

"So it's just Darren?" I asked.

"Yes Master," the daemon replied. "He does wield a club though."

"What?" I exclaimed.

"He has found a fallen arm of a tree and does intend to use it as a weapon," Durchial said.

Now that wasn't fair. If it was just a straight up fight, maybe Adam would be okay without any interference from me. However, walking unarmed into a fight like that needed my intervention.

"Master, I know you are thinking of appearing, but I must remind you of your rules," Durchial chided me. Sometimes, I really wish that I hadn't explained, in such detail, my limitations to the daemon, as he sometimes took a childish delight in stopping me from appearing to Gillian with all guns blazing.

"We need to do something to stop Adam from getting hurt," I told him.

He grinned a toothy grin at me and held up a hand. Shaking it slightly, five claws extended from the ends of his fingers.

"No Durchie, you can't kill him!" I groaned at yet another attempt by my little daemon helper to slice someone up.

I had run out of time to think, as Adam turned the corner and started to walk through the alley, not remembering about the arrangements he had made earlier with his former friend.

"So, you came after all then, chicken?" Darren sneered.

"What?" Adam jumped back, startled by the sudden sound of the ginger boy's voice. "Darren? Look I don't wanna fight you."

"Course not, 'cos you know I'll kick your pansy boy ass from here to home!" Darren chuckled.

"No, it's 'cos you're my friend, even if you've forgot that and I don't fight with my friends," Adam tried to explain.

"Well, if you don't fight back, you're just gonna get hurt more!" the bully stated and swung the small branch into Adam's side.

I felt the pain, heard the gasp and saw Adam drop his school bag to the round so that he could clutch his now throbbing side. He looked back up at Darren with tears threatening to spill.

"Come on Darren, please," he begged. "You're my friend."

"Not any more pansy," Darren announced. "You got Gary killed and I'll never forgive you for it!"

Darren swung the branch again, this time aiming for Adam's head. I was more prepared this time and caused a strong gust of wind to swirl down the alley, ripping the wooden weapon out of Darren's grasp. He stood for a few moments, watching it tumble away before shrugging and turning back, a look of determination on his face. I saw him ball up his fists and mentally, I urged Adam to do the same or, at least, take steps to protect himself. However, my young charge simply stood there, arms by his side, facing the ginger boy.

"I'm not going to fight you Darren," Adam repeated firmly. "If beating me up will help you grieve, then go ahead."

The boy was too good for his own sake, and safety, and I cringed as I saw Darren take a big swing at him. I waited for the sound of flesh striking flesh, to feel the pain of the punch, to hear the cry from Adam but nothing came. I looked at the boys and was shocked to see the pair of them frozen in place. A chill hit me from behind, and I heard a whimper from Durchial.
I spun around, and saw my little helper grovelling on his knees, head pressed to floor in front of a large figure, cloaked in black. Blood red eyes glowed from inside the darkness of the hood and, as I gazed up at the seven foot figure, I knew that I was in the presence of a mighty demon.

"Hand messenger, I have found thee at last," a deep voice boomed from within. "Where have thou been?"
"Mighty Highness, forgive your messenger," Durchial croaked in fear. "I was bested by the Protector and have been enslaved to his purpose."

Now that wasn't fair, putting all the blame on me! Well, actually I suppose it was, as I had bid him to my service, but I thought we had become friends at least.

"The Protector? This boy?" the figure bellowed in a voice that I'm sure would have rattled my teeth, if I had any physical form.
"That's me," I announced, trying to put on a brave voice in front of the darkness. "Protector Joseph, on a mission from Our Father."
"Your spiritual entity is no father of me or mine kin," came the response. "I am Horrodeon, Prince of Daemon and Leader of my race."
"What is your concern here then, Your Highness?" I asked, figuring that it couldn't hurt to be polite to the biggest, baddest demon there is.
"Foremost, I came to see where my hand messenger was, as he has been sorely missed," Horrodeon replied. "Secondly, I sensed the Soul Key was in need of help."
"The Soul Key!" I exclaimed. "You keep your hands off Adam!"

I willed myself in between Adam and the black robed figure. I was shocked as a shining blade appeared in my hand. I could feel the psychic energy flowing from it, and knew that it was enchanted to protect me against the Underworld.

"Fear not Protector, for the time of the Prophecy is yet to transpire," Horrodeon calmed me. "By thy Father's restrictions, thou art helpless in this situation, but I am not. I will not allow this creature to interfere with the destiny of the Soul Key, for I require it in time yet to come."

"What are you going to do?" I asked, now fearing for Darren, more than Adam or myself.

"This creature of Yeqon must not harm the Innocent," he told me and waved an arm.

The air shimmered around us, and time restarted. Darren's arm continued its swing but he swung too high, missing Adam by inches. As he turned back to face his former friend , he seemed to falter in his resolve.

"Go, creature of the Fallen, your mission stops here!" Horrodeon boomed.

Although I could hear him plainly, it was obvious that he was speaking in a higher frequency than human hearing could detect. However, watching Darren's face, he must have penetrated the barriers that Yeqon had installed, the ones that I had repeatedly failed to penetrate. A look of disgust appeared on the freckled face.

"You're not worth my bother!" Darren spat at Adam and brushed past him, bumping the younger boy hard on the shoulder as he did.

Adam rubbed his side once more and I laid a healing hand on him, taking away most of the pain. I knew I had to leave a small amount so that he didn't know I was there, but he didn't have to suffer. As he headed up the alleyway, I turned back to the two demons.

"Thank you," I said, simply, wondering why the Demon Prince was so helpful. "What's going to happen now?"

"Now, you will continue your mission, Protector," the tall figure replied. "Until we meet again, keep the Innocent from harm, for he is needed."

"What about Durchie?" I asked. "Can he stay with me?"

"He is useful to you?" Horrodeon queried. Seeing my nod, he motioned to the blue figure who was now standing between us. "Continue thy service to the Protector. Guard well the Innocent and thy reward will be bountiful."

"Yes, my Highness," Durchial bowed.

Warmth spread back into the alleyway as Horrodeon disappeared from sight. I shivered and turned to Durchial.

"Wow! That is some presence!" I gasped.

"My Prince is an imposing figure," Durchial grinned, showing his fangs. I could sense a relief from him that he was no longer in the vicinity of Horrodeon, and agreed with his unspoken thought to get away from any lingering effects of him.

Chapter Twelve

As shaken as I had been in the presence of Prince Horrodeon, I held out some faint hope in the fact that, not only had he protected Adam from Darren, he had also broken through Yeqon's barriers, something that I had consistently failed to do. However, the over-riding memory of his statement that Adam was still needed, that, as the Soul Key, he was the instrument to release the demons onto the human plane, burned in my mind. I had to find some way to protect Adam from Horrodeon, but the aura of power that he had given off in the alleyway felt far too strong for me to cope with.

As much as I pressed Durchial on matters regarding the Soul Key Prophecy, as soon as I mentioned his Prince, the little daemon shivered and silence followed. If I continued questioning, he simply vanished from my side. Even though I was supposed to be his Master, nothing I commanded would make him speak of Horrodeon, except in terms of awe and subservience. I guess that he was the equivalent to a God in their race and, knowing the power that even the lowest of the Angels of Our Father wielded, I wasn't too surprised that Durchie would be afraid of his leader. I certainly was!

One thing I did want to investigate was the sudden appearance of my mystic sword. Having been instructed in battle skills by none other than Saint Michael himself, I knew the power that a Heavenly Sword could wield against the creatures of the Underworld, so I rested a little easier in the knowledge that in times of dire need, I could call on such a weapon.

Time passed, as it is want to do, and the last couple of months of Adam's school year at King Edward's passed more easily. With Horrodeon's warning still ringing in Darren's brain, the bullying lessened and, to my shame, I also interfered in a way that Durchial had suggested, following a discussion with Edith.

"Master, one trick of the Fallen is distraction," Durchial explained to me, as we discussed tactics of Yeqon and his fellow dark Angels.

"Distraction? What do you mean?" I asked.

"When a good soul is on the path to blocking a plan of the Darkness, sometimes a Fallen can place an object of desire in the way, and the good soul no longer follows his chosen path," my helper explained.

"So you are saying I should distract Darren somehow to forget about hurting Adam?" I queried.

"Yes Master, it is an aeon old trick," Durchial replied. "Lord Lucifer is the master of deception and distraction, turning those of Your Father's ministry away from His teachings."

"So how would that work with Darren?" I asked.

"If you had him focus on someone else, he would forget about the Adam child," Durchial suggested.

"I'm not putting someone else in danger to protect Adam," I argued. "That wouldn't be right."

"Why not push this Darren boy into a love of a girl?" Edith countered. "That way, he will spend more time thinking about how to woo her and spend time with her and he will forget about causing Adam pain."

"But I can't make him love someone," I held out. "It's against free will."

"You told me some time ago that he already fancied a girl in the class," the old lady continued. "Give him a little push in the right direction and if the girl has anything about her, she will also frown upon any of his moves to hurt Adam."

"That way, if he wants to remain in her favour, he will stop?" I had a moment of insight into the deviousness of Edith's mind. Are all female minds this devious?

"It could also reignite the goodness that you once felt within the boy, saving him from the clutches of Yeqon," Edith advised.

When we were next with Darren, I was able to probe his mind through the chinks of Yeqon's barriers made by Horrodeon. I found that Darren still harboured thoughts about the small, blonde haired girl in his class called Tracey. I scanned her thoughts easily, and was pleased to find there had not been any otherworldly interference with her, yet. Despite her dislike of how Darren had been treating Adam, she still found him attractive, easily explainable as Darren was growing up to be a miniature version of his father, so it just took a little push one lunchtime to persuade her to ask him out. Darren, was overjoyed that he finally had attracted the attention of the girl and readily agreed. Soon everyone knew that they were girlfriend and boyfriend.

As Edith predicted, any time that Darren chose a public setting to try to embarrass or bully Adam was met with a sad look from Tracey, and it only took one day of her silence to him for the ginger boy to figure out that he had to be nice to Adam to remain in her favour. He continued his mission of hatred towards my charge when she wasn't around, but at least it bought Adam some free time during the school day. By making sure that Adam learned several routes home, having Durchial follow Darren from school to identify where he was lying in wait to ambush the brown haired boy, I was able to ensure that he made it home safely most afternoons.

As the school year came to an end, it was with a heavy heart that Adam said goodbye to his teacher, Miss Yeates. Louise, over the last few weeks, had grown more self-confident as her relationship with Jimmy blossomed, and she found herself wanting to spend more and more time with him, so much so that she decided to apply for a teaching position at Northbrook School. This was something that I was delighted to see, wondering why I didn't think of encouraging her to do so in the first place, but pleased that not all the good things needed my intervention. As Edith repeatedly told me, good things happen to good people and we just need to trust Our Father's plans.

That was all well and good but, in the important matters that related to Adam, I wasn't so willing to leave things alone, so it took just a couple of nudges with Mrs Henderson to give her blessing to Louise. A quick nudge to Mr Cross, a stern looking man who was the Principal at Northbrook Road School, encouraging him to accept her application and Louise was the new English teacher, and also Form Tutor. Someone, or something, somewhere was smiling down on me as I had a flash of foresight and saw that Adam would be placed into her Form Class.

Firstly, we had the school holidays to contend with and, this year, with no Darren or Gary for friends, I was worried about what Adam would do. I certainly didn't want him spending too much time with my sister, who took a cruel delight in denying him any pleasure at the merest opportunity. I kept pushing the conman spirit of Ben Grover for a solution, but he was running into brick walls. His main solution was one which Durchial agreed with, and that was to remove her from the scene, permanently, something that I wasn't willing to do yet.

Pete was assigned as Adam's mentor, for which I gave a quick prayer of thanks to all concerned, getting a ghostly chuckle in response from Zadkiel, and the two boys clicked instantly. All my fears of Adam being lonely vanished as the older boy met up with my charge and whisked him off to the park, to the cinema or simply to my parents' home. I felt a small thrill of pleasure as my parents' welcomed him in with open arms, and I was even happier when I discovered Jimmy was a semi regular visitor, having made a home visit to Pete to discuss the mentor project, and having my parents apologise for their attitude during the final years of my life.

All was looking good as Adam neared his eleventh birthday and I had almost started to self-congratulate myself once more, when John announced that he had proposed to Gillian and that they would be married within the next week.

"But Dad, I don't like her," Adam complained, while Gill was out of the room.

"Well son, it isn't about you," John replied shortly. "One day you will be grown up and moved out and I want someone to spend my life with."

"But she's horrible to me," Adam continued. "When you're not here she's nasty."

"What do you mean son?" John queried, a faint hope lighting in me that this could be a chink for me to work with.

"She makes me do all the jobs that we used to get people in to do, and won't let me have any time for me," Adam started before being cut off by his father.

"So she asks you to help out and you don't want to take responsibility?" the man snapped. "Gill said that you are ungrateful for everything that she does for you and, when she asks for your help, you are rude and obnoxious to her."

"No, it's not like that!" Adam shouted back, losing his cool at his father's stubbornness.

"Do not raise your voice to me, boy!" John hissed back at Adam, pulling him towards him. "You will learn respect, even if I have to beat it into you."

As he pulled his son over his knees, anger flared once more in my small charge.

"I'll never respect her!" Adam said through gritted teeth as he felt his father's hand connect with his backside.

I turned away, not wanting to watch as John spanked Adam a dozen times, hard, knowing that I was powerless to stop the interaction between father and son. As soon as John released his hold on him, Adam jumped up off his father's knees and rubbed himself to relieve the stinging pain. Tears welled in his eyes and, as I touched his mind, I found they were more for the betrayal he felt from John's attitude and willingness to believe Gill over his own son, rather than any pain he felt from the punishment.

As Adam turned to leave the room, I saw Gill standing at the doorway, an evil smile on her face. I could sense the animosity boiling between the two as they passed each other, and it was all I could do to calm Adam down to prevent him from saying something else that would further drive a wedge between him and his father. Gill, sensing another victory, made her way to John and kissed him noisily, making sure that Adam could hear.

"So how did he take the news?" she asked.

"Not well," John replied.

"Well, you know that he is a lazy little boy who doesn't want to do even the simplest of jobs to help out," Gill lied. "He actually threatened me with the kitchen knife earlier just because I asked him to help with the washing up."

Adam sprinted up the stairs to his room and leapt onto his bed face down. Punching his pillow repeatedly, I heard him muttering curses that he really shouldn't know, I knew that I had to do something about my sister fast, before Adam spilled his own anger out and did something that he would regret.

"Look brat, I'm going to marry your dad and there's nothing you can do about it," I heard Gill's voice from the doorway.

"Why?" Adam asked wearily, his eyes puffy from his frustration. "You don't love him."

"That doesn't matter," she replied. "He has things I need, and you are one of them."

She walked over to Adam's bed, sitting down and grabbing his arm in a painful grip.

"In three weeks, I am up for a promotion at work, and the only way a woman is going to get it is if she has a husband and family," Gill explained. "My boss is a sentimental old fool, and you will play the good son."

"No I won't," Adam rebelled. "When I meet him, I'm gonna tell him how horrible you are to me."

"I wouldn't do that if you love your father," she hissed. "He hasn't told you as he doesn't want you to worry, but he has an illness and, if he doesn't take these pills, he will die."

She held up a small bottle of tablets, which I tried to get a look at but failed. Shaking them in front of Adam, she continued.

"It wouldn't be good if he had a seizure and we couldn't find these tablets now would it?" Gill smiled at the boy whose face dropped in worry.

"What's wrong with him?" Adam begged.

"It's some brain condition, probably hereditary so you will need to start watching yourself as well," Gill chuckled. "I'd hate to see you have a seizure and fall down the stairs and hurt yourself."

She pushed him away and left the room. I willed myself downstairs to John's side and quickly probed into his brain. Sure enough, I found damage to his tissue. However, I also found traces of chemicals that didn't sit right with me.

"Think Joe, what's happening here?" I scolded myself.

"Fancy a cuppa dearest?" I heard Gill's voice, dripping with honey.

"Yes please love, and maybe one of those tablets," John replied. "I think I've got one of my heads coming on."

Gill walked in with a cup of tea and gave John a purple tablet, which he swallowed with a gulp of the hot brew. Seeing him grimace, I probed once more and found the levels of the mysterious chemicals in his system had increased. My sister was the cause of the seizures!

"Durch! Watch Adam!" I mentally yelled and phased myself out of the house. Not really knowing where to start, I found myself in the park outside St Paul's Cathedral. Casting my mind's eye around, I sensed a spirit close by.

"Hey, I need help to find someone, can you help?" I asked the figure who was skulking in the shadows of the building.

"Who are you? How did you know I was here?" a young voice asked. A teenage girl came into view. She had a pretty face and would have been considered attractive, I'm sure, apart from the criss cross scars on her arms that told me that she had taken the same route out of her mortal life that I had.

"I'm Joe, and I need to find a spirit called Ben Grover," I said as way of introduction.

"You aren't a Fallen One, I can sense that," she said, losing a little of her wariness. "I can sense Heavenly touch on you, yet you're not an Angel."

Not wanting to go into the whole story, I quickly explained who I was and, more importantly, what I was and, as soon as the term Protector came out of my lips, her whole attitude changed to one of helpfulness.

"Grover is a sneaky bastard," Hayley told me, having informed me of her name moments earlier.

"Tell me something I don't know," I replied. "He's been promising to help me for months, but nothing yet."

"He's been promising me the secret of sensing the Fallen after I helped him get his hands on a copy of the Book of Yeqon," Hayley complained.

"What?" I gasped. "Yeqon has a book?"

"Well, yeah, all the Fallen do," she said. "It was forced on them by God after He cast them down, as part of their penance for serving with the Despicable One."

"What's in it?" I asked, wondering if this would give me any forewarning of his plans.

"The usual crap that the Fallen spout, you know, cursing their luck, the betrayal of the Seraphim who had pledged support and then withdrew it, and what they plan on doing to get back into Heaven and overthrow the Throne," she explained. "Though why Ben wanted Yeqon's in particular is unknown to me."

"That's who I'm fighting against," I told her. "I wonder why he wants it?"

"He said something about insurance, but then vanished and didn't pay up," she moaned. "Now, not only have I got the Chasers after me, but also the Satanic group that I stole the book from."

"Look, if you help me find Ben, I will give you the sensing gift," I offered.

"You? Only Angels, or the beings from the Underworld have that gift," Hayley accused.

"I have a daemon servant that I bested, and he has the gift and can teach you," I told her, skipping past a lot of unnecessary chatter.

"And all I have to do is find Grover?" she asked.

"Yeah, I need to find him now!" I urged.

"Okay, let's see," she started. "Isn't he normally hanging round that Communer?"

"Edith?" I asked. "Well I know he knows her 'cos she introduced me to him, but Edith would tell me if she knew where he was."

"Well, it's a good start, let's go see her," Hayley replied.

Focusing my mind, I found Edith at her home. Taking hold of Hayley's hand, I willed the pair of us to her side. However, instead of going straight to the old lady, I found myself hitting a barrier and we materialised outside in her little garden.

"What? Why didn't we go straight through?" I asked.

"Maybe it's because of the barrier," Hayley said. "As I'm not one of the chosen few to see her, maybe it won't let me through."

"That's a good point," I agreed. "I know that there are a few beings that would want to harm her, so we can't be too careful."

I walked through the barrier, seeing Edith sitting outside on her garden chair enjoying the sunshine.

"Hello Joseph," she greeted me, causing me to chuckle once more at the way she could sense me.

"Hi Edith," I replied, taking her hand and settling on my knees by her side.

As she turned her head toward the sound of my voice, I could see that the white milkiness of her eyes was now complete. Her body had finally lost its battle to retain her sight. However, many times she had told me not to fret over it, as she had a vision more beautiful, that of the ethereal world.

"Worry not young spirit," she told me, sensing my frustration at her refusal to allow me to try to heal her eyes. "It is part of God's plan, as is everything that occurs."

"Then Our Father best come up with a way to help me stop my sister, as she's poisoning John, and she gave a vague threat to Adam about doing the same," I whined.

"It is not your place to second guess Our Father's plans," she chided me, not for the first time making me feel like a naughty schoolboy in front of his headmistress.

"I need to find Ben to get him to help me break her hold on John, before Adam loses his father and becomes an orphan," I told her.

"He has been a little distant for some time," Edith said. "Why have you come to me child?"

"I met this girl, Hayley, who has had dealings with him as well and she suggested you as a starting point," I replied.

"Where is this girl, and I take it she is a soul yet to Pass Over?" the old woman asked, her insight as spot on as ever.

"It looks like she cut herself like I did, and I found her in the park next to St Paul's," I explained. "She says she can't come through the barrier around your house as she isn't from Heaven, or been invited. Is that like the vampire thing?"

"Far too many films that corrupt the clear thinking of our youth today," Edith muttered under her breath, but loud enough so I could hear it. As I giggled, she started to whisper an incantation, which I assumed would allow Hayley in.

As she finished, Hayley suddenly appeared at my side. Introducing her to Edith, I saw a sneer appear on the pretty girl's face while, at the same time, a look of horror flashed across Edith's before returning to one of serenity and peacefulness.

"Well Despicable One, I see we finally meet," the grandmotherly figure hissed at the girl.

"Long has this appointment been delayed, witch!" the girl answered in a deep voice, not girly at all. In fact one that reminded me a lot of. . .

"Yeqon!" I gasped, springing from my knees but found myself frozen in mid-stride towards him.

I watched in horror as the figure of the pretty girl morphed into the beautiful young male who I had seen on the first day of my death. He circled me, as if to ensure that I was immobile before turning his attention to my aged advisor.

"Long have I, and mine, tried to break through this barrier of yours, witch," he said harshly. "Little did I know that all it would take was just a simple deception and fluttering of eyelids, and the Protector here would be such a push over."

"Seek not to cast the blame on the young one," Edith countered. "You think that I could not sense thy presence through my barrier? The foulness of your spirit doth contaminate the very soil around thee."

"But was it not for this over eager puppy, he would not have led me to thy abode witch," Yeqon argued. "I hope that you have prepared yourself, for today you will meet Your Maker."

"Long have I known my destiny and my appointed time of departure to Our Father's Kingdom," Edith told him calmly. "It is a day long overdue, for my work was not yet complete."

"Edith! Do something, call someone!" I shouted out.

"Nah my young one, for today is the day of my journey to Our Father's side," she said softly. I watched as she pushed herself up and out of her chair and turned towards me.

"Enough! Say your goodbyes to your witch, Protector, for you have her no longer," Yeqon snarled at me.

I watched, helpless, as he moved to cover the short distance between them, approaching her from behind. As he got close, his form changed into the demon that chilled my very essence and, despite being shielded from my view by Edith's body, I saw his arms bend into a shape that I knew wasn't good. I cried out in shock as two points of burning light burst from Edith's chest, her body stiffening in pain, her hands stretching forward towards me.

"Oh, my Joseph!" she gasped, stumbling forward, dropping to her knees.

Pain, anger, hurt, fear, sorrow, overwhelming sorrow shot through my body and I felt raw power in my mind blow apart the grips that the Fallen One had placed on my essence. The glowing silver sword appeared in my right hand as I turned on the demonic form of my opponent who, with a snarl in my direction, disappeared from my sight.

Hearing a soft sigh, I focused back on Edith's crumpled form, catching her upper body in my arms as she finally fell to the side, her strength ebbing away.

"Edith, I'm so sorry, I didn't know," I sobbed, tears flowing freely down my face.

"Worry not, young one, for today was preordained," she told me, taking my hands in hers.

"Let me heal you, Edith," I begged. "I know that I can."

"Not today Joseph," she replied. "Do not fear, for I am content that I have fulfilled my role in Our Father's plans."

"But I still need you!" I cried. "I don't have the knowledge that you have, the faith that you have."

"You should, young one," Edith said, her voice getting weaker with each spoken word. "It was the strength of your faith that saved you from immediate damnation, and there are a lot of beings that have placed their faith in you to complete your mission, Our Father being one of them."

"But I don't want you to go, to die," I whimpered, knowing that I could not stop what was going to happen, but maybe if I wished or prayed hard enough, someone would listen.

"It is my time, young one," the old woman whispered. "Know that you have done well and are loved."

Before I could say anything else, I saw that her chest failed to rise for her next breath. Her eyes, still cloudy white were focused behind me and a gentle smile was on her lips.

"I love you too Edith," I said, gently placing her hands onto her chest.

I felt a light touch on my shoulder and, knowing that I could feel the presence of Ezekiel, amongst others, I turned to ask them to look after my friend as she made her way to Heaven. I found myself staring into the deep blue eyes of the most beautiful young woman that I had ever seen. If I thought that some of the female Angels that I had met during my training were attractive, this young woman was, in my opinion, how the perfect Angel should appear. Her long blonde hair curled around her shoulders and a robe of white covered golden shoes. As she straightened her shoulders, wings of silver feathers extended out, much to her delight.

"I never knew that they would feel like this," the Angel giggled, her voice strong and pure, yet familiar to my ears.
"Edith?" I asked, knowing for sure it must be her.
"My young friend," she said. "Mourn me not, for I am in my rightful place."
"I'll miss you Edith," I cried into her gown as she took me into her arms.
"As I will you, little one, but know that I will be watching you," she told me.
"Communer, it is time," Ezekiel announced.
"One more moment, please," she answered. She took hold of my face in her hands and, for a moment, I thought she was going to kiss my lips but instead, her kiss found my forehead.

My essence tingled with power and, shocked, I looked into her eyes. She winked at me and I heard her voice in my head telling me that she had passed some of her abilities to me. I felt a hand on my shoulder and looked up to see Jackson, smiling at me.

"You're going to be okay Joe," my former tutor told me. "Now you know how to call on your sword, you have passed into a higher phase of your abilities."
"But I still can't break through Yeqon's barriers," I argued.
"Didn't you just smash his hold on you with ease?" he countered, smiling knowingly.

With that knowledge in my heart, I turned to bid farewell to Edith and the chorus of Angels who had come to welcome her into Our Father's Kingdom.

Chapter Thirteen

Edith was gone. The source of most of my knowledge of the ethereal world and, more importantly, my friend was at peace, her place in the battle between Heaven and Hell now complete. My heart ached in sorrow, but also swelled with the understanding that she was being rewarded for a long life given over to the service of Our Father.

As I reappeared in Adam's bedroom, Durchial immediately mewed in what sounded like sadness, as he sensed my loss. My attention focused on the sleeping form of Adam. Despite my grief, I still had a mission to complete, that of protecting this young boy from the horrors of Yeqon.

I watched over him that night, surprised that, at one point in the evening, John came into the room to make sure that his son was covered by his duvet, pausing to stroke Adam's hair in a loving manner that belied his previous outburst earlier that day. I still held out hope that I could break him free from my sister's influence, although this was rapidly diminishing with the now imminent wedding.

At first, I had a thrill of excitement at the thought of Gillian having to step onto the consecrated ground of a church, but that was soon dashed by John. He announced that he had booked a registry office for the service, because of the speed with which they wished to tie the knot. Adam, not at all thrilled by the plans, was at least cheered by Pete agreeing to attend for moral support, the older boy being fully aware of my charge's dislike of his soon to be stepmother.

As the day arrived, it seemed only fitting that someone up on high was casting their own disdain for the union as the heavens opened with a deluge of rain, threatening to cause localised flooding but, somehow, the cars carrying the various wedding guests arrived safely at the council building. Resplendent in black top hat and tails, John and his best man Kevin, a colleague from his bank, stood at the front of the small crowd of well-wishers. Adam, forced into his own miniature tuxedo stood to one side of his father, his blue eyes flashing in disgust as Gill made her triumphant entrance, wearing a flowing red dress.

Gillian's original plan to have Adam trail her into the room as her page boy was immediately shot down by the boy and, for once, John had sided with his son, much to his new bride's displeasure but, sensing not to push her luck, she still won a small victory by having the small boy as the ring bearer.

The service was plain and simple and, as a civil ceremony, the registrar only invoked the name of the government and not that of Our Father, as I am sure that He certainly would not wish to allow the marriage to happen. As the happy couple made their way into the wedding car to travel to a local hotel, where the reception was to be held, a perverse logic formed in my mind. John was now my brother in law, making Adam my nephew and with Pete now adopted by my parents, they were now sort of related as step uncle to step nephew. At least some good came from this union. As all traces of my sister had been wiped from my parents' house and her name had not been mentioned since Pete had been living with them, I was sure that neither boy would realise.

Despite Adam's previous assertion that he would not play the good boy in front of Gill's new boss, Adam's good manners came through when he met the tall businessman. They had a shared interest in rugby. Soon, he had Adam and Pete in fits of laughter as he regaled them with stories of misdeeds and scrapes he had got into as a youngster, on tour with his local rugby club.

As the evening wore on, Adam started to tire, so Pete suggested that they make their excuses. They were allowed to leave the party and head to the room that John had booked for them. Pete had been allowed to stay over after a joint request from the boys but, jokingly, issued threats of punishment, such as no X-box for a week, if he misbehaved.

As the two boys undressed for bed, Adam turned to his older mentor, studying the teen for a moment.

"Pete, do you think I'm gay?" the young boy asked.

"What? Why?" Pete replied, his mouth a little agape at the question.

"Well, Darren kept saying all through last year that I was a pansy, and that his Dad knows how to spot them and he said that I was one," Adam mumbled.

"Well, I think at the moment you are too young to know either way," the taller boy said, running a hand through his neat blonde hair.

"How old were you when you knew?" the ten year old asked.

"Crumbs, I can't really remember," Pete replied, scratching his head. "It was after I ran away from home, so it was definitely after my twelfth birthday."

"Why did you run away?" Adam asked, wanting to find out more about the teen, who he was beginning to hero worship.

"That's not a great story, and one I don't really want to remember," Pete answered, sadness creeping into his voice. "Let's just say that my old man was a drunk, and used to like taking his anger out on me with his fists, amongst other things."

"I'm sorry," Adam said, putting his arms around the teen to hug him in apology.

"Look, it doesn't matter if you're gay or straight," the older boy told him. "If you are a good person, then why does being black, being a girl, or being gay make a difference to how people see you?"

"But Darren says that gays are perverts and damned to Hell," my little charge replied. "I don't wanna go to Hell."

"Darren was that ginger boy in your class?" Pete asked, and receiving a nod in confirmation continued. "I think someone needs to have a word with that boy, or he is going to grow up hating the world."

Now that was something I completely agreed with. Having spent the last three years of my mortal life in a world surrounded by hatred, I knew first-hand how incredibly hard it made the lives of those who were bullied.

"Come on, let's hit the sack," Pete yawned, his own tiredness catching up with him.

"Okay," Adam agreed. He hugged the older boy once more. "Thanks."

I watched over them as they climbed into the separate twin beds and, as they said goodnight to each other, Pete flicked the light off and the room was cast into darkness.

The next two days were as busy as I could remember in the Zegers' household, as the preparations were made for the honeymoon. Of course, Gill had insisted that only the two newlyweds went, and discussions were underway as to where Adam would stay, while they were on their ten day cruise. Adam desperately wanted to stay with Pete but, as soon as Gill found out that the teen had been adopted by our parents, heated arguments about whether he could have any further contact with his mentor ensued, causing Adam to back down on the subject of staying with Pete. The fear of losing him completely stifled his comments back to his new stepmother, so it was with some trepidation that I followed Adam and Gill as she drove him to her friend's house.

As they approached the house I quickly scanned it, and the thirty something woman who opened the door to welcome them into her house. I was surprised to find no trace of Yeqon anywhere and allowed myself to relax slightly, as it seemed that the woman was simply that, just a woman doing her friend a favour. However, with my recent mistake of not spotting that the girl Hayley was in fact Yeqon, I set Durchial the task of watching over the house like a hawk.

As tempted as I was to follow Gill and John on honeymoon, I left them to it, concentrating instead on tracking down Ben. I eventually caught up with him a couple of days before the married couple were due back, having found him at Edith's grave.

"I'm really going to miss the old crow you know," he said as I approached him.

"She's gone upstairs you know," I replied.

"That was always going to happen, Joe, she was far too good for this world," Ben answered. "I'm just surprised that He didn't call for her sooner."

"She said she still had work to finish, which is why she stayed," I told him. "She looked really pretty when she turned into an Angel."

"I saw pictures of her in her heyday and yeah, by damn she was a fine looking gal," Ben said, a chuckle catching his voice as he stroked the white marble headstone.

"So, have you found anything out for me?" I asked. "It's getting urgent now because Gill has now married Adam's dad."

"I've dug around in every nook and cranny of darkness that I could find, without getting caught, and the only thing I've come up with is the prayer to stop the power of a succubus," Ben advised me.

"A succubus? What's that?" I asked.

"A female demon who gets her powers by, ahem, using sex as a tool," he explained.

"But Gill is human so how would that work?" I queried.

"She may be in human form but, if she has been seduced by the Fallen, they could already own her soul which, in theory, makes her non-human unless she seeks full redemption from a priest or vicar," Ben said. "Look, it's the best I've found, short of killing her."

He handed me a scroll which, when I unravelled it, gothic script showed the incantation.

"It was written in the eleventh century, shortly after a rumour about Pope Sylvester II confessing his sins on his deathbed about how he had used a succubus to keep himself in power," Ben stated.

"A Pope?" I was flabbergasted! "Really?"

"Well, the only confirmation was a story written in the Twelfth Century by a guy called Walter Map, and most of his stories were just that, stories," he grinned. "But it's the best hope you've got."

"Fine, I'll try it as I'm all out of ideas when it comes to my sister," I said gratefully.

"Um, now the matter of payment?" Ben asked.

"I haven't forgotten," I said.

I called Durchial and after ten minutes of the two of them talking, Ben walked over to me.

"One last thing, for the prayer to work, it has to be said by the victim of it," he said, before vanishing from my sight.

"Shit! How am I supposed to get John to read it and mean it?" I wondered more to myself than anyone else.

"Maybe the time spent with her will make the John man come to his senses," Durchial proposed, though with as little faith in that as I had.

As I reappeared next to Adam, I was pleased to see that Vanessa, Gillian's friend, was once again spending time with him, this time playing scrabble, testing the young boy's spelling skills. All of my initial fears that she would be part of Gill's plans to continue to cause Adam grief had proven untrue, and I found myself wondering how someone like this lady could befriend such a creature as my sister. It was a question I could sense Adam was also pondering but, although he had been unable to see Pete during the time spent at Vanessa's due to distance, he was happy enough that he wasn't being treated like a slave or serving boy so he had kept his questions to himself.

The day came when John and Gill arrived back from their cruise, and my first glance at them took me aback. Gill looked full of life but John seemed fragile and continually leaned on his new wife for support.

"What's wrong Dad?" Adam asked as he sat down in the lounge, Gill in the kitchen ordering in a delivery from the local Chinese restaurant.

"I've not been feeling well recently son," John started. "I had a couple of funny turns while we were on the ship, which could just be sea-sickness."

"Gill said that you were taking pills," Adam said, concern in his voice.

"It's nothing to get worried about Adam," John tried to reassure him. "It's just some headaches. The doctor says I'll be fine."

I needed to have words with this doctor! I saw Adam stiffen slightly as he felt Gill's hand on his shoulder.

"Now then Adam, let's not tire Dad out now," she said with a hint of fake concern in her voice. "Why don't you come and help me in the kitchen."

"I wanna stay with Dad," he complained, shaking her hand off his body.

"Now then son, go and help your mother," John said softly, rubbing his temples as if a migraine was coming on and he just wanted to be left in peace.

I sensed the anger and hatred boil inside Adam as his father told him to address my sister as 'his mother', but in a show of self-restraint, he bit his lip until he had followed Gill into the kitchen. She turned to look at him, a self-satisfied smile on her face.

"Well then son, let's get the table ready for dinner shall we," she instructed, honey dripping through her voice.

"I am not your son!" Adam said through clenched teeth.

"Look boy, I'm your mother now, whether I like it or not, so you are in the same boat as I am," Gill snapped at him. "If I'd known you were going to be such a brat, I would never have started up with John."

"Well, you could always leave," Adam suggested.

"Not likely, not now," Gill laughed. "I've got too much invested to let that happen."

She pushed plates into Adam's stomach, making him groan at the brief, but sharp pain before taking them from her and setting them on the round wooden kitchen table. He quickly walked over to the cutlery drawer, not wanting to risk a similar passing of items with sharper edges. Once the table was set, Adam sneaked away and up to his room. Unbeknownst to my sister, Pete had given him an old mp3 player so that Adam had some music to listen to whilst reading one of the many books that now adorned his walls.

"Master, I was thinking," Durchial said, appearing at my side startling me. He was getting sneakier at doing that recently, a trait that was beginning to worry me after the encounter with Horrodeon. "Maybe you could put the spell into one of the Adam boy's books for him to find."

"Good idea Durch," I started to agree, before seeing Gill make a fuss over John, giving him a drink of water and another one of those tablets that I knew was the cause of his illness. "However, I can't see John believing him that Gill is evil and needs exorcising."

"If you don't act soon, Master, it may be too late for the John man," the little daemon warned.

And there was my problem. How could I persuade John that my sister was a creature of evil, one that needed banishing, without revealing myself to him. The rules of the agreement burned in my mind, rules that already had been bent by Gary knowing of my existence before he died, of Adam's diminishing memory of me, but one that still existed. I simply was not allowed direct physical involvement with any member of the Zegers household, on pain of having my powers restricted for any given period of time.

Over the next few weeks, Adam kept a low profile, away from his stepmother. His eleventh birthday was celebrated without fanfare, only Pete, along with Harry, Jessica and a couple of other children who were Adam's age and now being mentored by the older students, celebrated with any gusto. The day before the actual day, Pete had arranged for them to go ten pin bowling, always a favourite of the blonde haired student, and something that allowed the six youths to talk, eat junk food and generally have a good time.

For the first time since Gary's death, Adam allowed himself the freedom to enjoy himself, something that had been sorely lacking but now, free from Darren's taunts, I found my charge more relaxed. I touched his mind, gaining easy access past that shining white barrier, which was lowered, and gave him my own birthday greeting. I was pleased for him when Vicky, one of the two kids his age, swallowed her own fear and gave Adam a peck on the cheek as they left the bowling arena. Adam, knowing he was under the watchful eye of Pete and Jessica, flushed bright red and stammered a thank you to her for her card and present.

As the two boys settled down in Pete's bedroom back at my old house, permission having been surprisingly granted by Gillian to allow a sleepover, Pete turned to the brown haired boy.

"So, Vicky seems to like you!" Pete half teased, half confidence building with Adam.

"Yeah, well, who knows what girls think!" Adam blushed back.

"She's pretty," the teenager egged.

"I thought you only liked boys?" the birthday boy shot back, a grin on his face showing he was trying to deflect questions.

"Hey, just 'cos I don't like boiled potatoes doesn't mean I don't like chips," Pete countered.

"What? What the heck does that mean?" Adam asked, confusion showing on his scrunched up face as he tried to understand the deep meaning behind his older friend's words of wisdom.

"I haven't got a clue, but it sounded good," Pete laughed, grabbing the younger boy and tickling him until Adam cried for mercy, with threats of peeing all over Pete's bed if he didn't stop.

Both boys laid on Pete's double bed, panting to catch their breath as the laughter subsided. As they lay in a comfortable silence, I could see Adam sneaking glances every now and then at the older boy. I didn't need any psychic ability to sense that, while Adam was as relaxed and happy as I could remember for years, there was also a nervousness that rolled from his mind. It was a feeling I remembered well. I wanted to reach out to Adam, to stop him from making his next move, a move that had the potential to go so wrong for him.

I watched as he rolled over towards Pete and, with a clenched stomach, leaned over and kissed the older boy on the cheek. While I knew that Pete wouldn't reacted in the way that a homophobic bully would, I wasn't surprised when Pete moved away and swung himself into a seated position, facing away from Adam for a moment, a look of surprise on the teenager's face.

"Adam, what did you do that for?" he asked softly, turning back to face Adam, who's face had dropped like the proverbial lead balloon.

"I thought that if you were gay, and if I was thinking I was, then you would fancy me or something," Adam mumbled into his chest, his chin pressed firmly into his torso as he refused to look at the young man he held in awe.

"Adam, just because I'm gay, doesn't mean I fancy every guy I see," Pete started.

Seeing the young boy sob and turn away from him, rolling onto his front, his face burrowing into the pillow, the blonde teenager felt guilt rack through him as comprehension dawned about the rejection that the young boy must be feeling.

"Look Adam, I didn't mean it like that, please believe me," Pete said quickly, leaning back over to his friend, snaking his arms around the slim frame of the eleven year old.

"Well, what did you mean?" Adam sniffled.

"I might not be able to explain it properly so please take it how I mean it," the teen started. "I find guys my age or slightly older attractive and it's someone my age that I want to have as a boyfriend."

"So you think I'm ugly?" my little charge whimpered, my heart going out to him as I felt his self-confidence plummeting.

"God no! You're a cute boy, but that's the problem for me," Pete replied. "You're just too young for me."

"So if I was older?" Adam asked.

"Who knows? You're a great lad, smart and intelligent, and when you let yourself enjoy yourself, you can be so funny and witty that it makes my sides ache," the older boy answered. "In ten years' time, the age difference between us won't matter but at the moment it's huge, and besides, you're still at the age where you are discovering yourself."

"What do you mean?" he asked.

"Look I'm not going to insult you and say that you're too young to know if you are gay or not, because stuff I've been looking into says that it can start at any time, and kids are realising younger and younger these days," Pete explained. "But it may be a phase, it may be that you think you owe me something, or that you want to be like me, but aren't really, so I want you to really think about it before committing yourself to coming out."

"Okay," Adam replied. "I'll think about it, but I'm still glad you're my friend!"

"I'll always be your friend Adam," Pete said, giving him a friendly hug.

With the heavy discussion out of the way, and some printed leaflets about teen sexuality in his bag for future reading, Adam settled down, and the two boys forgot all about the talk as they concentrated their efforts on slaughtering zombies by the score in the latest game that Pete had bought for his console. Eventually tiredness caught up with Adam, and the pair climbed into Pete's bed. Adam, still feeling a little uneasy after the discussions, edged himself to one side of the bed, before a calming hand from Pete pulled him back towards him and they snuggled together as friends.

After one of my mother's world famous big breakfasts had conquered the boys' morning stomach grumbles, Adam gave his thanks and farewells, he headed home, his backpack slung over a shoulder, carrying his clothes, cards, presents and the all-important pamphlets. I smiled to myself as I walked beside him, revelling in his happiness, while still keeping my mind sweeping the area for unexpected surprises.

As he turned the corner to his home street, he stumbled slightly at the sight of an ambulance and police car parked outside the Zegers' home. With a scream of despair, Adam broke into a sprint as he saw two yellow and green uniformed paramedics carrying out a stretcher that had a black body bag lying on top of it. I followed Adam as he ran up the driveway, I saw my sister being comforted by her friend Vanessa, whilst talking to a policeman.

"What's happened?" Adam cried out. "Where's my Dad?"

"Oh Adam, I'm so sorry," Gillian sobbed. "Your father, he's, he's, he's gone."

"Gone where?" Adam asked, hoping against hope that he had gone out and wasn't the one currently being loaded into the ambulance.

"He's died," my sister wailed, pulling Adam towards her, wrapping her arms around his frame.

I almost believed that she meant it sincerely, that she cared that John was dead and how it would affect Adam. I almost believed that she was comforting him as the shock of her statement broke past his disbelief and tears streamed down his pale face.

"No! He can't be dead!" Adam yelled, squirming to get free of her hold on him, but my sister showed a strength that belied her frame and held him tight.

"I'm sorry officer, but as you can see, my stepson is very upset," Gill said, turning to the uniformed man by her side. "Maybe we can continue this later?"

"Of course Mrs Zegers," the tall policeman said. "Once again, please accept my condolences for your loss."

Gill ushered the sobbing Adam into the house, allowing Vanessa to close the world out and lead him into the lounge. Despite his feelings for his stepmother, Adam had no choice but to hold onto her tightly as his young frame shook with sorrow as he cried onto her shoulder. I was surprised to see Gill softly stroke his back, trying to soothe him, to allay his fears and sorrow.

"Here's a drink for both of you," Vanessa said, returning to the room with two mugs of tea.

"Thanks Nessa," Adam mumbled, wiping his nose, trying to get his emotions under control.

"Drink up son," Gill instructed.

For once, Adam let the name slide and took a large sip of his tea, eyes widening as he did.

"I put a little something extra in to help calm the nerves," Vanessa said, pulling out a small bottle of whisky from her handbag.

"Well, I think we all need a bit of calming," Gill agreed.

"So what happened to my Dad?" Adam asked, his voice catching as he talked.

"He was complaining of another headache, so I told him to go for a lie down," my sister explained. "He couldn't sleep so he took a sleeping tablet. The next thing I knew was, was..."

A tear rolled down my sister's cheek and I found myself wondering if this could be an act, or if she did truly mean her sorrow.

"When your stepmother went to wake him for breakfast, he wouldn't wake up sweetie," Vanessa continued for her friend. "I'm afraid he'd passed away in his sleep, but at least it was a painless way to go. He is free of pain now."

Adam nodded sadly, and got up. Giving Vanessa a hug, he announced he needed to go and lie down to think and remember his Dad. Receiving a nod from Gill, he slowly made his way upstairs, pausing at his father's bedroom door, seeing the unmade bed, tears welling his eyes once more. He turned away and lay on his own bed, covering his face with his hands.

"Master, the Gillian sister woman is not telling the truth," Durchial said, once again scaring the beejesus out of me.
"Flipping heck Durchie, you've got to stop doing that!" I told him, gathering my thoughts. At least I wasn't going to have a heart attack or anything! "What do you mean, she's lying?"
"It's true that the John man had his bad head and went to bed, but the Gillian sister woman gave him the pill to hibernate," Durchial explained. "When he was in slumber, the Gillian sister woman used one of the pillows and covered his face until the John man stopped his breathing."

I was stunned. I knew that Gillian could be an evil bitch, manipulating those around her, and the fact that she had been giving John pills that had caused his illness was bad enough, but to sink so low as to commit outright murder? I looked over at Adam, sadness pulling at my heartstrings as I realised that Yeqon was now responsible for the death of both of his parents, leaving him an orphan. I wondered what would happen to him now. I couldn't see my sister playing the happy stepmother so, unless her plan was to torment him, I could only assume she would put him into social care.
The day passed slowly, Adam only venturing out of his room when hunger or nature called. Vanessa had kept Gill company for the day, preparing food for her distraught friend and my young charge, before leaving for home as the day turned to night. Adam, giving the lady a big hug of thanks, turned to his stepmother and in a moment of shared sorrow, gave her a goodnight hug.
As I watched him slip into a troubled sleep, I pondered the new situation and how my sister would react. I tried to scan her mind, to see if I could pick up any hints of her future behaviour, but, despite Jackson's assurance that my powers were stronger, I still found the red barrier of Yeqon's mind firmly in place within Gillian.

The night passed almost trouble free as I guarded Adam from any nightmare that may have tried to encroach on his slumber. However, it was the real world that I should have been preparing to defend him against. As sunlight fought its way through the closed curtains in Adam's room, I saw Gillian open the bedroom door and walk quietly over to his bed. For a moment, there was almost a motherly look on her face, before she shocked me by sliding herself underneath the duvet and into Adam's bed.

A flash of thought spilled from her mind, and I felt sickened by my own flesh and blood as my link to Adam meant that I felt her hands on his body. Anger boiled inside me and instantly Durchial was at my side.

"Master, the rules, remember the rules," he hissed at me.

"Fuck the rules," I spat. "I'm not going to stand by and let her molest him!"

My link to Adam must have made him aware of the hostility I felt towards my sibling, as he stirred in his sleep before shaking himself out of his slumber. Now fully aware of what my sister was doing, he tried to free himself, only to be held down by the supernatural strength of Gill.

"Let me go!" he yelled.

"Shut it brat!" she hissed in his ear, grabbing a handful of his hair, pulling his head backwards towards her.

"I've just found out that the rat bastard father of yours had not done what he promised and he has left his will as it was, leaving everything to you," she snapped. "So, you and me are going to get very close now. We're going to spend every waking minute together. As your guardian, I control your money but have to have your little stamp of approval for certain things, so I'm going to make you deliriously happy and you are going to agree to every single request I make to spend your money."

"I hate you!" Adam cried, but gave up his struggle as pain from the handful of grabbed hair overrode his desperation to get away from her.

I felt his horror and disgust, his self-loathing as he submitted to my sister and I could stand by no longer. My purpose was to protect Adam, and by God's truth, protect I would. I braced myself and phased into the human spectrum, the sword of burning light appearing in my right hand as I did.

"Leave him be, Gillian!" I said sternly, raising my voice to a volume that would break through her wanton mind.

"What the fuck?" she gasped as she turned and saw me, her eyes widening in recognition. "Joe? Is that really you?"

"Yes it is, now leave Adam alone!" I commanded.

Seeing her tighten her grip on Adam, who was staring at me with eyes the size of dishes, I strode across the room and grabbed her arm, whispering a cantrip that made electricity spark through her body.

"Fuck!" she yelled, pushing Adam away from her. He jumped up, pulling up his pyjama bottoms and ran to hide behind me.

"Joe, please help me!" he begged.

"Don't worry Adam, I'm not going to allow her to hurt you any longer," I reassured him.

Turning back to my sister, who had leapt out of Adam's bed to face me, I raised my hand to deflect the three books that she had thrown toward me in quick succession.

"What are you doing here Joe?" Gill asked. "You should be in Hell!"

"Well, guess what, I'm not!" I replied. "I'm here for justice and your payment is now overdue!"

"Revenge? How terribly unlike you brother," she laughed. "And I guess you haven't changed in death either have you? Hanging around boy's bedrooms?"

I ignored her insult but knew that I needed to let her know why I was there.

"I'm here to protect Adam from the likes of you, sister," I said, venom dripping off my voice as I acknowledged our relationship. "As for revenge, that's not my thing. I fully accept that what I did was wrong."

"Then why are you here?" she hissed at me. "I sold your soul to the Devil! Has he had enough of your foul presence as well?"

"What?" I gasped, startled by the revelation. "What do you mean?"

"Where do you think I got my power? My ability to seduce even the most dedicated husband comes from my prayers for power," she explained. "I made a trade, there was this lad, older than me but still young, and he promised me power in exchange for my soul. I bargained with him and offered him you instead."

"What? Who? When?" I was flabbergasted that, even when I was alive, she was willing to see me dead.

"That doesn't matter now," Gill replied. "I've got my hands on the kid and, as such, the money that it brings!"

"You have him no longer," I hissed. "I said I was here for justice, and that is for Adam, and for John."

"My Dad?" Adam whispered, before turning to face his stepmother. "You killed him?"

"Of course I did," she cackled. "Why would I want to put up with him, when I can control you, and have more fun with you in bed? Once I train you up, I will have a few years before I have to get rid of you and move on to my next slave."

"Well, sister dearest, your free ride stops here!" I said through clenched teeth, as the thought of Adam becoming a slave to her desires fuelled my determination even more.

I moved slowly towards her, covering the distance with sure steps, my sword held low in front of me. I saw her grab at a pendant around her neck and she cried out in a language I didn't recognise. Feeling the temperature begin to drop within the room, I hesitated no longer. I thrust forward with the sword, feeling no resistance as it ran through her body. Gill gasped loudly, her eyes widening in shock as she stared at the silver sword that had penetrated her chest.

"Joe? What are you doing?" a voice behind me gasped.

I turned to see a red haired Angel staring at me, open mouthed.

"Taking care of a demon," I replied, pulling my sword back to my side.
"You cannot kill, Joe," Uriel admonished me. "You are not one of Our Father's chosen, so this is a sin!"
"She was going to abuse Adam in the most horrible way," I argued. "My mission is to protect him, and I will, even if it means killing her."
"But this is cold blood Joe," Uriel explained.

We both turned at the sound of a whispered plea from the fallen form of my sister, surprised that she was still alive. Desperately fumbling with the pendant that had broken off after my attack, I sensed that it was the source of her power, having recalled that I had never seen her without it. Uriel strode quickly towards her.

"Gillian Zegers, I am Uriel, Angel of Justice and Retribution and you are found guilty of the murders of seventeen souls, the latest of whom demands justice to protect his son," he bellowed. "Your time on this realm is over."

His own shining sword appeared and he slashed downwards, ending my sister's life. Uriel turned to me, noting my quizzical expression.

"By my intervention, your actions in your sister's death are no longer applicable," he told me.
"Thanks Uriel," I replied, relieved that my overspill of anger wasn't going to cost me.

A howl suddenly echoed through the room and Adam squealed, running to his bed and diving beneath the covers. Six skeletal figures appeared, chains rattling in their hands as they wrapped them around my sister's dead body. They pulled upwards, and I gasped as I saw Gillian's shadowy form appear, prisoner to the Crawlers, as I had discovered they were called. Of course, he finally put in an appearance. In true demonic form, Yeqon circled the room.

"Joey, what's happening?" Gill's spirit begged.

"What's happening, my dear, is that it is time for my Lord to collect his payment," Yeqon replied.

"I owe you nothing!" she hissed, but her mouth dropped as the Fallen Angel transformed himself to that of the youthful seducer.

"You!" Gill gasped. "But we slept together years ago!"

"You were fourteen and very much a dark soul already remember?" Yeqon chuckled. "I gave you everything you wanted and in return you owe me a soul."

"I gave you his!" she cried, pointing at me. "I got him to kill himself so that you could collect."

"Unfortunately another collected him before the transaction was complete," Yeqon snarled, before returning his mouth to his charming, trademark smile. "You still owe us a soul though so, now it's time to pay. Take her!"

I tried to shut my ears to the cries of horror as the Crawlers disappeared downwards, towards Purgatory, dragging my sister's soul behind them. I turned back to my opponent, Uriel, who was studying me, and the quivering bedcover.

"I call a point of order," Yeqon announced in a deep voice.

"What?" I asked, confused.

"You can't!" Uriel stated. "You have your soul, let it go Yeqon!"

"Not this time, my old friend," the Fallen One replied.

"What's a point of order?" I asked.

"You have broken the covenant of the agreement of battle and, therefore, the balance needs addressing," Yeqon said.

Light and darkness filled the room. I turned and looked around me as I saw Angels of all forms appeared into my vision. As much as I was scared of Yeqon in any form, I shivered as Metatron appeared in Adam's bedroom. This certainly did not bode well.

"We acknowledge the point of order," the voice of God boomed.

"Then you know and accept the punishment? The restriction?" Yeqon requested.

"We accept a three month restriction," Metatron agreed.

"Ha! Your Protector has consistently broken the prime rule of the agreement, which we have allowed to slide, but to appear in front of the Innocent in such fashion," Yeqon started. "We demand twenty four months."

"Don't be ridiculous Fallen One!" Uriel jumped in. "He was acting within the boundaries of his charge, so punishment should reflect the fact."

"Actually, his boundaries excluded any interaction of the Zegers' household so, as soon as the bitch married Adam's father, she became a member of the household," a member of the host from Heaven intoned.

I turned, shocked that a member of my own team would side with Yeqon, but my face, and my hope, dropped when I saw that the Seraphim present was the same one with whom I had exchanged cross words in Saint Paul's all those years ago.

"Eighteen months," Yeqon countered, nodding at my betrayer in the midst of my Father's representatives.
"Nine months," Uriel offered. "And a bond to the boy."
"Twelve months, bonded and we have agreement," Yeqon replied.
"Agreed," Metatron announced.

The majority of the celestial beings vanished, leaving Yeqon, Metatron and Uriel. I looked around, worried and confused over what had been agreed, and what I had done to attract the full attention of both sides of the battle.

"Protector Joseph, you have been found guilty of breaking rule four point three of the covenant regarding the battle for the soul of the innocent child, Adam Zegers," Metatron started. "With the agreement of the representative of Lucifer, it has been passed down that you will be stripped of your powers for a period of one year, and any further interaction with the subject is forbidden."
"To allow you to fully understand your weakness," Yeqon hissed at me, an evil smirk on his face. "You will be bonded to the boy, so that his pain and torment is yours."

I felt pain erupt in my very essence. I tried calling out to Durchial to help me, but I felt nothing other my own voice rattling around in my head. I called for my sword to smite Yeqon, but was left empty handed, much to the amusement of the youthful being in front of me.

"Our presence needs wiping from the boy's memory, lest the covenant is compromised once more," Yeqon announced.
"Agreed," Metatron said, walking over to the hump underneath the blue duvet. He pulled back the cover, exposing Adam's shaking body. As he laid a gentle hand on the child, I heard the whispered cantrip blocking Adam's memories of the last half hour.

Yeqon, with a snide smile on his face, vanished from our vision. I looked at Metatron and, noting his displeased expression, turned away in embarrassment. I looked into Uriel's eyes, seeing sorrow shining back at me.

"Give me your hand Protector," Metatron commanded, and as I did, he placed it over Adam's outstretched hand.

Pain like nothing I had felt scorched my soul and I suddenly found myself with a weird double vision. I could see normally but overlaid on top of my sight, was that of Adam's.

"For the next twelve months, what he sees, you shall see," the voice of God started. "What he smells, so shall thee. What he feels, you will endure. Such is the punishment for breaking Our Father's Law."

Metatron vanished from my vision, leaving a sad looking Uriel standing next to me.

"You screwed up Joe," he told me. "Now, Adam will suffer for your folly, and you will feel every moment of it. I pray for both your sakes that the boy is strong enough to cope."

Guilt swept through me, as the full impact of my actions crashed into my mind. Uriel phased out of vision and I was left in Adam's bedroom, alone, with no power to achieve anything to help the boy who I had been charged with protecting. The good news was that my sister could no longer hurt him.

How bad could things turn? Surely nothing could get worse than losing his last remaining family member?

Over the next twelve months, I was to discover it could.

Chapter Fourteen

My heartstrings tugged for the third time in the five months since the deaths of John and Gill, as Adam was once again on the move to a new foster home.

Immediately after the police and ambulance were recalled back to the Zegers house, this time to collect the body of my sister, Adam was taken into care by a social worker called by the attending policemen. Given that he had no recollection of how Gillian had died, thanks to the memory wipe by Metatron, I watched as Adam was bundled off to an emergency foster placement with an elderly couple who had been fostering kids for years.

While the old couple had greeted him with kindness, for a week my young charge was almost zombie-like with his mind's inability to cope with the loss of his father, and the uncertainty of how he had come to be in his bedroom with the corpse of my sister. Recognising that Adams' needs were beyond their capabilities, the elderly couple were soon saying goodbye as Adam was moved across London to a middle aged couple, desperate to get approval for an adoption certificate.

And all I could do was watch, unable to influence the choice of the new foster parents.

Fortunately the couple, named Harry and Janet, were just as kind and responsive to Adam's needs in the days of his grief, and I felt a slight sense of comfort as I watched them with him. They stood by him as he attended the joint funeral of his father and stepmother, the sour memory of her actions now a retreating memory for him. They held him as he cried for his loss. Then his nightmares started.

And all I could do was watch, helpless with my powers restricted, unable to guard his nightly slumbers, unable to protect him from his nightly dreams.

For two months the couple worked with Adam, helping him come to terms with his grief, helping him adjust to life in a new school where he knew no-one, and trying to help him make new friends in their neighbourhood. Still mourning his loss as school restarted, Adam's unresponsiveness to the first forays of friendships by his new classmates labelled him in their minds as an odd child, and he soon wore the mantle of the lonely, quiet boy. You know the one. The one who sits on his own at the side of the class, talking to no-one, keeping his head down to concentrate on his work as, for the few minutes that he did, it blocked out the loss of his family. The one who finds a quiet part of the school to eat his lunch in relative silence. I saw so much of me in him, it hurt me to the depths of my essence.

And all I could do was watch, unable to influence the youths around him to give him a chance, to take the gamble to say hello, to help cheer him up.

I did start to worry myself into a frenzy when it became apparent that three boys from the year above had identified Adam as a target for their bullying attentions. With my lack of power, I could only stand by and feel the pain of each shove, each trip, each punch as they began their daily campaign of torment. I was relieved when it stopped almost as abruptly as it started, although the reason why concerned me, when the boys appeared one morning sporting bruises and cuts to their bodies. Unable to explain how they received their injuries, their parents were questioned by police but, with no credible evidence linking them to the boys' injuries, no charges were brought against them. However, any time that the boys approached Adam, all three stopped suddenly, seemed to have a change of heart and walked away with pained expressions on their faces.

Eventually, Janet and Harry's efforts started to pay dividends as I felt, through my forced bond, that Adam's grief was beginning to fade as he realised that he still had a life to lead. He was determined not to dishonour his father's memory and, one sunny October morning, came downstairs for breakfast, ready to take on the world.

However, just as Adam had begun to see daylight in his situation, the unexpected happened for Janet and she found she was pregnant as she turned forty. The couple had discussed the situation in depth, and had decided that they couldn't cope with looking after a new born as well as the troubled youth. They announced, with a heavy heart, that they had requested that the social worker begin looking for a new placement for Adam.

With a lack of willing foster parents in the area, the net was cast further afield and Adam was soon away from London, from Pete and any support that he still had, and found himself in the Midlands. A new set of young parents, Simon and Lorraine, still working through their own recent loss of a child found that helping others helped them deal with their own grief.

A new home, a new school and a new start was what I felt would help Adam, but once again, something or someone conspired against us. As Adam began to make friends in his new class, an accident at work left Simon disabled and unable to work. As they readjusted their lives to cope with the changes, once more the creation of new life, normally such a joyous occasion, was the cause of despair and, with the prospect of a new born baby and a disabled husband to look after, Lorraine announced their decision and Adam found himself leaving his third foster home.

And all I could do was watch, unable to call on any help, unable to reach Durchial, unable to ensure that my young charge found yet another loving home.

I watched as Mr Garsham, Adam's new social worker, picked up his bags to load them into the car while Adam hugged a tearful farewell to Lorraine, I felt a shiver run through my very soul. Desperately I tried to break the shackles around my powers so that I could scan the tall, dark haired man, but the barriers around my mind were too strong. I found myself in the back seat, watching Adam in the front next to the man as they drove away from the house he had started to call home.

"Well Adam," Mr Garsham started. "We've hit a stumbling block at the moment."
"What do you mean, sir?" the ever respectful boy asked.
"I'm afraid there simply aren't any placements open with families at the moment," he replied.
"So where am I going to go?" Adam queried, a hint of fear echoing in his voice.
"Don't worry, you're not going to be on the streets," the social worker chuckled, reaching over to ruffle the lengthening brown hair.

Adam frowned slightly, pulling down the sun visor so that he could straighten his messed up locks in the mirror. He turned to the man who, in a way, held Adam's future in his hands.

"There is a group home that has a space," he started but, seeing him frown even more, quickly continued. "Now I know what you're thinking, but it isn't a state run home, it's privately run by a businessman who has several homes across the country."
"Why?" Adam asked.
"Why what?" Mr Garsham countered, confused.
"Why does the bloke run them?" my charge questioned.
"I don't know exactly," the man answered honestly. "All I know is that the homes are very well equipped, fully staffed, and that the boys and girls that stay in them are happier than those staying in a state facility."
"Oh, okay, cool I guess," Adam conceded.

At least he was going to a decent facility I thought to myself. I had seen programmes on television, albeit some of them fictional, and the thought of Adam being in a downtrodden orphanage had worried me. As the car pulled up in front of a large house, I followed Adam out of the car as Mr Garsham introduced him to a small, rotund man by the name of Mr Bell, who was in charge of the house.

Bill, as he introduced himself to Adam, running a hand through greasy looking, short dark hair set all my alarm bells ringing, if you'll pardon the pun. I saw Adam cringe slightly as he shook the man's hand, wiping it on his jeans to remove the covering of oil from his palm.

"Well, let's show you around then boy," the podgy man said, clasping Adam on the shoulder. "Why don't you leave Adam's bags in my office and I'll sort them out later."

"Okay," Mr Garsham said. "Well Adam, enjoy your stay here, and I'll be back to visit you in a month, unless I have any joy with a placement."

"Oh, you won't need to find a placement," Bill started. "I'm sure that when you come back in a month, Adam will be begging you to let him stay."

"Well, each of the other three boys I have brought here have asked to stay, so maybe you're right," Mr Garsham agreed. Giving Adam another hair ruffle, the social worker turned and walked off towards the staff office.

"Let me give you the two minute tour of the place before the other boys come back from school, then we'll have a chat in the office about rules," Bill said, turning back to Adam with a smile. "I'll show you to your room after that and your roomie can give you the full tour later."

"Roomie?" Adam asked, almost looking up at the man. Adam found that he was almost as tall as the large man, something he found comforting.

As I watched, Adam was led from room to room, upstairs and down. There was a large kitchen with an impressive wooden table that looked like it could seat sixteen people easily. What I imagined had originally been a dining room had been knocked through into the lounge, creating a huge room. A large television adorned one wall, while three smaller screens, with varying games consoles, showed that there would be plenty to keep the boys occupied in the free time. Upstairs, there were eight bedrooms and three bathrooms. Six of the bedrooms had twin beds, all of which had various posters and clutter showing that indeed teenage boys were the occupants. Two other bedrooms were marked 'Staff only' and Bill explained that they were for the night care workers.

"And that is the door to the basement," Bill explained pointing out a locked entryway.

"What's down there?" Adam asked.

"Oh, just some equipment and the like," Bill replied. "It's off limits to you boys, unless you're told to go down by a member of staff."

"Oh, okay," the eleven year old responded. "What's that room?"

Adam pointed towards another door, again with a couple of locks clearly visible from the outside. Bill grinned as he opened the door, ushering the young boy inside.

"This is a room where I hope you won't be spending any time," Bill chuckled. "It's the time out room."

Adam stepped inside and, as I followed, I saw a room no bigger than maybe three foot square. It was bereft of windows, furniture, and well, basically anything! I looked up and saw that the only source of light was a small bulb, encased behind plastic, high on one wall. There was no switch, so I assumed it was controlled from the outside.

"This is where we have to put boys who get unruly and start picking on others, or not doing what they are asked to do by the carers," Bill explained. "Normally, a ten minute time out is enough to calm down any angry boy, and not many want to come back in again."

"What? You lock boys in here?" Adam gasped out.

"Only as a last resort," the man replied. "As I said, once a boy has been in here, he sees the error of his ways and doesn't cause any more trouble."

"Um, isn't it wrong to lock a boy up?" my charge asked. I was in total agreement.

"Let me ask you this, Adam," Bill started. "If one of the boys decided that he didn't like you, for any reason, and started calling you names, pushing you around or even hitting you, and the carers couldn't get him to stop by asking him to, wouldn't you want him to be moved to another room to calm down and not hurt you anymore?"

"I guess so," Adam said slowly.

"Well, as long as you behave and do everything that we ask of you, you will never see the inside of it again," the man smiled, patting Adam on the shoulder.

He led Adam away from the small cupboard like room and into the staff office, where he motioned for Adam to take a seat opposite him as he sat himself down behind the desk. Paperwork and folders littered the surface, and was a sure sign that the man wasn't particularly well organised. I glanced around the room, noting various calendars on the walls, some showing staff shift patterns and holidays, others with names against dates, mostly weekends.

Although I had lost my powers to protect Adam and influence those around him, my own senses were still on high alert. Call it paranoia, call it mis-placed trust in others previously, call it whatever the hell you want, until someone proved themselves trustworthy around Adam, I wasn't going to give them a free ride. And the feeling that I was getting from Bill didn't do anything alleviate my initial fear.

I listened as Bill ran through the rules of the house, telling Adam that he would be placed onto the work rota, which meant helping with the chores like washing up, doing the laundry and keeping the house tidy. I couldn't help but wonder about the occasional look that flashed across the greasy haired man's face as he looked at Adam, and his gaze kept flashing to the calendar that I spotted earlier.

Finally, the man allowed Adam to leave the office, handing him over to another care worker, this time a young man who looked like he had barely finished school, let alone gained the necessary qualifications to work in this environment. Carl, as the blonde haired employee introduced himself, showed Adam back upstairs and into a room that was only half as messy as the rest.

"Here you go kiddo," Carl said, his lean frame easing past Adam into the room. "This is yours. You have half the wardrobe, one of the cupboards and the bed on the left."

"Who else is in here?" Adam asked, wondering who he would be sharing with.

"This is Niall's room," Carl replied. "Irish lad, bit older than you, bit of a temper on him, so be careful not to disagree with him too much."

"I'll try not to," he assured the man.

"Well, I'll leave you to get unpacked," the young worker said. "If you need anything, just give me a call."

With a pat on the back, Adam was left alone and he looked around the room. Posters of Manchester United were stuck haphazardly on the wall above what he now knew was Niall's bed. Books were strewn across a table at the end of the bed and Adam carefully picked his way through t-shirts, socks and the occasional pair of boxers that had been left on the floor. Sitting on his new bed, I could tell he was pleased that the mattress was fairly firm, and that the bed didn't squeak or rock. He sat in thought for a few moments, and I could almost see cogs turning behind his eyes, before he gave himself a shrug and unpacked his clothes. Adam had always been a tidy kid, so it was no surprise as I watched him neatly fold his clothes into the drawers of the cupboard and hang up his shirts and trousers.

As he was putting the last of his clothes away, he had a quick flick through the rest of the wardrobe, to see if he could gauge how big his new roommate would be. He pulled out a pair of Niall's trousers and held them against himself, giggling slightly as he did. The legs of the trousers were a good three or four inches past his ankles and waist was four inches wider, so he assumed that Niall would be at least two years older than him.

Shouts from downstairs and a slammed door startled Adam, and he quickly re-hung the trousers and sat down on his bed, as he listened to what sounded like a herd of elephants making their noisy way up the stairs to the top floor.

"Did you see Freddie bash the Connor brothers at lunch?" a high pitched voice squeaked.

"Well they deserved it," a second voice countered, this one a little lower with a definite Irish lilt to it. Niall?

"I know, but Freddie is gonna get it from Bill when Mr Dennison rings him," the squeak said.

"Well, I'll back Freddie up 'cos I saw Danny Connor punch Adrian in the back of the head," the Irish voice reported. "That's what started Freddie off. Oh. Hello. Who are you?"

The two boys, whom the voices belonged to, appeared at the door to Adam's new room. Adam glanced over at them. The Irish voiced boy was most certainly taller and older than Adam, as my charge discovered when he stood up to greet them. Shocking red hair running past his shoulders drew both Adams' and my attention. I looked into his sparkling green eyes, seeing intelligence behind them, and a body that was well built without being muscular.

"I'm Adam, just got here," my charge introduced, holding out a hand.

"Niall," the older boy said, rolling his hand into a fist and holding it out. Adam quickly picked up on the idea and copied his motion, bumping it in greeting.

"I'm Brandon," the smaller boy offered, a toothy grin appearing on his face. Nudging the taller lad, he said, "cool, you're not gonna be able to boast about being in a single anymore!"

"Um, look, sorry about spoiling that for you," Adam apologised, casting a glance at the freckled faced smaller boy.

"Don't listen to the squirt," Niall laughed and gave the blonde haired boy a push. "So, what's your story?"

I casually listened as Adam explained the last few months to the boys, getting pats of sympathy before they gave their own abridged histories. Brandon had run away from home at the age of ten after being beaten by his drunken father one time too many. He had survived on the street for three weeks before being picked up by the police and handed over to social care. Two years later, his father was now in prison and Brandon in the home, waiting to see if there was a family willing to take him on.

Niall was a little more involved. He explained that he was now fifteen and had been in 'the system' since he was born. The son of a drug pushing father and a drug addicted mother, he was born hooked on heroin. It took some time for the hospital staff to wean the new born off his dependency, and he was removed immediately from his parents care. A succession of foster parents and children's homes followed and, by the age of eight, he had fallen in with the wrong crowd. A list as long as Adam's arm of petty criminal offences followed, burglary, theft, shoplifting and drug possession as Niall remained with one foot just outside the Young Offenders Institutes.

"Best thing that happened was when I came here," the Irish lad smiled. "They helped me with my school work, I'm only a year behind where I should be now, and they give us enough stuff that I don't need to nick shit anymore."

"That's cool," Adam said. "It sounds like they really help you here."

"Yeah, all you have to do is, do what they say, go where they say and you're set," Niall confirmed. "I even have a load of money saved from the jobs so, when I turn eighteen, I've got enough to get me own place."

"They give you money for doing the jobs around here?" Adam gasped in surprise, remembering Gill's comments when he was forced to clean the outside of the house.

The two boys just gave each other a knowing look and nodded in answer to Adam's question. A yell from the passageway announced to Brandon that it was his turn to shower, so the twelve year old jumped up and ran off, leaving Adam alone with Niall. The older boy got up off his bed and started undressing, to change from his school clothes into casuals. Adam stared at him for a few moments, comparing the Irish boy to Pete and, with the memory resurfacing of his lost friend, I felt tears start to leak from Adam's eyes and, in an effort not to lose face in front of his new roommate, he turned away, put his head down and pretended to rummage around in his bag for a book.

"I take it Bill gave you the whistle stop tour?" Niall asked.

"Yeah, Mr Bell showed me round the place quickly," Adam answered, still with his head in his bag.

"Well, let me show it you proper, and I'll introduce you to the other guys as well," he offered. "Come on!"

Niall grabbed Adam's arm, leaving him no choice but to follow the red haired lad, not that he didn't want to anyway. A similar tour to the previous was given, except that this time, the lounge was occupied by seven boys fighting over the controls to the games consoles, and the kitchen contained brown haired twins, arguing over a recipe book.

"These are Larry and Lenny," Niall told him. "They both fancy themselves as chefs and, to be honest, they do cook well, so we leave them to it."

"I'm gonna be famous and on telly someday!" the twin called Lenny snapped back as Niall poked him in the ribs.

"Yeah! Crimewatch!" Larry laughed. "Just watch your valuables when my brother is around!"

"Piss off queenie!" the offended twin retorted, throwing an egg at his brother, who showed amazing dexterity, catching it without breaking the shell.

"Enough you two!" Bill scolded, raising his voice as he walked into the kitchen. "You need to prepare extra tonight as we have visitors coming."

"No problem Billy," Lenny told him. "We were gonna do lasagne anyway, and we always have leftovers."

"How many?" Larry asked, with a catch in his voice I identified as worry.

"Make plans for five as I'm not sure if Mr Mackay is going to stop," Bill told them.

"Who's getting the visitors?" Niall queried. Standing behind Adam, he gave Bill a questioning look I didn't particularly like. Whatever the question was, it was answered with a shake of the head.

"Jack, Kenny, Brandon and these two," the large man replied.

I saw both the twins expressions change from the happy go lucky pair that they seemed to be, to one of discomfort and slight distress.

"Come on Adso, let's go watch some telly," Niall nudged my charge, moving him out of the kitchen and the worsening atmosphere.

The boys spent the next couple of hours vegging on one of the sofas, watching a series of programmes on the various satellite channels, before moving on to one of the games consoles. Much to Adam's delight, they had the zombie slaughter game that he had played many times with Pete. As the memory of his friend came back, I felt sadness flow through his body. Niall picked up on it and, in an effort to stop the younger boy from descending into what looked to him like a fit of depression, launched a tickle attack.

One thing I had noticed over the last eleven years, watching Adam grow, was that he had proven to be susceptible to a tickle attack, especially around his sides. Given Niall's larger frame, my charge stood no chance and was soon screaming for mercy as the older boy sat atop him, his fingers finding new places to tickle that Adam didn't think possible.

Suddenly, Adam's expression and demeanour changed and he started frantically trying to buck the older boy off his body.

"Niall, get off me," Adam said sternly.

"Not yet, not 'till you cry uncle," the Irish boy laughed, not realising Adam's change of emotions.

"Get the fuck off me now!" the younger repeated, raising his voice slightly.

"Woah there!" Niall answered. "We're just having some fun."

"Fun or not, I want to get up," Adam huffed, a hint of what sounded like embarrassment and anger in his voice.

"Okay, okay," the red head said, and eased himself off Adam.

As Adam struggled to his feet, it became obvious to me what the problem was, and it didn't go unnoticed by Niall as the youngster ran from the room. Niall looked around at the other three boys in the lounge, but they were all occupied by whatever sports news was flashing across the screen. Niall sighed to himself and got up off his knees and followed Adam's path upstairs. Sure enough, Adam was face down on his bed. Niall sat heavily beside him.

"Look Adso," Niall started. "Just 'cos you popped one, don't mean anything okay."

"You saw?" Adam cried, a couple of tears leaking from his eyes.

"It was a bit hard not to!" the older boy giggled. "You should be proud of it."

"But I got it while you were touching me!" Adam sobbed.

"So?"

"So that means I'm a dirty perv, just like Darren's dad said so!" Adam sniffled.

"I don't know who Darren or his dad is, but trust me," Niall answered, stroking Adam's back gently, "there's nothing wrong with enjoying getting touched! Okay?"

Not getting a response from Adam, he repeated his question and finally seeing Adam nod, Niall ruffled the brown hair before casting a quick glance at the doorway. Seeing no-one around, he leaned down and pecked my charge on the cheek.

"You're a cute kid Adso, and if you do let yourself enjoy yourself, you'll make someone a great boyfriend," Niall stated.

Deciding he had done his bit, the teen left Adam to ponder on his words. I wished, for the hundredth time since the day my sister died, that I could get back inside Adam's mind, to reassure him that he was okay, that there was nothing wrong with him but, once again as I tried, I just couldn't force my thoughts outside my own head.

Sighing to myself, I settled down to watch Adam as he picked up a pencil and his sketching pad. As he started scribbling on the sheet of paper, I saw the hooded figure of Horrodeon appear on the page once more, this time the smaller figure of my little friend, Durchial, alongside him. Regret surged through me, as I realised I missed the little daemon more than I thought I would have. I marvelled once again at the skill that Adam showed as he sketched, the drawing showing that while Metatron may have wiped the memory of our appearance in his room, there was still some residual recollection in his subconscious of other instances. This time, Adam was doodling the aborted fight that he had had with Darren, all those months back.

Eventually, Niall re-appeared in the room, this time with a downcast Brandon. The older boy whispered urgently into the twelve year old's ear as he placed an arm around his shoulders. Niall looked up at Adam and told him that he needed to wash up before dinner, so the young boy quickly disappeared to the bathroom to do the business and the three boys headed downstairs to the kitchen.

As the boys all took their seats, Niall quickly introduced Adam around the table. Bill came into the kitchen followed by five men. One look at them, and I took an instant dislike to all of them, but more so the first man through the door. Something tugged at my mind when I watched him ease his muscular frame into a chair at the head of the table.

As Lenny and Larry, helped ably by two other teens, served up the meals, I placed myself behind the grey haired man who sat talking to Bill. I noticed him glance at Adam several times during the course of the meal, but I couldn't tell what his interest in Adam would be. Most of the boys laughed and joked around, occasionally being told to keep it down by Bill, but I noticed Brandon and the twins weren't joining in the fun.

Finally, the meal was over and with three of the boys, including Niall, tasked with clearing the table, the remaining boys got up to make their way out of the kitchen. The five boys that Bill had mentioned earlier headed out of the room, closely followed by the four men who had come to visit them, and for a moment Adam paused, wondering if to stay and help Niall, or head into the lounge with the other three boys.

"Ah, and this is Adam," Bill announced suddenly, clapping the youngster on the shoulder and turning him to face the grey haired man. "Adam, this is Mr Mackay, the gentleman who runs the homes."

"Nice to meet you sir," Adam politely offered his hand, all my senses screaming at me to grab him and get him away from the man.

"Such a polite young lad," Mr Mackay said. "I think you will fit in very well here."

As he completed his statement, he moved his hand to stroke Adam's cheek. Pennies dropped in various places in my mind, and I pulled back an image that I had taken from a very scared Pete when I found him in the alley way all those years ago. This was the man that he had run away from, the man he was so scared about. This was the man who had ordered Pete's death.

I tried to push the man away from Adam, but only found myself passing through him as I lacked substance to my form. I growled to myself, wishing that I could call on Uriel, on Durchial, on anyone, to protect Adam.

"I think I would like to visit with this young man and introduce myself properly," the man said. "Would you like that Aaron?"

"Adam," my charge corrected. "My name is Adam."

"Oh, I'm sorry," Mr Mackay apologised, insincerity showing in his voice. I think he really couldn't give a damn what Adam's name was. Remembering the reason why Pete had run away from the clutches of the man, I screamed at the world to help my boy as the man firmly placed a hand on his back in an effort to guide him out of the kitchen.

"Mr Mackay," I heard an Irish accent call across the kitchen. "Maybe you'd like to visit me today? It's been a while since we've had some time to, um, talk."

I saw the man's eyes flick between the two boys and, nodding at Niall, he took his hand from Adam's shoulder and told him to run along to the lounge to watch television. I decided there and then that, if it was in my power to award a sainthood, Niall would be a worthy recipient. He obviously knew what was going to happen, and rescued Adam from it at the expense of himself.

I sat with Adam for the remainder of the evening, the pair of us not concentrating on what was on the television. Adam half-heartedly responded to Freddie's attempts to engage him in conversation, but I could sense he was worried about his new roommate. It had only taken a brief glimpse of Brandon, crying and limping away from the basement door back to his room, helped by Carl, for my charge to figure out what the visits were all about. He may only be eleven, but he was rapidly growing up in the world around him.

As the so called visitors left, one by one, Mr Mackay was the last out of the door, he paused to observe Adam for a few moments before heading out, then the boys were told that it was bedtime. Amid a few grumbles, mainly from the three boys on the games consoles, all the boys headed upstairs. Adam tentatively opened the door to his shared room to see Niall already in bed, lying on his front facing the wall.

"Are you okay?" Adam asked softly, as he heard quiet sobbing from the older boy.

"Yeah, I'm okay, go to sleep," came the reply.

"Do you want anything?" the younger boy asked. "A drink or something."

"Just go to sleep Adso," Niall replied, turning over to tell my charge to get into bed before Bill came round checking.

Both Adam and I let out a horrified gasp as we saw bruises on the Irish boy's face, back and arms.

"What happened?" Adam asked, a little naively.

"He gets, um, aggressive, at times," Niall answered, a brave sad smile crossing his lips. "Don't worry about it, I'll heal, I always do."

"He was going to do that to me wasn't he?" Adam stated more than questioned.

"Yeah kid, he was," the older boy confirmed. "Look, I'm not going to be able to protect you for long, so you need to get ready for it."

"Why?" my boy asked. "Why do you let them do it? Why don't you fight back?"

"'Cos they're stronger than me, and they're gonna do it no matter what I try to do," Niall replied. "If you struggle and fight, they just slap you around and still do it to you anyway."

"But at least you're not giving in," Adam started, to be interrupted by the harsh look on his new friend's face.

"I ain't ever given in okay!" he hissed at the younger boy, who stumbled back onto his bed, surprised at the venom in the Irish boy's voice. "I do what I have to 'cos it's the only way to survive here. Boys go missing if they cause too much trouble."

"M m m missing?" Adam stuttered.

"We get told that they've either been moved to other homes, or been adopted, or fostered but no-one ain't ever heard off them again," Niall explained. "Mr Mackay is a bastard, he's evil okay. If there was a devil, really a proper one and not just make believe, then he'd be it."

"What do you mean?" my charged asked, fear evident in his voice, something that Niall picked up, which instantly changed the older boy's attitude to one of concern and worry for the younger boy.

"Look, I ain't gonna lie, 'cos you're gonna find it all out sooner rather than later," the Irish lad said. "He rents us to men for money. We have to do whatever they want."

"You mean sex stuff?" Adam cried out, the repressed memory of Gillian bursting past any barrier that had been erected around it.

Niall got out of bed and, ignoring the fact that he was undressed, perched himself next to the eleven year old, hugging the crying boy to him.

"Some of it ain't that bad, I mean, we get to keep some of the money," he said. "As soon as I've got enough, I'm out of here, whether I'm eighteen or not."

"Would you take me with you?" Adam asked, his eyes the perfect imitation of a puppy.

"I won't be able to afford to look after you as well," Niall replied honestly, sadly.

"What if I get my own money?" my charge queried, remembering the trust fund that John had set up. "My Dad left me money."

"That will be gone by tomorrow," the red head told him softly. "As soon as your social worker signed the form placing you here, they became your legal guardians so they will have access to your dosh."

"They can't do that!" Adam yelled.

"Shush, you'll bring Bill around and, trust me, you don't want him around you at night," Niall explained, shivering, looking at the closed door, praying it stayed shut. "I had been given a payout when my old man snuffed it in prison, 'cos the guards killed him or something, but that was robbed before it even hit my bank."

"So how am I gonna get out of here?" Adam cried softly.

"Just do what they say, everything that they say, keep quiet and smile at your social worker and keep stashing the money they give you," Niall gently told him. "Come on, let's go sleep. We've got school tomorrow."

"Niall?" the eleven year old asked nervously. "Could I sleep in with you, just for tonight?"

"Sure thing squirt," the Irish lad smiled, hugging Adam in comfort once more and they settled down in Niall's bed.

For once, I didn't need to guard his dreams as it seemed the presence of the fifteen year old kept them at bay.

Chapter Fifteen

The next few months were an abject lesson in the hard school of life, and everything unpleasant that it could throw at Adam. As Niall had predicted, the older boy's efforts at shielding the younger one from the seedier side of the home were short lived, and it wasn't long before Adam was receiving his own trips to the basement, or days out with the shady volunteers who came to visit the boys.

I wept as the pain and suffering that my charge was forced to endure left him a shallow shell of a boy, afraid of shadows for who may be lurking there, and all the time I was unable to step in, unable to interfere. At first he did fight against it, rebelling against the so called 'care workers' in the house, only to be locked for hours on end in the darkness of the cramped time out room. The light that I had seen was always turned off as soon as the door was locked, robbing him of the sense of sight. The walls were soundproofed, mainly to stop any social worker calling by unexpectedly hearing the cries, shouts and sobs of any boy unlucky enough to be locked in. Time expanded and shrunk as Adam tried to figure out how long he was locked in.

Physical punishment always followed a time out, with belts, canes or simply Bill's hands and fists, all used to break the fighting spirit of a boy. In the end, after a joint beating from Bill and a visiting Mr Mackay, the men found Adam's weakness; threats of violence to the other boys and, especially when the weaker Brandon was begging for mercy as he was chained high off his feet, it was enough to break the resistance of my charge.

So Adam simply set himself a target of survival, counting any time away from the home, and the clutches of the men involved, as a partial success. Many times he thought about simply telling someone, anyone, but after witnessing one of the social workers who looked after the twins take them down into the now despised basement. The final straw to break his idea was when Adam walked in to his room, only to discover Niall with his headmaster. There was simply no-one that he thought he could trust with the secret of what was happening.

He tried starving himself to get taken to hospital but, after three days of refusing food, two of the older care workers held him down while a third force fed him until he vomited. A warning that any further display of rebellion would be met with further violence, to both himself and a random boy at the home, had the most of the boys bullying him into behaving. Niall tried his best to shield Adam from the worst of it. However, they had all gone through their own breaking process and none wished to relive it, so they simply waited until the Irish lad was absent to make their point known to my charge.

All through this, I had not seen any sign of Durchial. Whether it was because my powers were restricted that I couldn't see or hear him, or if he had now broken free of the control that I apparently had over him, I wasn't sure. I had not seen any Angels to offer me hope that things would improve, or that somebody else was trying to look out for Adam, and I had seen no sign of Yeqon either. I had thought that he would taunt me throughout the whole year, with me being powerless to stop any plans he set in motion, but even his non-appearance, I found disturbing.

I did have a few hints that my little daemon friend may still be around, with random acts of vandalism inflicted on the vehicles of the visitors to the home and, once again at school, no-one seemed to bother Adam and, by association, the other boys from the home. I did hope that it was Durchial, and not just some random, otherworldly being. I had enough on my plate to deal with as it was.

The school year finished with all the boys scoring highly in all subjects. I suppose that, no matter what else was happening at the home, one good thing to come out of it was that Mr Mackay refused to accept failure, and he expected all the boys to study hard. In a way, I guess he was trying to set them up for a life after the home but, while they were there, they were just another commodity to him, another tool in his underhand businesses. I regularly prayed for my powers to be returned, even if it was just to take care of him once and for all. After all, he had hurt Adam, he had hurt and damaged scores of other boys, he had even killed boys, not by his own hand maybe, but his control over his employees was so complete that they had no compunction in carrying out the worst of his orders.

As the summer holidays started, Niall and Adam were talking one night after lights out, their voices a faint whisper.

"Adso, I think I've just about got enough to go," the now sixteen year old told Adam.

"I haven't though, have I?" my charge said sadly.

"How much have you got?" Niall asked.

"I've only got about three hundred left 'cos Billy fucking Bunter Bell found my stash," Adam moaned, the loss of his savings four weeks previously still rankled him.

"I told you not to hide it in our room," the older boy chided.

"How much do I need to come with you?" Adam asked.

"I'm gonna go London, 'cos it's easier to get work there," Niall explained. "So, unless we stay on the streets, which I ain't ever gonna do, it means some serious cash to get somewhere to stay."

"I could do all the housework and ironing and stuff," Adam offered. "If you're gonna get a job, you need someone looking after the house and all."

"You wanna be my wife?" Niall giggled. "'Cos that's what it sounds like."

"Fuck off!" my charge retorted, a smile on his now flushing face showing that he didn't mean or take any offence. "I just meant..."

"I know," the Irish boy sighed.

"So, when do you think you'll go?" Adam asked sadly.

"Well, Mr Mackay is coming up this weekend, so not before then," Niall replied, his face a mask of thought.

"It's my birthday in three weeks, so maybe we could use that as a diversion," Adam suggested. "Freddie and Adrian went bowling with their friends from school without anyone from the home being there."

"So, if we ask to go out on your birthday, we could run away then?" the red haired smiled at the idea.

The boys fell asleep soon after, plots and ideas whirling around in Adam's thoughts as to how to approach the subject with Bill.

The next two weeks dragged slowly by for the two would be escapees. Every snatched conversation about their plans was carefully guarded, either at school or late at night, under the covers of one duvet or the other. With his impending escape now on the cards, Adam's attitude around the house brightened, as he thought of getting back to London, of finding Pete and, somehow, getting his former mentor to help Niall and him set up on their own.

Even the prospect of, what Adam had assured himself would be, one final visit to the basement didn't dampen his enthusiasm for his upcoming birthday. The care workers just put it down to a young boy's naivety and tried to create a party atmosphere in the house in the week leading up to the big day when Adam would turn twelve. I shook myself at the thought that, in some cultures, Adam would be considered an adult yet to me, he was still very much my little charge. I still had visions of the day he was born, being held in the arms of the young teenager that I had dragooned into helping deliver him into the world. My mind wandered as I wondered for a moment what had become of Jake Warburton. Had he realised his own dreams?

As well as looking forward to the boys carrying out their plans, and escaping the hell hole that they were in, I had another reason to look forward to Adam's birthday. It would mark the end of the twelve month punishment that I had been handed down, or up, depending on your point of view. I would finally get my powers back and be able to start protecting my charge in the manner to which I was accustomed.

Finally, the big day came around, Niall gently woke Adam. He winced as he saw, once again, the bruising to Adam's body, the result of the previous evening's 'entertainment', and I heard him swear to himself that, even if Adam didn't have enough money to leave, he would make up the shortfall. Not really understanding how or when it had happened, I could see that the young Irish lad had begun to love the younger boy. Whether it was brotherly or not, in a way, I didn't care as Niall had proven to me over and over that he would step in front of anything coming to harm Adam, if it was in his power to do so.

As Adam showered, I heard Bill's voice call Niall downstairs. Heated words were being exchanged and, as I made my way downstairs to see what was occurring, the unmistakable sound of flesh striking flesh rang out.

"Fuck you Bill," an Irish shout echoed around the house. "You promised that Adam and I could go into town for the day, and now you're backing out?"

"You don't run the home mister," a snarl from the older man retorted. "Just remember that. Fancy some time out?"

"No," I heard Niall whimper, his voice dropping to a whisper. "Anything but that!"

One thing I had discovered, and so had Adam and the care workers, was that Niall was desperately afraid of being locked in the dark, cramped time out room. As soon as it had become known, it was used as another threat to ensure Adam's behaviour.

"Well, I need you to go and deliver this envelope to the address written on it, wait for the response, and then I will allow Adam to open his presents when you get back," Bill told him, handing him a plain white envelope. Niall looked at the address and, seeing that it was only a quick ten minute run, nodded his agreement and was out of the door, hoping that he would be back before Adam finished his breakfast.

Adam slowly eased himself down the stairs twenty minutes later, having winced and grunted through the process of getting himself into clothes that not only looked like he was going to spend the day in the city centre, but also would be warm enough for their initial journey. Adam had argued for going on the train as it would be quicker and they would be in London within two hours but, when Niall had pointed out the price, he quickly agreed to the more dangerous, but cheaper option of hitchhiking with any lorry driver willing to take them.

As he entered the kitchen, he received several pats on the back and a couple of cards from the other boys. However, in line with the rest of the boys, birthdays were used mainly as an excuse to spend time away from the house, and the clutches of any of the care workers. For Adam, it was to be the day of his escape.

I had my own reasons for counting down the days to celebrate my charge's twelfth birthday, and that was the regaining of my powers. I had hoped against hope that they would be restored on the stroke of midnight, but it looked like I was going to be made to wait until the exact time that I had been punished. I wondered whether the boys could start out on their journey without me having to prompt anyone in the right direction. If they did indeed end up hitchhiking, I wanted my ability to scan the mind of the person offering the lift, to ensure that they would not be in any danger. However, even if it did not return, I was sure that the two of them could take care of any problem, Niall especially, as he had proven an able fighter at school, once released from any restraint that would cause trouble in the home.

"Where's Niall?" Adam asked the twins as they placed a bowl of porridge and a glass of orange juice in front of the birthday boy.

"Bill asked him to run an errand," Lenny started.

"Don't worry, he'll be back soon." Larry finished.

"So what have you got planned?" Brandon asked, still a little down as he had been excluded from the whispered plans made by the Irish boy, something that he had noticed more and more since Adam had come to the home.

"Oh, we're just going into the city, I think we're going to the cinema and then Niall said he's gonna buy me dinner," Adam replied, trying to make the day seem nothing more than a trip out.

"So why couldn't I come as well?" the small boy asked.

Through my link with Adam, I knew that he felt guilty for lying to Brandon, but Niall had insisted that their escape plan was kept completely secret, as Bill had proven, in the past, that he would use any means necessary to extract information from the boys, if he thought they were up to anything. Having experienced the full force of Bill's fists previously, Adam had reluctantly agreed knowing that, if Brandon didn't know anything, Bill would have no reason to hurt him.

"Sorry mate, but Niall just wants it to be us two," Adam explained, earning a whistle from Lenny.

"Looks like we've got a couple of lovebirds in the house!" the twin giggled, earning a punch from his brother.

"Leave him alone, Len," Larry complained, seeing Adam flush red at the thought. "You're just jealous."

"Am not!" his brother snapped, before making a sharp exit from the room.

"Ignore him," Larry told Adam, giving the younger boy a hug. He produced a small cupcake with a candle on the top. "Here, you should have a cake on your birthday."

"Thanks Larry!" Adam said sincerely, smiling at the thoughtfulness of the older boy as he blew out the candle.

"What did you wish for?" Brandon asked.

"No!" Larry yelled, startling both boys. "Never tell a birthday wish, otherwise it won't come true!"

How I wish I could find out what Adam had wished for, so that I could ensure it would. After the last twelve months of agony, I wanted to make sure that he had a period of happiness to make up for my mistake.

Adam finished his breakfast, and his cake at the insistence of the enthusiastic chef to be, before helping clear up the table, against the arguments of the two other boys. Explaining that he was at a loose end until Niall returned, he wanted to stay busy, more to take his mind off the imminent escape I felt. Eventually running out of jobs in the kitchen, he wandered into the lounge, challenging Freddie to a shoot 'em up challenge on one of the consoles.

I started to worry as the boys finished their fourth game, it now being over an hour since Niall had left on the errand for Bill. Leaving Adam in the safe care of Freddie, I moved into the head care worker's office just as he was finishing a telephone conversation.

"Just deliver it back here, by the bins out of the back," the greasy haired man ordered. "It will help drive the point home."

I saw him frown and he raised his voice slightly, a hard edge that I had heard on a few occasions creeping in.

"If you want to receive a visit from Mr Mackay, you keep up with that attitude," he hissed. "I'm sure that we can find another cleaner."

Sighing to myself that the big argument was just over the house cleaning service that he employed to deliver cleaning equipment for the boys to use, I made my way back to Adam, pausing as I saw Brandon being man-handled by Carl into the time out room.

"I don't know nuffin, I told Bill that!" the young boy cried as he was forced inside the small room.

"You were told to find out what they were up to, and you failed," the young care worker snapped, lashing out with an open palm, catching Brandon on the cheek.

Anger flared inside me as I wished, once again, that I was able to punish the evil being carried out in this house. I silently vowed that once my abilities were restored, and if I still had my little daemon friend around, I would let him loose on the men who were hurting the boys. I was growing to like Durchie's attitude of 'attack, slash, kill'. I wasn't sure if I needed to get permission from the powers that be, but after the revelation that demons work outside of the destinies set down, that seemed the perfect get out clause for me.

I felt distress from the lounge and moved quickly back to my charge's side. He had finally woken up to the fact that there must be something wrong, as it was easily past the time when his older roommate should have returned.

"I'm going to go ask Bill if he knows where Niall is," he told Freddie, handing the controller to Adrian, who had been waiting patiently to take his turn.

"Okay, laters," the older boy said, bumping his fist.

I watched as Adam knocked on the office door and was ushered inside. Taking the offered seat, and a can of cola, he sat while he watched Bill rearrange several files on his desk.

"Now then young man," Bill said pleasantly. "What can I do for the birthday boy?"

"I was wondering if you knew when Niall would be back?" he asked.

"Niall?" the large man asked, looking confused. "He'll be back later this evening I guess. My question to you is, why haven't you gone with him?"

"Um, what do you mean?" Adam replied. "You sent him to do something for you, and I was waiting for him to come back so we can go into the city like we planned."

"There seems to be confusion somewhere then, as he came back while you were in the lounge, playing with Freddie," Bill explained. "Niall got some things from your room and said he'd be back in time for supper."

"No! He wouldn't do that!" Adam shouted at the man. "He said we were going together!"

Adam jumped up from his chair, tears streaming down his cheeks as he listened to the man tell him unwittingly that Niall had changed their plans. He ran upstairs, ignoring the shout from Carl to walk, and threw open the door to their room. Although there were a lot of the Irish boy's clothes and belongings still present, it was obvious that things had been removed. Niall's large school bag was missing and, as Adam looked into the wardrobe, enough clothes to last a week had been removed. Crying out in frustration, he wheeled to the table that the boys shared for doing their homework. A couple of pictures were missing and the small silver dragon that Adam had bought his roommate for his own birthday was also gone.

I watched, unable to do anything, as the twelve year old threw himself on his bed, face down, hugging his pillow as the realisation that Niall had left without him dawned on him, his tears soaking the pillow he was using to muffle his cries. Something didn't sit entirely right with me. I just couldn't believe that the boy who had spent the last two weeks coming up with the plan for the pair to escape, the boy who had repeatedly offered himself in place of Adam, the boy who had nursed Adam's injuries, that he could so cruelly leave without Adam, crushing his hopes of escape.

I lost track of time as I sat next to my charge on his bed, trying to gently stroke his hair, his back, anything to give him any comfort. He ignored the requests of Lenny, then Freddie and finally, a teary Brandon, released from the time out room, to join them in the lounge but his silent form gave them the answer they didn't want to hear.

Eventually, a sweaty Bill appeared at the doorway. Pausing to study the small frame in a way that made my skin crawl, well it would have if I had any, he reached over and shook him.

"Come on Adam, time for dinner," he said.

"Not hungry," Adam replied shortly.

"Well I don't care if you are or not," Bill stated, smacking him hard on his upturned backside, causing Adam to rollover to protect himself. "Get up, wash your face and get downstairs before I have Jin drag you down there by your hair."

Adam looked over at the tall, bulky Asian worker who seemed to take a devilish delight in pushing the boys around, and was very free with his fists. He nodded at Bill and, having made a quick visit to the bathroom to clean the tear streaks from his face, he made his way downstairs. The kitchen was quite rowdy as the boys took their seats, the unclaimed chair next to Adam being overlooked.

I saw Bill and Jin talking quietly to one side as Lenny and Larry served up the meal. Several boys attempted to engage Adam in conversation but his muted, one word responses were noted, and soon he was left to eat in silence. I noticed Brandon glance several times at Adam, his eyes showing the sadness that was mirrored in my charge's demeanour. Eventually Bill presented Adam with a couple of gifts, new clothes that had been bought by the home kitty, and the boys all sang enthusiastically, if a little out of key, to whichever rude version of Happy Birthday took their fancy. This did bring a slight smile to Adam's face for the first time in a few hours, until Bill asked him to stay behind, as the rest of the boys filed out to spend their last couple of hours before bedtime in the lounge.

"I know it's your birthday and all, Adam," the fat man started. "But I need you to help me outside for a moment."

"Okay Bill," Adam sighed, knowing that he should normally be excused chores on his birthday but now, not really caring either way, the joy of his birthday extinguished.

Bill put his hand on Adam's shoulder, making him cringe slightly and nodded to Jin to follow them out of the back door. As they approached the bins, Adam almost stumbled over a thick, heavy bag.

"We need to dispose of this, Adam," Bill told him. "I thought that you would be the perfect boy to help Jin empty it."

"What's in it?" Adam asked, as he took hold of one end of the bag and tried to lift it. The bag rolled slightly and Adam let his grip slip, causing Bill to frown at him.

"You'll see soon enough, but we need to empty it in the woods out the back," he told Adam.

Adam re-gripped the bag and with a firmer hold, picked up his end of the heavy bag, wondering what was inside that couldn't be thrown into the large wheelie bins. As they followed Bill through the back garden and out of the back gate into the small copse of trees that marked a boundary between the house and a dark, fast flowing stream, Jin dropped his end as they reached the edge of the water.

"Unzip it and open it up," Bill said into Adam's ear, holding his shoulder, almost painfully.

I watched with growing dread as Adam kneeled down by the bottom of the bag. As he unzipped, my fears were confirmed as a pair of trainers came into view. Trainers that were familiar to both me and Adam, as my charge had jokingly remarked on the smell several times in the past few months. Trainers that were not empty. Trainers that were taped together. Trainers that were moving slightly.

With a yelp, Adam quickly unzipped the bag, crying in relief as he uncovered the bruised and battered form of his Irish roommate. Blood flowed freely from cuts in the redhead's hair, streaming down his pale face. Eyes were unfocused as the teenager groaned and moaned through a gag that was tightly bound through his mouth.

"Niall!" Adam yelled, cradling his friend's head gently, before running his hands down his friend's body to find hands that were tied together. "Bill! Jin! Help me free him."

I almost wept as the innocence of the boy came to the fore. Of course, he could not think that, even after everything he had been subjected to by Bill, the man would be capable of this. Hands seized Adam from behind and he started screaming for help, before a large fist slammed into his jaw, stunning him into silence. Adam's legs wobbled and he fell to the ground. Leaning up against a tree, he watched the tall Asian pull the Irish boy out of the bag.

"This is what happens to boys who disobey Mr Mackay," Bill explained to Adam, who looked on in horror as Jin's foot connected with Niall's stomach, causing the older boy to cry out through his gag. Jin picked up the boy's legs and removed a knife from his belt. For a moment, I thought he would kill him there and then but, instead, he sliced the tape around Niall's legs and ankles. My relief was short lived though as, with a hard stamp, I heard the snap of the leg.

Adam's cries were easily muffled by Bill's thick hands, and he struggled against the tight grip as Jin repeated his stamp on Niall's other leg. High pitched squeals followed as I saw the so called care worker break both arms. Finally, three hard punches to the Irish boy's face silenced the painful echoes of sound as Niall was knocked unconscious.

"You understand now that, no matter what you plan, no matter how you think you can escape…" Bill whispered into Adam's ear. "You're ours until we get bored of you."

He pushed Adam towards the broken body of his friend. Adam, crying hard, laid his hands on his body as if he could possess the power of faith healing.

"Push him in," Bill commanded.
"But he'll drown!" Adam gasped.
"That's the idea. Push him in." Bill repeated, but seeing Adam shake his head, he rushed forward and slapped Adam hard across the face. "If you don't push him in, I'll have Jin do it, and then fetch Brandon and we will try again. We can stay out here until we run out of boys, if you want."

Fearful for the other boys, but unable to move, Adam shrieked in horror as Bill motioned to the bulky man, and Jin moved towards the body by the edge of the river.

"No! I'll do it!" he cried. Knowing he had no choice, he leaned forward and kissed the Irish boy's face, tears dripping onto the blood streaked face, he whispered silent prayers for forgiveness, Adam rolled his friend and, with a splash, Niall's body was quickly swept away by the fast current, pulling the boy's body under the water.

I watched as my charge collapsed on the ground, sobbing uncontrollably as the realisation that, not only was Niall gone forever, but that the men knew about the escape plan. Someone had heard, someone had told, and I felt a resolve form within Adam to discover that someone. I racked my own memory but could not see how any of the other boys could have overheard. Even if they had, there was only one boy who would tell Bill, that being Adrian, his current favourite, but he had been laid up in bed with the flu for over a week.

"Pick him up and put him in the basement," Bill instructed Jin. "Chain him up and we'll tell the rest of them he's gone on a visit for a few days."

"Will I get to hurt him again?" the Asian asked, his dark eyes shining brightly in the moonlight. That comment ensured that he would now be higher up my shit list.

"We'll have to wait and see what Mr Mackay says," Bill replied. "He told me he has plans for the boy so, until he tells us, we better not harm him too badly."

I followed the men, who carried Adam's limp body, as they took him downstairs and tied him against a frame, his feet on tiptoes, arms straining to hold his weight. As Bill disappeared upstairs, Jin unleashed a stinging slap to Adam's face, rousing him from his state of shock.

I felt the pain flow through me as Adam struggled against his bonds, pulling at his shoulders as he tried to free himself. He sagged down after a couple of minutes, to the laughter of the Asian, but the pain was still coursing through my essence. As I thought about the intensity of my agony, I realised that this was no normal pain, not one linked to Adam's anyway. It was like a burning of my soul, almost how I imagined a daemon would be affected by stepping on holy ground.

My mind erupted with power as understanding flowed through me. I was on the opposite to church grounds! This home must be on a site dedicated to evil. My powers were back and, as such, my soul was now being tormented by the unholy influences around me.

Reaching out to Adam's mind, I gently stroked him and with a word, put him to sleep. I waved my hand in Adam's direction, loosening the straps around his arms and legs, and eased him to the floor. Turning back to an open mouthed Jin, who was mutely staring at the sight of Adam's body apparently floating to the floor, I willed my sword to my side. Remembering, at the last minute, the rebuttal from Uriel, I called out.

"Durchial! Attend me!"

"Master! Finally!" the little daemon almost joyfully greeted me, as he appeared in my vision.

"Where have you been?" I asked, nearly hugging the blue figure in delight, as I saw my friend for the first time in a year.

"When your powers where blocked, you lost daemon sight, Master," Durchial explained. "I tried to make contact but failed. I let you down, Master."

"Rubbish!" I quickly stopped the small figure from looking downcast. "It was my mistake that led to it, so I'm to blame."

"Master, we should quickly depart for my presence can be detected," Durchial told me, looking around. "I was not able to break the barriers surrounding the home until you summoned me. A mighty Angel protects this evil place."

His words stunned me on two counts. Firstly, that he was now aware that evil was something not to be impressed by and, if he could change, maybe so could other demons? Secondly, an Angel was involved with this place! I heard him growl and realised that Jin was making a move towards the prone figure of my charge.

"Durch, stop him, but don't kill him," I instructed and watched as the face of my servant lit up in glee. Springing forward with a slash of his talons, he sliced through the hamstrings of the Asian monster, causing the man to yell in pain as he collapsed to the ground, his legs not able to support him.

I phased myself into his view, pulling my sword from its scabbard.

"This is a warning!" I boomed to him in as deep a voice as possible. "Your time of torturing boys is over. Protect them from any future pain and you shall live. Continue and die!"

As I finished, Durchial appeared at my side, growling and extending his claws to drive home the point. I guess that being around me for the last few years, the little daemon had picked up on human traits and was perfecting his acting ability.

As I bent over to pick up Adam's sleeping form, I heard a deep bell ring out, a low sound that reverberated through my essence. Turning quickly, I saw darkness fill a corner, and I was shocked to see Mr Mackay step forward. With a snarl, he shimmered and a figure that would remain in my nightmares appeared. Tall and slim, long dark hair and flashing black eyes set against a translucent skin, I would have described the figure as beautiful if it were not for the angry expression on his face, and the dark, black wings on his back. I could sense the overriding evilness seep into the air around him.

"So, we meet at last Protector!" he hissed at me. "Yeqon told me you would be hanging around here somewhere."

"Looks that way," I answered, holding my ground. "You have the advantage, or maybe I do, as you obviously know my name and what I do, but I haven't a clue who you are."

Durchial squeaked at my side, my attempt to goad the Fallen One bringing a look of contempt on his face.

"Master, that is Balthazar, General of the armies of Lucifer, chief advisor to His Darkness," the daemon explained to me.

"Okay, now, what do you want?" I asked.

"The boy," Balthazar replied, although I already knew that would be the answer. "He is mine and, on his thirteenth birthday, I will hand his soul to my Master."

"Over my dead body," I countered, raising my sword.

Could I really fight and kill an Angel? I guessed I was about to find out. Balthazar drew his own sword, black light glowing from it. He rushed forward, his sword held high and it was all I could do to parry his first blow, the shock running up my arms as the power of the Angel forced me backwards. Blow after blow rained down, and each time I managed to get in a block, deflecting the sword away from me.

"Is this the best that Heaven has to offer?" he taunted as a change of direction to his swing caught me unawares and sliced into my side. Dark pain erupted as the mystical weapon unleashed its evil essence as if it was coated with poison.

"Master, remember your training," Durchial cried, as he protected Adam's body from the loose swings of our weapons.

Training! The training I had received from Saint Michael! Yes, Balthazar was a power, but no-one was stronger than my former teacher. I had just about survived that and, with a surge of confidence, I caught his next blow on the edge of my sword and slammed the hilt into his face. Michael may be a Saint, but he isn't that much of one!

Catching the Angel off guard with my sudden attack, I followed up with combinations that had been drilled into me during my time in limbo. As Balthazar tried to counter, I added in my own moves, having watched hundreds of samurai movies during my life, and finally I nicked the arm of the shocked Angel.

"What's wrong Balthy?" I sneered, my confidence at a high. "Never been blooded before?"

"I will have your soul, Protector!" he snarled. "I will shred it over the fires of damnation and watch you burn before reviving you to do it all over again."

"Gotta defeat me first," I smiled, as another slice appeared on his left arm.

I picked up my pace of attack and, with a high low combination, forced my way past his defence and felt an electric jolt shuddered up my sword and arm as I pierced his chest. Mouth agape, the Fallen Angel stared at me in disbelief, as if he couldn't believe that I'd beaten him. His body shimmered and, in the dark flash of an explosion, he vanished.

"Did I kill him?" I asked Durchial, slightly surprised myself that I had indeed, bested him.

"Nay Master," he replied. "According to my Prince, only a Sainted One can cause the existence of a Fallen to cease. You have banished him from this site, however. He can never return to an Earthly site if defeated in battle."

"So the boys will be safe here now?" I queried, more in hope I suppose than in belief.

"I'm afraid not Master," Durchial replied. "His minions can still enter freely."

"Then I need to get Adam out of here," I told him.

I looked down at the sleeping boy, wondering how to achieve this. I tried to reach into his mind, but ran into the white barrier that I had encountered before. This time, however, I struggled to get through, barely making it past his defences. I planted the need to continue with his escape plan, despite the loss of Niall. I awoke Adam with a nudge, and he looked around the basement sleepily, rubbing his eyes. They widened when he saw Jin unconscious at the foot of the stairs. He jumped up and made his way quietly to his room, avoiding any of the care workers on duty.

Grabbing his already packed bag, he slipped a photo of Niall and himself into his pocket, before bidding a silent farewell to his room. Again, with stealth bordering on the supernatural, he crept past the sleepy eyed care workers and let himself out of the front door, which I had managed to unlock to allow his escape. I eased the lock back into place to cover his tracks, and he was away into the night.

Durchial scouted ahead, stopping a couple of drunken youths from approaching Adam as he made his way to the back fence of the nearby motorway service station. Showing his athleticism, he easily scaled the wire mesh and landed softly on the grass. Heading over to the main building, he saw a family of seven getting out of their SUV, the younger kids sleepily straggling behind their parents. Adam made his way across the car park so that he was a couple of yards behind them, and followed them into the building, any outsider thinking he was a member of the large family.

Once inside, he headed to the shop and bought several packed sandwiches and bottles of water, his conscience telling him to pay rather than steal. As I touched his thoughts, I could tell he was already resigning himself to committing certain petty crimes until he found his way to safety with Pete.

All of the time that I was watching him, I was mind scanning the customers trying to find Adam a safe ride. I almost set Durchial on one greasy looking lorry driver when I read his thoughts, but was pleased when his phone rang and he lost sight of him. After Adam relieved himself in the toilet, I forced a driver, who looked to be in his early sixties, to bump into Adam gently and, after exchanging their apologies, it became obvious to the driver that Adam was a runaway, and he offered him a lift. Prodding Adam to accept the offer, he was soon gawping at the large truck that Eddie, as he introduced himself, was driving.

"Now look kiddo, I'm easy going and have been around long enough to know that every runaway has a story that they make up, and the real one they don't want to tell," he started. "All I need to know is that you haven't got any drugs or weapons on you, and you can curl up in the back while I drive."

"I don't do drugs mister," Adam reassured him. "You can check my bag if you want."

"No, I trust ya, you've got an innocent face," Eddie smiled, patting Adam on the shoulder.

And with that, Eddie, Adam, Durchial and I were on our way back to London. Back home. A home still to be found for my charge, but one I was going to make sure was a safe home.

MICHAEL ANDREWS

Chapter Sixteen

True to Eddie's word, Adam was left to sleep for virtually the whole journey, not that it was too long anyway. After all, London was just a short three hour cruise in the lorry from the services near Birmingham. As he pulled into a layby just short of his destination, the elderly man woke Adam with a gentle shake.

"Well, this is as far as I'm going, young one," he said softly, watching as Adam wiped his brown eyes to rid them of the tears that still leaked from his eyes with the memory of the events in the woods.

"Where are we?" Adam asked and, as I looked around me, I saw that we were just on the outskirts of West London. My parents lived just beyond the East End, so there was still a good trek ahead of him.

"Just west of Staines," Eddie told him. "You know where that is?"

"Yeah, I think so," he replied. "Thanks for the lift Eddie, and thanks for not, you know!"

I saw Adam gesture towards his lower regions, and I saw Eddie's expression alter to one of disgust.

"Look here kiddo," he said, pulling my charge into a hug. "I ain't like that, but some guys are so you be careful out there okay!"

"I will," Adam replied.

"Have you got somewhere to stay?" the old man queried. "Or are you just going to be on the street?"

"No, I'm going to go and find my mate," Adam said confidently. "He got adopted and I've been round their house loads, so I know where it is."

"Well that's good then," Eddie said, reaching over to ruffle Adam's brown hair. "I would have offered for you to stay in my cab for the night, as I'm parking up after my delivery. I've got an early pick up so I'm staying the night down here."

"Thanks Eddie, but I'm gonna be okay," Adam replied.

Adam got down from the truck and, with a small wave goodbye, he started walking towards a signpost showing directions to the city centre. It was still the early hours of the morning, so there was virtually no traffic in the quiet neighbourhood where Eddie had dropped him off.

Despite that, I still had Durchial scout ahead and, with my abilities now restored, I took the opportunity to try to re-establish contact with Adam's mind. As the deadline of my punishment passed, my forced link with my charge had vanished and so I needed to touch his mind once more to know his thoughts, his feelings, his emotions. However, seemingly all traces of my presence were no longer there and as I tried to ease myself inside, I came up against the white barrier I encountered late yesterday evening.

I pushed against it, and felt it push back and for a moment I feared that Yeqon had gotten inside my charge, but when I felt the soul of the barrier, it was one hundred percent Adam. The boy's mind had reacted to my absence and built up a protective barrier of his own, one that now was keeping me at bay as well. I frowned to myself but thought that if he now had an extra layer of security from Yeqon, then it could only be good.

Being away from London for the last few months, I had forgotten just how big the city was. Adam seemed to have been walking for hours when the first rays of sun peeked over dark grey buildings and as I rose up to get my own bearings, I realised just how far Adam had to go to reach the safety of my parents and Pete. Touching his shoulder, my suggestion to rest made it past his barrier which interested me. Adam looked around and found a bench by the side of a small roundabout and took a seat. He pulled out one of the packed sandwiches and as he munched away, keeping the morning breakfast pangs at bay, I tried experimenting with what I could do.

Anything that would cause the boy no harm easily made it past the barrier, so things like telling him to rest, to eat, and watch his step, I could influence. When it came to decisions about the future which to his mind were unclear, this was where I started to run into problems. When Durchial appeared at my side, warning me that there was a small gang of older youths on the corner of an intersection a couple of streets away, my suggestion to Adam to take an alternative route was met by the white wall, until he saw the hooded boys standing outside a shop, sneering comments at people who passed them by. Keeping his head low, he turned left at the street before and quickly made a small diversion around them.

Now that people were on the move, I introduced the idea of the London Underground to the boy's mind. As it was a Sunday, no-one would pay any attention to a boy his age being on his own as he hopped onto the Tube. He was simply a twelve year old out to visit a friend in another suburb of the city and, in true London style, most people ignored the smaller boy who was sitting quietly, hugging his bag to his chest, trying his best to ignore those around him. But his eyes told a different story, as they were constantly on the move, checking out anyone who came near him.

I had to shut down my own mind scans as the underground train got busier and busier. The sheer volume of noise of the thoughts of the masses threatened to overwhelm my ability to surf. I suppose it's okay for Our Father to be omnipresent, and to be able to listen and see everybody's prayers but, to a mere former mortal like myself, not a chance!

So I was more than happy as Adam got off the train at the required stop and made his way back into the outside world. Looking around, we both recognised the street that was just a five minute walk from my childhood home. The closer he got to my street, the quicker his pace got, and the happier his face became until finally, Adam turned the corner, only to give a cry of despair.

The complete row of houses where I used to live was gone. Trees and grass lined the way as part of the regeneration of the area from the recent Olympics Games. Looking around, there was no sign of anything I recognised. I watched as Adam slumped against the wall, his body sinking to the ground, just as his dreams of a reunion with Pete sank without hope.

"Master, I could try to contact a tracer daemon," Durchial offered, as I stood there, watching tears leak from Adam's eyes once more.

"A what?" I asked. "A tracer demon?"

"Yes Master, there are times when humans back out of deals with the Fallen, and our kin are tasked to find them," he explained. "We have a sub-breed that specialise in tracking."

"But won't that bring us to the attention of either Yeqon or Horrodeon?" I questioned.

"Yeqon, no," Durchial started. "My Prince, yes."

"Then let's not," I told him firmly. "I want to keep Adam as far away from him as possible. As Adam is the Soul Key, I'm not putting him that close to someone who wants the key."

"As you wish Master," my little daemon bowed. "But I think you are mistaken."

"Noted, but it's my decision," I ordered. "Now, enough of that and let's see about getting Adam somewhere safe."

I suggested to Adam's mind that he needed to move from the spot where he was sitting before he attracted the attention of any wandering pedestrian or policeman. He certainly did not need to fall under the scrutiny of the police having just run away, sorry, make that escaped from the home.

I watched as he picked himself up and made his way to the edge of the grass, looking around as if trying to figure out what to do next. I felt when he made a decision, and he then headed back towards some empty buildings a couple of streets away. He forced open a window at the back of a closed down office, and climbed inside. A quick scout of the place showed that, despite it being closed, there was still water in the toilets so he quickly stripped himself and had a stand up wash, using some soap he had stolen from the home and dried himself on a towel, once again lifted from the bathroom at the home.

He hid his bag in an abandoned desk drawer before walking from room to room to see what he could find. A store room yielded a heavy spare curtain, which I could tell he would use as a blanket but, other than some notepads and pencils, which Adam happily stashed so he had some sketching materials, he found nothing of any use. Adam sighed to himself as he made his way back to the office where he had felt the most secure in his new hideaway.

As darkness fell and Adam was forced to go to sleep due to the lack of light. I left Durchial to watch him and willed myself high above the city. I always found it peaceful, away from the voices and thoughts of the population and, as the streetlights came on lighting London up like a Christmas tree, I settled in to think about what to do next.

The most obvious choice would be for Adam to find the nearest social worker and, with my powers restored, I could make sure he was fostered by a safe family. However, after the shock of seeing the twins being abused by the man who was supposed to be looking after their welfare, I knew that Adam's barrier would not allow me that option.

The next choice was to try to find Pete and my parents. My initial reaction was to send Adam to the school but, as it was the summer holidays, that was pointless. Also, Pete would have now finished his exams and gone on to his A-Level college. I guess I could find out which one but again, as it was the summer holidays, it was fairly pointless.

My only real option was to stay by his side and keep him safe, and to somehow try and find my parents, if they were still in the city.

Daylight broke and Adam woke with a start, once more crying out Niall's name as the nightmare of his role in the Irish boy's death weighed heavily on his soul. My light touch succeeded in slightly reducing his guilt but still burdened with his heavy heart, Adam ventured onto the streets to explore his surroundings and see what he could do to survive.

Adam wandered for hours, stopping to look in shops and windows. He walked through busy market places and tried to get the layout of the area. A couple of times he was shooed away from shops by suspicious owners, far too used to seeing young boys enter their premises only to shoplift when they were distracted. He did manage to make a few purchases, mainly snacks and a pillow before settling down at a small café and having a hot lunch, stuffing himself full with sausages, eggs, bacon and mash potatoes.

Finally, he decided he could walk around no more and headed back to the office. I felt a slight alarm as the window through which he had climbed out was open. I felt Adam's fear as well, as he remembered shutting it behind himself and, as he crept through the quiet building to the office that he was using as his base, he cried out in despair when he saw his belongings scattered over the floor. He ran to the desk where he had hidden his money, not wanting to take all three hundred pounds out onto the streets, only to find it empty.

"Master, what is the Adam boy to do now?" Durchial asked, appearing at my side suddenly.

"He's going to have to get money from somewhere," I replied. "Otherwise he isn't going to eat."

We watched as Adam slumped to the ground, pulling his homemade blanket over himself and cried himself to an early sleep. As he slept, I ventured out into the neighbourhood and was shocked at how many children there were sleeping rough on the streets. Whether the number had increased dramatically since I had died, or if I was just oblivious to other people's misery as I wallowed in my own, I couldn't answer but thinking that Adam needed allies to survive these first few days, I spent my time scanning each kid as I came across them.

I very nearly had to stop after the first half a dozen, their stories ripping at my heart as I discovered some had been thrown out of their homes for getting pregnant, for being gay or simply for being born and unwanted. Others had ran away after suffering abuse similar to Adam, and the rest were kids who had just slipped through the net of the system.

I found two brothers, sleeping in a cardboard box under a bridge, who I thought would be ideal candidates to help my young charge. I planted the idea in the elder that they could go to the office building to sleep, instead of in the unsafe environment of the outside, and he awoke with a start.

"Deano, wake up," the blonde boy said, shaking his younger brother.

"Huh?" the younger boy mumbled.

"I've just thought, we could go sleep at that office block you saw the other day," the older boy explained.

"'Morrow!" Dean replied, trying to turn back over.

I gave both boys a nudge to wake up fully and, with a look of disgust tinged with the obvious love he had for his older brother, the younger boy finally agreed to move through the streets towards Adam's base. It was clear that the boys were brothers, and that they had been on the streets some time. They easily avoided the drunks, the crazies and, to be frank, the perverts that preyed on the young kids during the night and climbed through the same window that Adam had been using.

"Let's find a quiet office and we can sleep in there," the older boy told his brother.

"Okay Tommy, but I'm hungry now," Dean complained.

"Well you're gonna have to wait until I can steal something tomorrow," Tommy replied, opening the door to Adam's office.

"Wait Tommy," Dean whispered, grabbing his brother's arm. "There's someone in there."

The boys crept in slowly and upon seeing Adam's youthful face poking out from the curtain, a soft snore escaping his lips, they grinned at each other and made their way inside.

"Should we wake him so he doesn't freak when he sees us?" Dean asked.

"Nah, let him sleep," Tommy said, grabbing a pen and one of the sheets of paper. I watched as he scrawled a note onto it and rested it by Adam's head. It simply explained that they were there, not to worry, and they were asleep as well.

I watched over the three as they slept, and with the dawn chorus of birds chirping away, Tommy was the first one to wake. I didn't need my powers to hear his stomach rumbling, and a quick scan showed it had been several days since he had eaten anything more substantial than half eaten leftovers scavenged from café tables or rubbish bins. I saw him look over at Adam's rearranged bag, with the sandwich packs inside, and the look of longing on his face broke my heart.

He picked himself up and, for a moment, I thought he would simply take what he wanted but instead, knelt by the side of Adam's sleeping form, gently nudging my charge awake in a way he thought may not scare him. As Adam's eyes fluttered open, he yelped and tried to move backwards, but was hushed by the older teen.

"Hey, hi there," Tommy said in as friendly a voice as he could muster. "I'm Tommy and that's my younger brother Dean over there, still sleeping."

"What do you want?" Adam cried out. "Just take whatever you want but don't hurt me."

"Don't worry mate," Tommy soothed. "We're just crashing like you were. I got fed up of sleeping under a bridge."

"So you've run away as well?" Adam asked, calming a little.

"Kind of, long story, don't like telling it," the blonde haired boy said quickly. "Same with you I guess?"

"What do you mean?" my charged queried, worried.

"Well, your eyes say that you've seen and done shit that you'd rather not of, so I won't ask."

"Thanks," Adam smiled at him, the first smile I'd seen for a couple of days. He giggled as he heard the older boy's stomach announce its hunger once more and, being the kind kid that I had grown to love, Adam showed no hesitation in offering to share the sandwiches he'd bought.

The boys sat discussing life on the streets, or rather Tommy and a now awake Dean explained to Adam what they had done to survive the last nine months, stealing and begging, and Tommy, with a downcast face admitted to performing the acts for money that Adam had become all too familiar with.

"Look Tommy," the twelve year old said, a streak of defiance in his voice. "I had to do shit like that at the home where I've run from, and I ain't ever gonna do it again. Forced or not. I'd rather kill myself."

"I'll never do it either Ad," Dean announced. "But only 'cos Tommy says I shouldn't."

"So what do you nick?" Adam questioned. "I did have three hundred quid, but I got robbed yesterday so I've only got a tenner left. I need to get some money."

"Well, we steal off the market stall when they ain't looking, so we get our fruit like we're supposed to," Tommy started.

"Yeah! Our five a day!" Dean giggled, pulling out a bunch of bananas from his bag.

"Where did you get them?" his brother asked.

"The market, like you told me to," he replied, confused.

"Why didn't you tell me you'd got them?" Tommy demanded. "I nearly stole Adam's food 'cos I was so hungry!"

"Hey!" Adam shouted at the pair as they looked like they were about to fight. "It doesn't matter now does it? He's got them, so let's eat them before they go off."

As they ate the fruit, Tommy explained that, if they couldn't get enough money from begging, they did resort to stealing. Their favourite tactic was Tommy barging into their victim, snatching either a handbag, wallet, or anything of value and in the process of apologising, accidently bump into his brother who would be wearing a hat or some other form of disguise and hand him the prize. That way, if the victim realised that they had been stolen, when Tommy was caught, he had nothing on him to mark him as the thief.

In scenes reminiscent of Fagin's hideout in Oliver Twist, the boys spent the next couple of hours teaching Adam the intricacies of how to pickpocket, some of the efforts causing all three to fall to the ground in laughter at the weak efforts put in. Finally, Adam felt confident enough to try his hand at breaking the law and they headed out into Old London Town.

They scouted through the markets, working in tandem, two of them distracting the stall owners whilst the third lifted pieces of fruit, random snacks and, at Tommy's insistence, Dean bundled a couple of pieces of so called antique jewellery into his coat pockets so that the boys could pawn them later to one of the more unscrupulous traders.

With Dean's ability to melt the hearts of any old lady walking past and gain the odd fifty pence or pound coin, they made their way to a small greasy spoon café and as they counted out the money they had made, they discovered they had enough to have a decent hot meal and could put some away to save for days when they didn't have such a good day.

As the boys sat eating and talking, joking about anything that could lift the gloom of their lives, I noticed Tommy stiffen slightly in his seat. I followed all three boys gazes to see a middle aged man enter the café and take a seat at a table, two away from the boys.

"Do you know him?" Adam asked.

"Yeah, he is, um, one of the guys, um," Tommy spluttered, his face glowing red as comprehension dawned on Adam.

"Don't do it, Tommy," he said.

"Look, I've been with him a few times before, and he's okay," Tommy stated unemotionally. "He pays a lot for next to nothing."

With that, the older blonde got up and headed towards the toilets. They were single door entry that locked behind them and, as he passed the man, I saw the man get up and follow him into the toilet.

As much as I wanted to intercede, I decided that I needed to concentrate on Adam. Tommy seemed to accept what he was doing, and if it helped get some extra money to look after my charge, then so be it. I guess that my enforced absence from providing protection for Adam, from the harshness of the world, not only had made him grow up quickly, but had also changed my viewpoint of the world. I now knew that I was no longer the knight in shining armour who could right every wrong. I was now the experienced soldier who realised that sometimes collateral damage had to be endured to win the greater battle.

Dean tried to keep Adam occupied in conversation, with only a small amount of success and, as Tommy reappeared at the table, he smiled wanly at Adam and answered Dean's questions about the thirty pounds he had just earned.

"Look Adam, you don't have to like it, you don't have to do it," Tommy hissed into his ear as he grabbed Adam's arm as they left the café, "but sometimes it is the easiest way to earn decent money fast."

"Let go of me," Adam growled, shaking his arm out of the grasp of the older boy. "You can do it if you want, I just don't want to take any of that money from you, okay?"

"We're not gonna agree on this are we?" Tommy asked sadly, and seeing a shake of the brown haired head, added. "Well, it's the best way to make money fast."

"You want some fast money?" Adam snapped back. "Here, I'll go get some."

As I reached out unsuccessfully to his mind to try to stop him, the brothers watched with mouths agape as Adam set off towards a couple who were walking along, minding their own business, chatting about whatever seemed to be taking their fancy. I had a sense of foreboding as Adam picked up his pace as he approached them from behind and, with an outstretched hand, grabbed the loosely held handbag from the brown haired woman. He carried on his path at full speed, and I heard the man, a tall blonde haired figure, call out the world famous "Stop, Thief!" as he set off in pursuit of my charge.

I reached out with my mind to try to persuade the man that it wasn't worth the risk of the chase but my mind reeled in surprise as I touched him. Ideas, situations, all sorts of outcomes flooded through my thought processes until I was brought back to Adam's flight with a bump, as the boy, looking over his shoulder instead of where he was running, collided with the black uniformed bulk of a policeman. The policeman had angled himself to ensure that he didn't bounce off him and held on tightly to the now struggling Adam.

I looked around and saw Tommy and Dean had disappeared, obviously not wanting to be implicated themselves, and I couldn't blame the boys as they had only met Adam that morning.

"Now then sonny Jim, what have we here?" the deep voice of the policeman asked.

"Sorry for bumping into you sir, but I need to get back to my mother," Adam gasped out.

"I suppose that's your mum's bag is it?" he asked, holding Adam's arm in front of him.

Adam was just about to answer when the blonde man finally caught up with him, followed not too far behind by the woman my mind now introduced to me as his wife.

"I believe this scamp stole your handbag?" the policeman asked the lady.

"Yes he did," she started before gasping in recognition. "Adam? Adam Zegers? Is that really you?"

Adam produced the most realistic double take that I had ever seen, and his mouth dropped in surprise.

"Miss Yeates?" he whimpered.

"Well, not anymore, but yes, it's me," Louise said, pulling Adam into an embrace and out of the grip of the policeman.

"I take it you know the young man?" he asked Jimmy, who's own face now had the dawning recognition himself.

"Yes we do, we've been looking for him for some time," he replied. "If it's okay with you, we'll take him from here."

"And why should I allow that sir?" the officer asked.

"My wife and I are both teachers at his school, and have been concerned for his whereabouts for some time," Jimmy responded, pulling open his wallet showing the officer his driving licence and his teaching union membership card. "We don't want to press charges, so there really is no need for you to be burdened by a load of paperwork that you would need to complete, just to see him walk away anyway."

Seeing the truth in Jimmy's statement, the policeman gave Adam a small ticking off about watching where he was running and how lucky he was to have been found by the pair. I wasn't sure if he actually heard much of it, as he was locked firmly into a death grip hug by his former teacher.

"Let's go and grab a coffee shall we?" Jimmy said to the pair of them, ushering them out of the middle of the street where they were beginning to attract attention.

Sitting in a large coffee shop, the teachers tentatively asked Adam about where he had been and realising before he had answered too many questions, that he had suffered some horrendous abuse, quickly changed to the subject of where he was staying now.

"I was looking for Pete but his house is gone!" Adam sniffled into his hot chocolate.
"Yes, the Harris's sold their house under the regulations for the redevelopment of the area," Louise told him. "They live just around the corner from us now."
"From you?" Adam queried.
"Louise and I have been married for about three months now," Jimmy explained. "So Miss Yeates is now Mrs Johnson."
"Cool!" Adam smiled. "I'm pleased for you."

Louise reached out and patted his hand, in a manner that showed she would have made a wonderful mother, if only nature hadn't been so cruel. As much as I wanted to plant the idea in their heads about taking Adam in, it seemed that for it to be a truly safe home for him, and a decision that they would not regret, I knew they needed to make the choice unaided. Fortunately luck, or someone upstairs, was on the same wavelength as Adam was soon walking with them towards their car, Louise's hand resting gently on his shoulder as they started their journey home. Stopping briefly to allow Adam to collect his few meagre belongings, including his photograph of Niall, they made the short trip to a tree lined street and a nice three bedroomed house. Adam was given the quick tour and, as they sat in the lounge, the discussion about his future began.

"Well, the first thing we need to do is call Social Services to let them know where you are," Jimmy started but seeing Adam's expression darken and his body tense, my best friend reached out a hand and rested it on Adam's shoulder. "I take it you had a bad experience with them?"
"Yeah, Mr Garsham was okay I guess, but the guy in charge of Lenny and Larry was one of the men who, you know," he stammered.
"Well, I think if I can pull the right strings, you will end up really liking the lady who would be in charge of you," Jimmy reassured him.

"Why? How do you know and how could you pull strings?" Adam asked, a look of hope, tinged with disbelief on his face.

"The Be A Friend project is still going really strong, and has helped identify some cases where children have been hit, or worse, by their parents," Louise explained. "Jimmy, along with Pete, is right at the forefront, and he has got to know the supervisor and several case workers who have helped children in bad situations."

"Well, if you think you should call them, I guess it's okay," Adam said timidly. "If I don't like her, I can always run away again."

"It won't come to that I'm sure," Jimmy smiled, stepping outside the room to make the call.

Louise turned the subject to a scholarly nature, to take Adam's mind off the situation, and was pleased when he told her that he had gained high marks in his end of year exams. The subject of their wedding, followed by the sad memories of John's funeral were discussed and, before they realised the amount of time they had spent talking, a doorbell interrupted their thoughts.

"Ah, hello Mrs Vickers," Jimmy's voice rang out from the hallway. "Yes, he is in the lounge with Lou."

The door opened and I could sense the anxiety and worry flowing from my charge until the form of a lady so familiar appeared in the doorway.

"Helen!" Adam shouted, jumping from his seat and running to envelope his former nanny in a bear hug.

"Adam, I'm so pleased we've found you!" she cried, tears streaming down her face as she kissed her former charge on the top of his head.

"That's two of you who have said that now," Adam stated.

"Come, sit down," Jimmy said. "Tea?"

Receiving a nod he disappeared into the kitchen, returning minutes later with a full tray as the two ladies explained their anguish and sadness over John's death, followed by their efforts to maintain contact with Adam, as he was shipped from family to family.

"So, Jimmy, Louise," Helen started, interrupting the latest flood of chatter from the four. "You have indicated many times that you want to be considered for fostering. Is that still valid?"

"Of course it is," Louise replied. "There isn't any chance that maybe? Is there?" The look she gave Adam showed the deep affection she still held for him.

"Chance of what?" Adam asked, not quite realising.

"Let me get the form from my briefcase," Helen instructed, reaching inside her leather bag. Putting it onto the table top, she told the adults to sign on a particular line.

"What's going on?" Adam queried, having seen his former foster parents sign forms like this before.

"Well kiddo, Lou and I want to foster, and maybe eventually adopt, as Lou can't have a child herself," Jimmy started.

"And we want to foster you if that's okay?" Louise completed.

No answer was needed as I watched Adam break down in tears as he realised that, for once, he wasn't being forced onto a family, onto a couple. They actually wanted him in their home and indeed had been searching for him. After many hugs between all four, Helen eventually left the new, happy family to enjoy the rest of the evening.

If the previous year had been abject horror, the next few months were the complete opposite. Firstly, as Adam settled into the Johnson's home, his loving personality shone through as he felt more secure than at any time since his father had been murdered. Within a couple of weeks, he was reunited with a shocked but very happy Pete as my parents returned from a holiday abroad with their adopted son.

School restarted, as it always does, and Adam very quickly gained a group of friends, Vicky especially pleased to see him back. However, a quiet word from Jessica one day curbed the young girl's enthusiasm for gaining a boyfriend, to simply making a best friend, much to Adam's relief.

There was an uncomfortable meeting early in his return to school when he bumped into the red headed Darren Walford. I was immediately on my guard, ready to protect him, but the former bully simply nodded in his direction and moved on. I reached out to touch Darren's mind and was surprised not to encounter any barrier. It seemed that the encounter in the alley way with the demon Horrodeon had finally removed the compulsion to bully him, and Adam was simply left alone.

As the year passed on, Adam, and I, started to get excited at the prospect of Jimmy's parents visiting from Japan. Even though Jimmy had left to return to the United Kingdom, they had stayed out there, enjoying their retirement in the Land of the Rising Sun. However, the first set back in months occurred when Mr Johnson, ever the joker, broke an ankle falling from a tree as he was trying to teach his next door neighbour's grandson how to scrump for fruit, and so their trip was postponed.

Once again, I began to feel myself falling into a zone of comfortable safety, one that I tried desperately to keep myself out of. At one point, I even persuaded Durchial to try to ambush me, to try to sneak past the defence barriers that I placed around my charge, just to keep me on my toes. Uncomfortably for me, my little daemon friend eluded me on several occasions, but calmed me with his reassurances that it was simply because he knew tricks, as he called them, that the Fallen did not. With him as back up, there was simply no path through the pair of us for Yeqon to gain access to Adam.

As Adam's thirteenth birthday approached, I stepped up my efforts to remain on alert. New pupils would randomly appear at the school, looking to cause trouble for my charge, but my careful deflections of their attention, or their fellow pupils blundering into situations set up by the newbies, gave Adam all the protection he needed. A carefully placed bottle of whisky in the drawer of Adam's history teacher, who had suddenly started to find fault with him for no reason, at least no reason known to the rest of the faculty, soon removed him from the school, and Yeqon's latest attempt to remove Adam from the safety net of his group of friends, failed.

I constantly monitored the house and gardens for any trace of demonic activity and, despite a scare a couple of weeks before Adam's thirteenth birthday where I felt the overwhelming presence of Horrodeon for a few moments before the heavy atmosphere lifted, I was comfortable that no otherworldly forces were present.

I did notice, however, that Jimmy and Louise had started becoming secretive in conversations concerning Adam. As smart as he was, Adam soon picked up on this, to the extent that he started to betray his moral fibre, and began trying to eavesdrop on the whispered conversations. Much to his dismay, he could only hear snippets which he couldn't string into sentences, but there was definitely a hint that his foster parents were looking at sending him away somewhere.

To my frustration, I couldn't anticipate it either. It was as though someone, or something, was keeping me from finding out as well. I complained bitterly to Durchial each night, but he simply shrugged and repeated his assurance that no Fallen One had entered the home.

As Adam's thirteenth birthday dawned, I watched as he awoke, stretching his slim frame as he remembered that he was expecting Pete to call round as they had plans to go to the cinema. I felt his mood swing rapidly as emotional memories flooded through his mind as he remembered his last birthday, with the fake plans of a cinema visit with Niall, a day that left the Irish boy drowned in the stream behind the home. Adam opened his bedside drawer, removing the photograph of the two boys that had been taken on a trip out. He gently kissed the image of the red head who had done so much to protect him, before saying a quiet prayer in memory of the boy he thought he loved.

He slipped his dressing gown and slippers on and headed down the stairs, knowing that Louise had promised him a breakfast full of sugar and syrup and everything that the goody goody chefs on television said was bad for children. He approached the kitchen door, his slippers padding quietly on the carpet floor.

"So that's the form is it?" Louise's voice said.

"Yes dear, this is the one," Jimmy replied. "It finally arrived in the post this morning."

"And we are sure that it's okay to send Adam?" the woman asked.

"I know it will be hard, but we agreed to do this," Jimmy reminded her.

Adam paused behind the kitchen door, his mouth dropping open as he heard the two adults talk.

Chapter Seventeen

As Adam paused at the door, leading into the kitchen, he heard Jimmy and Louise continue to talk softly, discussing the teenager. He knew it was wrong to eavesdrop but, over the last couple of years, had learned that in doing so, he found out so much more than people would be willing to tell him.

"So if we sign this," he heard Louise say, "then we can send him on his way?"

"Yes dear," Jimmy replied sadly. "We both need to sign it to make it official."

I saw tears well in Adam's blue eyes as he took a couple of steps backwards. This was wrong. Adam didn't understand that his foster parents would not be so callous as to get rid of him on his thirteenth birthday.

I could feel the confusion, the self-pity, the anger rolling out of the troubled teenager. I tried to enter his mind, to soothe him and reassure him, but the protective barriers that he had been building around himself were now firmly back in place and I could no longer break through. In despair, I watched as he turned and ran, through the hallway and opened the door leading to the basement.

I caught glimpses of his mind and, in horror, I realised that this was the time. After everything we had been through, after all the pain and torment, all it had taken was those two sentences from the adults that Adam had come to love and trust, the feelings of rejection that he felt, had broken him.

"I'm not being sent to another home," Adam cried to himself as he hurtled down the stairs. "I refuse to become someone else's play thing."

As he reached the bottom of the stairs, I felt the air shimmer as the ever reliable figure of Durchial appeared.

"Master, I can feel a nexus approaching," the blue demon announced to me.

"I know, I think this is it," I said. "In these next few minutes, the battle will be won or lost."

We looked on as Adam found the rope that he had previously discovered whilst playing amongst the congested boxes. A noose was quickly knotted. He slung the rope over the wooden beam in the ceiling, securing it with the expertise of the Boy Scout he had once dreamed of becoming.

I tried to touch his mind, to break his barriers, to show him all my love, but the white wall was impassable. In desperation, I sent a mental shout to James and Louise, warning them of the lad's danger. I felt a surge of success as my former friend dropped the cup of coffee he was drinking and ran for our location.

Adam pulled a chair into position and, with deliberate sureness, slipped his dark haired head through the loop of the noose. His hands reached up to tighten the rope and he stood for a moment, eyes closed.

Without having to sense his arrival, I cursed at Yeqon.

"Well, well, well," the beautiful figure of the Fallen Angel started. "It looks like we will have a final reckoning at this moment."

"Yeqon, please, let me break through to him," I begged.

"And why should I allow that?" he sneered. "After all, my Lord Lucifer is quite fond of all those tortured souls that he would have to give up to Him."

I was at a loss, but had hopes of saving the teen as I saw James come running down the stairs.

"Adam, Stop!" James shouted.

"Why?" he cried. "Just so that you can send me away again?"

"What are you talking about?" James asked, stunned at his question.

"I heard you and Louise talking about the forms," Adam replied.

Time froze.

"And here it is, my unworthy opponent," Yeqon whispered at me, circling the two humans, one ready to commit his soul to Hell, the other willing to save it. "All of your efforts, all of your persuading others to protect him, and it now comes down to your former friend, the one who deserted you, the one who left you to rot in that festering hole that you called home."

"No!" I shouted back. "Jimmy didn't leave me, he came back for me. It was just that I wasn't strong enough to hold on for him."

"And yet, once again, he is here, witness to another death as his own rejection of the boy drives him into the arms of my Lord," Yeqon snarled.

"He's not like that, I know it," I said, pleading more with myself than anyone else.

"Shall we play out the next scene?" the fallen angel asked and waved a hand to unfreeze time.

"We were talking about your birthday," James pleaded, trying to reassure him.

"Liar," Adam shouted.

"You said you wanted to visit my parents in Japan," James tried to explain. "Well, we need to get you a visa for the trip."

Time froze once more.

"Hhmmm, will he believe the lies that the unreliable one spins?" Yeqon asked. "How many times has he already been let down by the pair?"

"Those weren't James' or Louise's fault and you know it," I snarled back. "You were the one behind Gary's abduction and death, you were the one who turned Darren against him, everything bad that happened to him was you."

"And so you see, my unworthy opponent," he replied calmly, "at the end, in all things, I am triumphant."

Durchial whimpered as he stood by my side.

"As for you, demon spawn, I will enjoy feasting on your essence once you are returned to the Second Realm." Yeqon shimmered and the youthful figure dissolved into the red and black demonic form that was forever etched in my nightmares.

"Master, make a bargain for the boy," Durchial whispered. "Allow yourself to go willing to the Fallen in place of the Adam boy."

"But why would he accept that?" I asked perplexed. "If Adam commits suicide, he gets us both anyway."

"But one soul already passed, willingly given, will cause greater joy for the Fallen than two souls dragged down to Purgatory," Durchial advised.

"But Adam is the one he needs, the Soul Key," I nearly sobbed out. "Why would he want me in place of that? I mean, it will allow them to break free."

"It is worth the risk, Master," the little demon answered. "What is the worst that could happen?"

I considered it for a moment, and knowing that, should Adam fall, I was doomed anyway, it was all I could do to save the soul of the boy I had been charged to protect, the soul of the boy that I loved unconditionally and had vowed to die for.

"Yeqon, a bargain," I offered. "My soul force willingly for his."

Yeqon stopped circling the frozen mortals and looked over at me, his eyes narrowing as they studied me.

"You offer yourself in replacement for the Innocent one?" he asked. "Why should I accept?"

"It's me that you really want isn't it?" I countered, trying to bluff. "After all, you were the one who set my parents against me, the one who owned the soul of my sister, the one who caused me to suffer through everything when I was alive."

A sparkle of light illuminated the basement as a silvery figure appeared.

"Joseph! No!" the form of my Uncle Dylan begged.

"Stay out of this, angel!" Yeqon growled at him.

"Joe, if you do this, if you give your soul away for a second time, there can be no redemption for you in this cycle," Dylan warned.

"I don't care," I sobbed, knowing that I had to do this. "I said I would protect Adam at all costs and so I will."

"You are committed to this?" Dylan asked me.

"Yes," my simple reply.

"Yeqon, do you accept?" my uncle asked, offering my soul to the Fallen One for all eternity. "If you do, you give up your right to the soul of the Innocent and everything that goes with it."

"Most definitely," Yeqon replied, shimmering back into his youthful form, a smile broadly showing on his face.

"Then done," Dylan announced, and his form disappeared from sight.

Time unfroze.

"Really?" Adam stammered. "I can go visit them in Japan?"

"It was meant to be a birthday surprise for you later, kiddo," James told him.

Adam slowly lifted the noose from his neck and jumped into the open arms of the man who was his foster father. James caught the teen, embraced him and kissed his forehead.

"Don't ever do that to me again ok," James chided him.

"I won't, I'm sorry," Adam replied.

As Adam stated his commitment to James, I saw a dark hole open at the base of the wall opposite me. I could sense an over-riding feeling of joy, of relief, of overwhelming thanks as I saw black shadows fly up and out of the earth. As the forms hit the basement, they shimmered and turned into figures of blinding light and shot up and out through the basement ceiling, disappearing from view.

I felt a thrill of success run through my soul as I realised that the Lost Youth, the ones who I had been charged with saving, were escaping the pits of Hell and the clutches of the Fallen.

"And now my young soul, I believe you have an appointment with this," Yeqon whispered in my ear, having moved behind me unseen.

Pain erupted in my side and I looked down in horror as the dual pronged spear, the one which Yeqon had threatened me with so many times over the last fourteen years, pierced my body. The shockwave of my agony rippled through the basement and suddenly the visible boundaries between the human realm and that of our unseen realm were ripped apart.

I saw Adam and James's eyes widen as they realised that they were not alone.

"Joey?" I heard the older man gasp in wonder.
"Go!" I shouted. "Get out of here! Durch get them away!"

I saw my little helper pop to their side and try to pull them away from the scene below.

"You've lost Yeqon," I snarled as I felt the Fallen Angel twist the embedded spike in my side. "Adam will never be yours!"
"Do not worry about them, Protector," Yeqon hissed at me. "It was you that I wanted all along!"

Electric jolts coursed through my body as he twisted the spike in my body. Out of my peripheral vision, I was happy to see Adam run out, up the stairs, while James lingered at the top, watching helplessly as Yeqon cranked up the pain in my soul.

"What do you mean it was me?" I croaked, gritting my teeth to fight the pain.
"Why do you think I spent so much effort turning your parents against you?" he asked. "Your sister was already a dark soul, so a little nudge ensured she followed my desires."
"But by trading me for Adam, you lose the wager," I said triumphantly. "That's worth my soul to release the rest."
"The rest of the souls will soon be ours once more," he sneered. "Now that I have the Soul Key in my grasp."
"Soul Key?" I gasped out. "Adam is the Soul Key! You've lost Yeqon."

The sneer did not fade from Yeqon's face as I expected it to and, as I looked around, I saw Durchial's head bow.

"Durch!" I shouted.
"Yes my Master," the demon said, appearing at my side.

"Tell him, tell him Adam is the Soul Key," I begged.

"Oh no, my Master," he replied. "You are the Soul Key. You have always been the Soul Key."

I heard the chuckle from Yeqon as my fears began to crash down on me, extinguishing the triumph I had felt just moments ago.

"Durchial, you have done well," Yeqon commended the blue demon.

"I have delivered him as required, Fallen One," Durchial replied, bowing to the figure that still held me, impaled on his spear.

I had been betrayed. All the time that I thought the little demon was aiding me, he was setting me up.

"Why?" I cried at him.

"It was my role, my Master," he replied, his white fangs showing through his grin. "And one that I am pleased to have fulfilled."

"And now, it is time for the Fallen to reclaim our rightful place in the Kingdom of Our Father!" Yeqon exclaimed.

The air shimmered once more and, suddenly, we were no longer in the basement but in an endless meadow of green grass. The aroma of flowers of every variety filled the air.

"Attend!" Yeqon cried out, and the meadow was filled with celestial beings. All had wings, coloured black denoting their status as the Fallen.

I struggled to try to get away from my victor but, with a sneer, he pushed me to the floor, finally releasing my body from the painful embrace of his spear.

"Stay there, you worthless slime," Yeqon commanded me, as a being of undeniable beauty strode forward.

"Yeqon, my most faithful follower and general, you have done well," the figure congratulated.

"My Lord Lucifer," Yeqon replied, bowing reverently to his master. "Here is the Soul Key."

"Ah yes, the Key to our entry back into the Father's Kingdom," Satan said, bestowing his full attention on me.

He waved his hand in my direction and I felt myself being lifted up, as a tree suddenly sprouted up from the soil beneath me. Vines grew out of the tree and wrapped themselves around my arms, stretching them out across the branches while more secured my legs against the trunk.

"How apt, you remind me of someone who sacrificed himself before for these worthless souls," the figure in front of me said.

"Yeah, well, Jesus saved humans from you, and so have I!" I shouted as the vines tightened their grip, causing me to wince in pain.

"Well, if you wish to be like Him, you seem to be missing something," Lucifer told me.

He held out his right hand and, to my horror, a burning white spear appeared. With a look of pure evil in his eyes, he gripped the weapon with both hands and pushed it into my side, piercing my body. Pain erupted in my soul and a prayer of mercy escaped my lips, one that I knew would never be heard.

"He cannot save you now, young soul," Lucifer told me.

"What will happen to me?" I sobbed, tears streaming down my face as the agony reached the core of my soul.

"I will mould the essence of your soul into the Key and with it, unlock the Gateway to the Golden Staircase," the bane of Christianity told me. "It will open and remain so for all eternity, your soul trapped as it tries to shut. I understand the pain you will endure will be… intense."

Laughter rang out from the multitude as I gulped, scared witless, looking around for any chance of salvation but knowing there was none. I had committed myself to this path, and now the whole of Heaven would pay a heavy price.

Lucifer came forward once more to lay his hand on my head. He started an enchantment that I couldn't fully understand, but caught the occasional word and recognised it to be the language of Archangels. I remembered a discussion between Saint Michael and Metatron during my training when they had lapsed into the archaic language. This was the oldest language ever to be heard upon the Earth and all the realms around it.

I cried out in pain as the Dark Lord started the drain of my life force, of my soul into the palm of his hand. As I desperately looked for help, I saw the Golden Staircase appear.

"My followers, the time is upon us," Lucifer crowed. "Today, we reclaimed our rightful position not at the right hand of Our Father, but on His very throne. Today, we will rule in Heaven!"

Cries of triumph echoed across the plain as the Fallen Ones celebrated their victory. My heart ached in defeat and, as I prayed for forgiveness once again to Our Father, this time I knew that I was damned.

I saw shining white figures appear at the bottom of the stairs. An old form came forward, his silvery beard almost reaching his chest.

"Peter," Lucifer greeted the figure. "Move to the side and I shall spare thee."

"You know I cannot allow thee to pass," Saint Peter replied.

"I have the power," Satan sneered. "The Soul Key is mine to wield and I shall reclaim Heaven! Demons, attend!"

As the darkened form of Lucifer strode forward, a host of demonic forms filled my vision as far as I could see. There was no way that Heaven could withstand this, I was sure.

"Fallen Ones, halt thy advance," a voice familiar to me shouted. "I cannot allow thee to pass into thy chosen realm."

"You are my servant, demon," Lucifer spat. "Get out of my way."

"I cannot, for you are not my master," the small voice said.

With my last strength I raised my head to see the small form of Durchial appear next to Saint Peter. Despite the knowledge that he had betrayed me at the last, I couldn't help but cry out in horror as Lucifer held his hand forth and shot a beam of energy into the chest of my little friend. Somehow, the time we had spent together must have created a bond between us because, as the beam hit Durchial, pain erupted in my chest.

Light surrounded the small demon, so bright that it bleached out even the vision of the Golden Stairway. It grew in size and intensity and, as the host of beings either shielded their eyes or looked away, a mighty thunderclap of sound and a sonic shockwave threw the Host to the ground.

I turned my head, agony shocking down my spine, expecting to see the blasted and charred remains of Durchial. However, he was there, standing tall, no longer the small demon that I had grown to love. In place of the diminutive figure was one of awe inspiring beauty. Fully six feet tall, muscles rippling underneath his blue and black skin, Durchial stood proudly in front of Lucifer and his Fallen.

"Out of my way, spawn of the Second Realm," Satan cursed at him. "Follow, my Generals, for tonight, we shall feast on the Souls in Heaven."

Unmoved, Durchial held out his hand, and this time it was Lucifer whose advance was halted.

"I call thee, my Prince," Durchial bellowed, "For the time of reckoning is now."

The air shimmered besides Durchial, and I was stunned to see the dark cloaked figure that I feared for so long. The second being that I had been determined to protect Adam from.

"Prince Horrodeon," Lucifer greeted. "Your presence is unnecessary."

"Be that as you may think, Despised One," the prince of demons replied, "but there is a matter of contracts to complete."

"There is nothing in this moment that requires my attention, daemon spawn," Lucifer spat back at the demonic lord.

"Oh, I disagree my Lord Lucifer," Horrodeon countered. "Durchial!"

The blue demon I had long associated with being my friend, appeared at the side of his former master, holding a scroll of parchment which, while it looked brand new, I could sense the archaic psychic energies emanating from it.

"And so should the Fallen Ones accept the Soul Key from the Guardian, then the agreement is complete," Durchial announced. "The Soul Key so willingly given shall, once again, allow daemon kin to follow their journey."

"Yes, so?" Yeqon snarled at my former servant and friend. "You have delivered him and now we can attain the freedom we deserve."

A low chuckle come growl spread across the meadow, chilling me to the bone, well, it would if I had any. I looked at the demons and saw Horrodeon raise himself to his full height. A myriad of colours swirled across his body.

"Soul Key, hath thee given thyself willingly unto the Fallen in place of thy chosen charge?" the prince of demons bellowed towards me.

Sensing this was the final chance to allow Adam to forever escape the clutches of those who wished to hurt him, I nodded my affirmative.

"And lo, with the willing sacrifice of the Soul Key, in accordance to the terms of the agreement, Daemon kin is freed from thy unholy bindings and are free once again to roam the galaxy."

A cry came from all around me as the multitude of demons multiplied in my vision, all of them with cruel expressions and, I assumed, a hunger for human souls, which would fit in with the plans I'm sure that Lucifer had for my former kind.

"Fine," Lucifer snarled at Horrodeon. "So you are now free to feast on the human scum. Enjoy yourself for, tonight me and mine dine in Heaven!"

He started towards the open gateway of gold, only to find his passageway blocked by half a dozen younger demons.

"Oh, my former Lord Lucifer," Horrodeon started, "how little does one read the prophecies, he who relies upon them to deliver him from the underworld."

"What do you mean, slave?" Lucifer spat.

"If you read the prophecy correctly, you should know that the Soul Key, given freely and guided by daemon kin, shall release our kind to roam the universe once more, and to be restored to all our former glory," the prince of demons said.

"And?" Satan replied, frustrated that his progress to the Golden Gateway was being interrupted.

"Our power was always to be restored by the Soul Key, if willingly given, to save a soul unselfishly," Horrodeon explained. "Protector Joseph has done just that, and so we are now free of your enslavement."

This is it, I thought to myself. The moment that the Fallen reclaim Heaven, and leave Earth and the human race to the mercy of the demons. I bowed my head once more, waiting for my soul to be claimed and moulded into the key of the destruction of the human race.

"My Master, fear not," Durchial whispered to me, enclosing my body within his strong arms. With a gentle, but firm pull, he released my entrapped body from the vines. Shocked and surprised, I turned to him. I could not believe that he was no longer the small blue demon that had accompanied me for the previous decade, but was now a fully grown demon, resplendent in his beauty.

"Durchial, you betrayed me to the Fallen, and now my kind will suffer for eternity," I cried.

"No my Master, I guided you to save our kin, and protect yours," he replied.

I looked over at the figures of Lucifer and Horrodeon, facing off in front of the Golden Staircase.

"The Soul Key, willing given shall, once again, restrict the Fallen to the Second Realm as the act of unconditional sacrifice by the terms of thy Father Lord overrides all previous sins," Durchial explained, standing by his Prince.

"As such, Lord Lucifer, thee and thy kind are once again cast back into the Abyss," Horrodeon cried.

"This cannot be!" Satan exclaimed. "We won the battle!"

A hole of utter darkness appeared behind the host of Lucifer's angels. As hard as they battled to stay within the meadow, one by one they were sucked back into, what I imagined was, Purgatory.

"But the Soul Key was ours to exploit!" I heard Yeqon scream, as he followed his fellows into the gateway.

"He was never yours, despicable being," Durchial announced, appearing once more at my side. "The Soul Key was always our being, our salvation and, at his command, he shall confine thee and thy kind to Hell once more."

I looked up at the fully grown Durchial, my soul pounding, my essence leaking from my very existence.

"Durchie," I croaked. "What do I need to do?"

"My Master, with thy strongest will behind you, you must banish the Fallen back to Purgatory," the tall blue demon told me.

"Then, I curse thee Lucifer, Yeqon and the rest of the Fallen back to Hell, where you belong!" I cried out.

Inhuman shrieks echoed across the meadow as the gateway to the Second Realm closed behind them. The meadow disappeared and, once again, I was back in the enclosed basement, the rope that had threatened to end Adam's very existence still hanging from the beam. There was only Horrodeon and Durchial standing in front of me.

"But what of your kin being unleashed on humans?" I asked.

A deep chuckle came from beside Durchial. Horrodeon had come witness his final triumph.

"My young, precious spirit," the lord of demons started. "It was never our wish to become trapped upon this realm of planets."

"I don't understand," I replied.

"Our kin are travellers, and for aeons we have traversed the universe, but we were drawn to the beauty of your planet," he explained. "Not only the architecture of the planet itself, but the light source of the human soul."

"So now you want to feast on them?" I snarled. "Not if I can do anything about it."

"Nay, my young feisty spirit of the being called Your Father," he replied. "We were observers who got too close and were trapped. Trapped when our craft was damaged. The Fallen Ones rescued us, but bound us to slavery. For millennia we have looked to escape, and finally you have given us the key to our continued existence. We are now able to be raised to our Exultance."

"I read about that, and I thought it meant that you were able to roam our realm," I said.

"No, young soul, it is the name of our vessel, awaiting us to continue our journey of exploration," Horrodeon told me.

"So you are now able to leave Earth, and us, behind?" I asked.

"Yes, and you will be revered amongst our kind, my Master," Durchial added. He placed his hand on my shoulder, and I could no longer hold back. I brought him into an embrace and let loose with my emotions. Tears racked my soul as I realised that not only was Heaven saved, but so was the human race.

"So why did they not realise what would happen?" I asked.

"The Fallen are so full of their own self-importance that they cannot understand how a lowly figure can impact the destiny of the universe,"

Horrodeon explained. "Your God sent his son Jesus Christ to fulfil this purpose once before, and now you have followed in his footsteps, freeing an enslaved race and saving your humankind."

"I don't understand," I said.

"Durchial was willing to forgo his normal growth so that he could guide you to where we needed you to be," Horrodeon explained.

"But I thought you were just a hand messenger?" I asked Durchial.

"My father relies on his sons to be his messengers," Durchial replied, grinning at me. "And as his youngest son, who better to escape under the view of the Fallen?"

"So what happens to me now?" I asked. "Uncle Dylan said that I could not now enter Heaven as I have given up my soul twice."

"We are bound by the laws of the Gods of the worlds that we visit," Horrodeon said sadly. "As such you are not permitted to cross into your Maker's Kingdom within this cycle of life."

The full truth of his statement hit home. Despite my willingness to sacrifice myself to save Adam, I thought maybe, just maybe, there would be a get out clause that would save me. Surely after everything I had done, God would still allow me into Heaven, but with the confirmation coming from Horrodeon, no longer to be considered a demon in the human sense of the word, I was once again, left in limbo.

"Father, can we not allow Protector Joseph to travel with us?" Durchial asked.

"That is a possibility," Horrodeon agreed. "It is upon you, Protector. We can show you sights that no human has ever seen. There are planets out there with trinary ring systems that are more beautiful than any diamond on earth."

I glanced around at my surroundings, taking in the view of the messy room, clothes strewn everywhere. My eyes were drawn to the stairs. Of course, Jimmy was there, frozen, waiting and praying for my safe return.

My Jimmy. My best friend. The man I had chosen to take on the responsibility of looking after Adam. The man I would trust with my soul.

I sighed. As fantastic as the opportunity sounded, I knew that I could not leave my own planet, even if it meant staying in limbo. Durchial, so in tune with my own feelings sensed this and once again approached the tall demon prince.

"Father, we have the power," he said,

"It is dangerous, my son, and can only be attempted with a fully compliant spirit," Horrodeon replied.

"But he deserves to be given the chance," Durchial begged. "He has freed us, and he is my friend."

I looked at the tall, yellow horned blue figure and, with tears welling in my eyes, I embraced him as he ran to me and hugged me.

"Protector, you have been told that you are barred from entry to your Maker's Kingdom in your current cycle," the demon prince started. "If you are willing, I have the power remove you from this cycle and place your soul into a new cycle. One that will have the opportunity to claim its place in Heaven."

"Really?" I asked.

"However, there is a cost," he warned me. "Your soul will need to be completely cleansed of this life cycle. You will lose all memory of your life, of your encounters and of your friends."

"I understand," I replied. "As much as I would love to follow you across the stars, my place is here. I want to go home."

"And so you shall." Horrodeon announced.

He motioned for me to kneel before him. As I did, Durchial once again rushed forward to embrace me.

"Joseph, my friend, I apologise for the deceit that I was forced to follow, and I plead your forgiveness."

"Durchial, there is nothing to forgive," I told him, tears still falling from my eyes as I realised that I was saying farewell to the closest friend that I had had since I had chosen to end my life. "You have helped me look after Adam and keep him safe and, for that, I will always be thankful."

"It's been fun though?" the demon grinned at me, once again showing his fangs, and now, knowing that they were not threatening in anyway, I could only nod in agreement.

"It's been great fun, Durchie," I said.

Even though I couldn't see it, I knew that their craft had approached. I let my mind open for the last time, and found the outer shell of the ship. Of course the craft was called Exultance so, once again, their prophecy was to be fulfilled. They would indeed be raised above all others, into Exultance.

"Are you ready, Protector?" Horrodeon asked.

"I am, your Highness," I replied.

He laid his hand upon my head and my vision was blinded by light, beyond which I could not see. I felt my body shrivel and compact and, in a moment of panic, I wondered if they had told me the truth, but then I found myself in a warm place. I couldn't see anything as my eyes would not yet work. I could hear a steady thump thump, thump thump, which lulled me into a deep sleep. One that would last for nine months.

MICHAEL ANDREWS

Epilogue

Nine Months Later

Two figures ran down the hospital corridor, slowing down to a brisk walk only when they came across a green clothed orderly or the stern looking face of a nurse. They came to a junction where the elder of the two, a man in his mid-thirties, studied the signs. He ran his hand through his blonde hair, his blue eyes searching for the information he needed.

"It's this way son," he said to the teenaged lad at his side.
"Are you sure?" the dark haired teen asked. "I mean, you were sure that you had the right way last time, and we ended up in the x-ray room."

The man chuckled and ruffled the lad's hair, causing a groan from him. He studied his reflection in a vending machine and palmed the stray hairs back into place.

"Yes, I'm sure tiger," the man said fondly. Putting his arm around the teenager's shoulders, he turned him and pointed. "Look, there's the sign for the maternity ward. Let's go and see Louise."

The pair walked towards the grey doors and, as they reached them, they saw a man who looked to be approaching his late thirties coming through the door in the opposite direction.

"Ah, you've finally made it," the blonde haired doctor said with a smile.
"Yeah, doofus here kept telling me to go in the wrong direction," James said, poking Adam who responded with a pout before giggling.
"Well, can I be the first one to congratulate the pair of you," the doctor said, offering his hand to the man who pumped it, a broad grin on his face. "Both mother and child are doing fine, and I know they are looking forward to seeing you."
"Thank you Jake," James said to the doctor he had got to know over the last few months, as the medical staff had closely monitored the progress of the baby. "Thank you for everything you've done."

"Yeah, thanks Doctor Warburton," Adam added.

They pushed through the door and headed towards the private room that held their waiting family. As they approached, Adam slowed down, almost stopping. James turned to look at the boy who was now looking downcast.

"What's wrong kiddo?" he asked.

"Well now that you and Louise have the baby, are you still going to want me?" Adam asked, his hair falling across his features, hiding the tears welling up in his blue eyes.

"Of course we do, why would you think that?" James responded, pulling him into a hug. The youngster limply shrugged his shoulders.

Sensing what was a potentially life defining moment for Adam, James knelt down on one knee so that he could be on a level with the lad. He reached his hand out to lift the boy's now tear streaked face.

"It's just that before, whenever someone took me and then had a baby, they got rid of me as they didn't need me anymore," the thirteen year old sobbed.

"Listen to me, son," James said firmly. "Lou and I made a promise to you when we took you into our home didn't we?"

"Yeah but..." Adam started before being interrupted.

"Yeah but nothing, kiddo," James said, looking the boy straight in his eyes. "Louise getting pregnant was a wonderful and totally unexpected surprise. We had been told that she could not have children, which is why we had decided to foster. When we took you in, we knew that you were the one that we wanted to become a permanent member of our family. We love you and want you to be our son, and nothing has changed that. We have had to wait for the probationary time to pass before we can ask you, but now is as good a time as any. Lou and I would dearly love to adopt you and make this a permanent thing, if you do. What do you reckon kiddo?"

Adam backed up slightly, a small smile of hope forming across his lips. "You really mean it, you want me forever?" he asked, a longing in his voice betraying his anxiety.

"Yes we do, forever and then a day past it," James replied.

"Sure, of course I want it, oh thank you so much!" Adam squealed in delight, launching himself into the man's strong arms.

Tears flowed freely down Adam's cheeks once more but this time, the happiness shone through. James placed the lad back on the ground and, with an outstretched hand, he took Adam's hand and the pair walked into the hospital room where a blonde haired lady, looking well despite the delivery of her newborn child, smiled adoringly into a bundle of clothes held in her arms.

"I take it by the squeal outside that he said yes," Louise asked.

"Yeah I did, um, Mother," Adam gushed, trying out the word for the first time in his life, initiating a glow of love from the woman.

"Is this him?" James asked.

"Yes James, this is our son," Louise replied, turning the baby in her arms slightly so that the pair could see the newborn for the first time.

James picked up his son for the first time, gazing into the open brown eyes of the newborn child. A shock of recognition shivered through him as he saw eyes stare back at him that he thought were long gone. With a look of wonder he turned to his new son to be.

"Here Adam, come say hello to your brother," the man formerly known as Jimmy told the boy.

The dark haired Adam reached out and gently took the child into his arms. A smile grew across his face as the baby looked into his eyes and smiled his first smile back at the formerly troubled teen.

"Hi Joe," Adam said. "Welcome to the family."

THE END

ABOUT THE AUTHOR

Michael Andrews is a Birmingham based author and poet whose debut novel 'For The Lost Soul' has become an international seller. 'The Empty Chair' shows his passion for trying to help solve the issue of bullying and was his second book released. 'Under A Blood Moon', 'The Howling Wind' and 'The Cauldron of Fire' are the first three books in The Alex Hayden Chronicles, his new paranormal series.

Find more about Michael at his website www.michaelandrews.co.uk

Follow Michael on Twitter @forthelostsoul

Printed in Great Britain
by Amazon